YELLOW JACKET

A FRANK HARPER MYSTERY

GREG ENSLEN

GYPSY
PUBLICATIONS

Published in 2018, by Gypsy Publications
Troy, OH 45373, U.S.A.
www.GypsyPublications.com

First Edition

Enslen, Greg
Frank Harper Mysteries Series
Yellow Jacket / by Greg Enslen
ISBN 978-1-938768-79-8 (paperback)

Edited by Diana Ceres
Cover by Jennifer D. Lucano
Cover Design by Pamela Schwartz
Cover photo by Oleg Dudko

For more information, please visit the author's
website at www.GregEnslen.com

ACKNOWLEDGMENTS

This book, like my others, was a team effort. The Frank Harper in my mind is a fighter, and he keeps getting himself into new situations and new trouble. I feel like he's on a journey, and each book is like a particularly complicated episode of a TV show that's running in my head. Welcome to the show.

If it weren't for the assistance of some amazing people, there would be nothing to this book but a pile of blank pages. I come up with some ideas that are pretty out there, and these people help keep me grounded and on track. Anything great in this book is probably a result of one of their suggestions, whereas any mistakes and miscalculations fall squarely on me. For this book, I researched a variety of things, including introductory beekeeping, elements of basic criminal law, the symptoms and signs of OCD, and basic trial procedures, and for those who helped me out in those areas, I thank you.

To my outstanding team of Beta readers—**Cherie Baker, Dee Gillis, Beverlee Smith** and **David Violette**—thank you so much for reading this and my other books early and giving me your valuable feedback on the characters and plot. Each of you has truly made what I've written better, and I can't thank you enough.

To my wife **Samantha**, who has to listen to me talk endlessly about Frank Harper and my plot ideas and how things are going to go and who will die. She doesn't roll her eyes too often, and I'm grateful for that. I can't imagine what people who overhear our conversations at Sam and Ethel's or Coldwater Café might be thinking when they hear me saying things like "I need to kill off this person," or "what if he gets kidnapped and tortured?" My apologies to my fellow patrons and thanks, Sam, for your great ideas and your insight. And your patience.

To my parents, **Albert and Dee Enslen**, for reading and re-reading this book and making the plot and characters far more interesting. And thank you both for your unwavering support of my writing career. I'm still working on buying you a new house with proceeds from my books, but the next time I'm in Florida, the donuts and coffees from **Tasty-O Donuts** on 14th Avenue are on me.

To my editor, **Diana Ceres**, who vastly improved this book by giving it a rigorous edit. Diana excised the fluff, kept Frank sounding like Frank, and chastised me when appropriate to keep me on point. And she had a great idea for the ending...

To **Judge Frances McGee Cromartie** for taking time out of her schedule to walk me through the complicated criminal proceedings and the phases of a trial in Ohio and Montgomery County. Without your expert direction, the details and order of the trial outlined in the book would have been much less realistic—and I would have missed several crucial details. As always, any errors in this area of the book are my doing, not hers.

To **Robert Dorsten** for teaching his beekeeping class at the Tipp City Public Library. I learned a lot about the basics of this fascinating occupation. And thanks to Lisa Santucci and the rest of the staff of the Tipp library for holding an interesting variety of free and inexpensive classes.

To **Ruth Ann Peck** and the other members of the **Wright Writers of Dayton**, my regular book group. Thanks for making me a part of your organization, which has celebrated writing and writers in the Dayton area since 1977. Thank you for your feedback and insight.

To the people of **Tipp City, Ohio**. I've based Cooper's Mill on the town where I live, and many people have embraced our fictional residents and even ask me questions about how they're doing, especially Frank.

Most of all, I'd like to thank my **readers**. You buy the books and send me feedback and post reviews on Amazon and email me with the things you liked—and didn't like—about my novels. I can't tell you how honored it makes me feel to know that somewhere out there, someone's running alongside Frank Harper or one of my other characters, enjoying one of our adventures. In this crazy, mixed-up world, I'd like to think I'm doing a little good.

— Greg Enslen, April 2018

YELLOW JACKET

PROLOGUE

"Sir? Sir? Can you hear me?"

Joe Hathaway felt rough movements along his body. Hands, grabbing at his arms and legs. Coming out of a fog of pain, he felt cold and wet. Something was wrong with his legs.

His neck, face, arms—everything hurt.

People were working to pick him up, grunting, lifting him into the air. He felt them plop him down onto a soft surface. People were yelling. Not at him, at each other. More hands moved over him, cutting him free of his clothes.

His legs felt like they were on fire. That pain, more than anything, woke him. Joe finally came to and moved his head. His neck sang in pain. He tried to lift his arms to cover the light, but they felt like blocks of ice.

A shadow moved over him. Joe realized someone was shining a bright light into his eyes.

"Sir!"

Joe blinked at the light and saw a black woman leaning over him, wearing a doctor's mask. He tried to say something to her but there was something wrong with his mouth and throat—they were blocked.

He tried to tell her, but his voice wasn't working. He realized they had probably put tubes down his throat to help him breathe. Joe kept his eyes fixed on the doctor. He grunted, and she looked at him again, this time without the flashlight. Her eyes caught his, and she looked at him.

"Sir, can you hear me? Do you understand me?"

He grunted.

"Joe, you've been in a serious car accident. Do you understand?"

He nodded slightly. Other gowned and masked people moved around the doctor. Bright lights hung from the ceiling behind her.

"We're gonna take care of you. I need to check your responses," she said to him. She waved the light in his eyes again, then said something over her shoulder to a person out of his sight.

"Okay, Joe," she said, leaning back over him. He felt someone pushing on each side of his head with something stiff, strapping his head down. "You won't be able to move your head," she said. "Gotta keep your neck from moving. We're gonna get you fixed up, okay?"

He grunted. The doctor patted him on the chest and disappeared.

Joe stared at the lights above him and tried to remember. There had been a loud noise, a train. A horn, blaring right next to him. He remembered being in a car. Racing down snowy roads, the sounds around him strangely muffled.

And then a train. Massive, racing at his car. It should have been louder. For some reason, he could barely hear the locomotive, even though it was only twenty feet away. He'd felt the jolting impact and spun through the air. In slow motion, he saw the train and the other cars and a tree and the snowy ground surrounding all of them. And then his car came to rest in a ditch.

Joe had been racing, trying to get away. It was all fuzzy in his head, and the hospital noises made it harder to remember. But Joe was sure of a few things. He'd been trying to get away from someone. The cops were after him. He'd shot at them. After rigging the ice shanty to sink. Joe had hoped to shoot at them and scare them inside, where the house would sink under the ice and look like an accident.

He remembered thinking there was no way he could shoot the two distant figures on the ice. It was just too far away, even for him, the best shot in three states.

It had been a great plan. He'd spent so much time digging holes around the perimeter of the ice shanty, grinding circles with the rusty auger down into the ice until the cold lake water splashed up onto his gloved hands. The weight of the men, combined with the weight of the furniture, made it inevitable that the ice floor would give way, plunging the men and everything else in the hut into the chilling water of Trapper's Lake.

But the men hadn't hidden where Joe had wanted. Instead, they had fled the ice shanty, running and hiding even as the ice broke and the shanty sank into the lake. Joe had seen a figure running across the frozen lake in his direction, and Joe ran through the calculations in a heartbeat. He had no other choice but to climb into the front seat of his car and flee, leading to the car chase and his horrific wreck.

The doctor popped back into his field of vision, shouting at someone. "Get that femoral artery stitched now!" Joe was looking up at her, but she wasn't looking at him. Her forehead dripped with sweat.

Joe felt someone moving his legs. He winced—it felt like he'd walked into a campfire. He could feel the heat on his legs, flickering over his skin.

"Stay with us. Joe! Look at me!"

He glanced up at the doctor and grunted. She probably thought he was passing out. She didn't know his mind or how it worked. Even as his body was failing, his brain still wanted to figure out what happened with the train accident. His mind went to work, ignoring the pain and recalculating the accident, projecting the distance to the train and investigating his inability to hear it approaching. He searched for answers and suddenly he knew.

He'd deafened himself.

Joe had copied the DC snipers and built a shooting position inside the trunk of his car, giving him a private and unhampered view out of the hole he'd punched in the rear of his vehicle near the license plate. When the time was right, Joe had fired his weapon several times from inside the trunk. Even though he'd made sure to wear ear protection, it must not have been enough.

Someone was digging at his leg, stabbing it.

His mind turned over, reworking the problem. He hadn't used enough ear protection, apparently, and sounds afterward had been muffled. Joe had been temporarily deafened by the gunshots in an enclosed space. That explained why he had not heard the train until it was too late. Joe remembered Frank Harper, the ex-cop that had run across the lake and chased him in his car.

That man was a real pain in the ass.

Joe had had all the other cops fooled. The murder in Indiana had been meticulously planned to look like an accident, and it had worked. The local cops weren't even classifying it as a murder, and the case was closed.

The other murder, right here in town, had been set up so perfectly, everyone had assumed the victim had moved away. Joe had made it look like Tom Mercato had left his wife and started a new life in Chicago. Instead, Joe had kept Tom's body on ice in his garage.

But then that idiot Frank Harper had come along. He'd been hired to deliver some papers to Tom Mercato, but Harper had figured a few things out. Soon everyone was looking for Tom, scaring Joe into finally moving the body. One thing had led to another and Joe had ended up at the lake, trying to trap Harper and another cop in a sinking ice shanty.

Harper was the fly in the ointment—

"JOE! LOOK AT ME!"

Joe looked up at her and a hint of a smile spread across his lips. He could tell she was surprised and saw her relax. She had no idea he was just deep in thought. She probably thought he was passed out, or dying.

No, Joe was just thinking, his mind whirling with ideas and possibilities, plans and schemes.

"Good," the doctor said. "Stay with me. Your legs are pretty messed up. We're trying to make sure you keep both. The rest of your injuries are manageable. Do you understand?"

He grunted. Joe understood things she didn't, concepts that were completely foreign to her. She had no way of knowing, but he was the smartest person she would likely ever encounter. He knew loss. He knew how to kill. And he knew about revenge.

"Joe, we need to set your bones, and it's going to hurt like hell. We're going to give you something to numb the bottom half of your body so we can operate."

Joe felt something like cold ice rushing into his back. He shook his head as much as he could against the restraints. He didn't want to go under—Joe needed to think.

The doctor nodded. "We're not knocking you out. Just relax."

Joe grunted, and she disappeared from view. He went back to ruminating on Frank Harper and the train and the accident. Joe ignored the people working around him and the slow loss of feeling in his legs. He thought about his options—options he wouldn't have had if he were in jail. Or dead.

Joe would need weeks, maybe months, to recover from his injuries. Healing, physical therapy, the whole nine yards. In that time, Joe could formulate some kind of plan. A new plan. Something that would let him get away with the murders or get his revenge on Mr. Harper. Or both.

CHAPTER 1
Good News

Ex-cop Frank Harper sat at his desk in his office in Birmingham and smiled. It was Monday morning, June 18, and this stack of folders marked CALLAHAN on his desk would make five. Five cold cases solved in a little over six weeks.

That had to be some kind of record.

Over the last few years, Frank Harper had worked in the Cold Case division at the Alabama Bureau of Investigation (ABI), a statewide arm of the state police. Frank had recently gotten sober, and it seemed to be helping. A lot. For the first time in years, he was taking his job seriously.

He leaned forward and typed the final paragraphs of the email he was working on. It was to the last surviving member of the Callahan's, a once-close-knit family from southern Alabama that had been struck by tragedy fourteen years ago. It had been a horrific case, one that had made headlines back in the day. It had also dragged on for far too long, with ups and downs and arrests and disappointments. For the past six years, it had been a cold case. And Frank had cracked it. He hoped that, with this letter, Tessa Callahan might finally get some closure.

He sat back from his desk, running his hands through his hair while he tried to think of the right words to type.

"You about done with that one?"

Frank glanced over and saw Detective Murray parked at his desk across from Frank's. Murray was the closest thing Frank had to a partner. They both worked for Tim Collier, a class "A" prick who rarely had a kind word for either of them. Frank and Murray got along fine, which made putting up with Collier that much easier.

Frank nodded, leaning forward and typing a few more words. "Just emailing the daughter again."

"The Callahan's?"

Frank nodded.

"Good to close that one," Murray said.

Murray didn't elaborate. He didn't need to. The Callahan murders were famous in the annals of Alabama crime—or infamous, to be more accurate. It had been a late-night home invasion in 1998 that had targeted a wealthy family in Dothan, a town in southern Alabama. Father and mother beaten to death. Five children killed in gruesome fashion. The sixth child, the eldest daughter, had been beaten and raped and left for dead. Just the fact that she had survived at all was a miracle.

There had been leads in the original case, to be sure, and the first investigators had worked it nonstop for nearly a year, tracking down leads and visiting Georgia and the Florida panhandle to interview witnesses. After a year, investigators finally charged a suspect with the killings, but there wasn't enough evidence to even put him on trial, much less convict him.

Over the years, the Callahan murders had become something of an urban legend in southern Alabama. Many kooks had confessed to the crime in the intervening years, but none of them were serious suspects. For Frank to come along, years later, and solve the case was nothing short of a miracle.

In the end, it was a jailhouse confession that broke the case open. One of the things they did in cold cases was to work with the Alabama corrections officials, along with those from other states, to review any rumors or reports from the prison system related to cold cases. Criminals were always talking, bragging about something they may or may not have done. A smart inmate knew they could trade potential information to the authorities for time off their sentence, so new information often trickled out of the prisons and back to law enforcement. Most of the time it was bogus.

In this case, though, a dose of bragging from one of the inmates in a prison in Tallahassee, Florida, had turned out to be true. The prisoner, Merle Dallas, had bragged to his cellmate about something related to the infamous case—not an uncommon occurrence, considering the notoriety of the crime. But then he'd mentioned more things, aspects of the crime scene that might have been guessed but could only be known for certain by two parties: the police investigating the crime or someone who'd been at the undisturbed crime scene. He knew things that could only be known by someone involved in the home invasion itself—or the frantic investigation afterward.

The cellmate passed along his information to a prison guard, who filed it away in the inmate's file, forgotten. The information should have been reported, but for some reason this bragging had been discounted and forgotten. Years passed before Frank came along and reviewed every scrap of evidence in the case, including the prison files from all suspects involved. In Merle Dallas' cellmates' prison records, Frank had discovered a mention of the half-confession. Frank had been intrigued and tracked down Merle Dallas, who was back in jail, having been released and then jailed on another, unrelated crime. Frank interviewed him and was immediately suspicious. There was just something "off" about him.

After the interview, Frank tracked Dallas' location at the time of the murders, placing him in the area. Frank got a warrant for a DNA sample, which came back as a match to some preserved hairs found at the original crime scene. It was enough to finally justify a trial. The grand jury would be considering the evidence starting next week, with a trial to follow, hopefully. For the first time, someone would stand trial for the Callahan murders. Frank had no idea if they would convict Merle Dallas or not, but at least there was a chance the Callahan family might get justice—and Tessa Callahan some closure.

"Well, it's not closed," Frank said after a long pause. "Not yet. But at least it's going to trial."

"Right," Murray said. "Hope they convict the son of a bitch. When does it hit the press?"

"Tomorrow," Frank said, returning to the email. "I gave her a heads-up last week."

"She'll be happy to hear about the trial," Murray said.

Frank nodded, unsure of how much to tell Tessa Callahan about the case itself. Fourteen years ago, back in the time of the Callahan murders, Dallas had run with a gang of idiots out of Dothan. The rest of the gang had long rap sheets, but Dallas had been new to the scene. He'd only involved in the gang's most recent robberies, as far as Frank could tell. The Dothan gang liked to roll over the border into Georgia or northern Florida, commit robberies in Valdosta or Tallahassee or Apalachicola, and high-tail it back over the border into Alabama.

Merle Dallas had a slight connection to the Callahan family—he worked at the country club where Mr. and Mrs. Callahan occasionally dined. He must have overheard someone talking about their large and opulent home in upscale Solomon Park. As far as the evidence showed, it appeared that the gang rolled the dice and decided to commit a robbery inside Alabama, something they'd never done before.

They'd also never killed anyone before.

The robbery had gone according to plan, apparently. The gang broke in, tied everyone up, and left with all the valuables they could carry. They fled the crime scene and, in a switch-up of their usual *modus operandi*, drove over the border into northern Florida to lay low for a while and split up the loot.

None of them realized that Dallas had apparently gone back to the scene a few hours later. And no one except Dallas and the victims knew the extent of what he had done, or why he'd carried out his bloody mania. Frank had pieced it all together, fourteen years later. Dallas had driven back over the border to the house, apparently worried that he would somehow be identified by the elder Callahan's. On his own, he'd decided to leave no witnesses behind. What he'd done to that family was horrific.

Detective Collier stepped out of his private office and studied himself in a long mirror on one wall. He turned and walked over to Frank's desk. A short, mousy man, Tim Collier was a snappy dresser, as vain as they came, and had the wide eyes of a basset hound. Frank was just happy to be off Collier's shitlist, where he'd resided until a few weeks ago. It wasn't long ago that Collier had suspended Frank for coming in to work "drunk and disheveled." Now, with all the case closures, Collier was Frank's biggest fan.

"So, that Callahan thing breaks tomorrow, right?"

Frank nodded. "Writing the daughter again. Giving her a heads-up on the announcement details, in case she wants to attend. You approved the press releases, right?"

Collier handed him several sheets of paper with markings on the typed text. "Just a few more changes," Collier said. "It's not every day the Cold Case division gets to make an announcement. You're making me look great for my bosses."

"Glad you're doing it instead of me," Frank said. "I never liked the governor."

Murray laughed from his desk. "Bet you didn't vote for her."

Frank just smiled and shook his head.

"Never mind that," Collier said, straightening his tie. "Just get those press releases sent over. I'm on my way there now."

"Yes, I will, sir," Frank said, then added with a smile: "You look nice."

Collier rolled his eyes. "Shut up, Harper."

CHAPTER 2
Stand Up

The small town of Cooper's Mill, located ten miles north of the sprawling city of Dayton, was abuzz with activity. It was the middle of June, and summer had finally arrived in earnest. The grass was green and, after a dreadful, bitter winter, people were mowing lawns and playing tennis and enjoying the weather.

In the historical downtown shopping district, shop doors stood propped open and customers were greeted warmly. Residents walked their dogs and stopped to chat with neighbors, catching up on local news.

June was always a busy time in town. The school year had just ended, and parents resigned themselves to three months of play dates and sports and low levels of productivity. On the upside, the local parks and swimming pools filled with giggling kids. Parents also had an excuse to set aside their work and simply relax for a few weeks. Summer was like that, at least in small-town Ohio. It was expected that the kids would run and play and get dirty while the parents stood around parks or playgrounds and chatted.

On the first Friday of each summer month, the community band and other groups performed free concerts on the corner of Main and Second. The locals were invited and reminded to bring their own lawn chairs. Only days ago, the new season of the local Cooper's Mill Farmers' Market had kicked off. Saturday mornings all summer, volunteers lugged heavy yellow barricades into the streets to close off Third Street to make space for food and produce vendors at the popular market.

On this Monday morning, June 18, members of the Cooper's Mill Police Department (CMPD) met to discuss the increase in crime that always seemed to bloom with warm weather. It was Chief King's theory that people were outside more and stayed out later in the summer.

King oversaw the local police department. In the town's small police station, he called his staff people together in the large room known as the "bullpen," located in the center of the station. He began another of his regular 10:00 a.m. "stand-ups," a short meeting to get on-duty staff up to speed on current investigations and time-sensitive information. He reminded them of the earlier summer curfew for the town's youth and the increase in panhandlers and loiterers.

At the end of the meeting, King answered a couple of questions and headed back to his office, one of the few enclosed spaces that ringed the bullpen. He answered calls, filed reports, and sent out a department-wide email on the local kids who, so recently in school, often started spending every day at the local parks and every evening either at the McDonald's on Garber Drive or at the local Dairy Queen on Hyatt and Main. Inevitably, some of the older kids started getting into trouble or got caught "parking" in the city parks after dusk.

Around 11:00 a.m., he gathered some papers and walked over to the row of new conference rooms. Last month, he'd overseen a remodeling of part of the bullpen. Now, the long wall of windows was sectioned off with another glass wall, creating a series of three modest glass conference rooms along the northern side of the building. He walked into the largest conference room and sat, joining Detective Luke Barnes, who had several stacks of reports and other papers spread out on the table.

"You ready?"

Barnes turned and nodded. "Sure we can't put this off another couple weeks?"

King shook his head. "Whitlowe's itching to charge him. What did you decide?"

"The three attempted murders are the easiest to prove," Barnes said, pointing at the thick folders on the table in front of them. "Deputy Peters and Derek Vole will testify, and I'm sure we can get Frank Harper up here for a few days to chime in as well."

Chief King nodded. "I already talked to the county. They'll pay for his travel and lodging."

"Good," Barnes said. "He was involved from the start, really. He'll be an excellent witness, along with Deputy Peters."

King nodded and leaned forward, grabbing one of the folders on Joe Hathaway. Joe had lived in Cooper's Mill for many years, and no one had realized he was a stone-cold killer. Chief King and the Miami County Prosecutor's Office were trying to decide which of several cases to take to trial first. The fact they had several cases to choose from showed how evil Hathaway was. Joe had killed two people, including a popular local man, Tom Mercato, in addition to the three attempted murders King and Barnes were discussing.

"I still can't believe this," King said to Barnes, shaking his head. "That kidnapping last year, and now a double homicide. It's like we're cursed."

Barnes nodded and continued to straighten his piles of folders. Barnes was a neat freak, which made him a good detective. He tapped the second pile of folders. "This is everything we have on the Mercato murder." The CMPD was still investigating Mercato's death. He'd been found in a local lake. Initially, it had looked like an accidental drowning. It was now clear that Mercato had been killed, likely by Hathaway.

And King and his men were cooperating with yet another murder investigation, this one being conducted in Indiana. Apparently, Hathaway had lured Mercato's girlfriend away with false texts from Mercato's phone. She was a local from Cooper's Mill, and Hathaway had arranged for her to have a car accident, killing the young woman.

"Shame about Gloria," King said. She'd been a young, vivacious greeter at one of the local downtown restaurants. "I liked her."

Barnes nodded. "I'm not sure what else to say to Whitlowe, sir."

"Just cover the cases," King said, seeing movement out in the bullpen. "It's up to him to decide." He stood and saw Kevin Whitlowe, the senior prosecutor for Miami County, crossing the bullpen toward them. King went out and greeted him, shaking his hand and directing him into the conference room.

"Kevin, thanks for coming in," King said, sitting. "You know Detective Barnes."

Whitlowe nodded and sat and looked around. "Nice, King. I like all the glass. I heard you guys were remodeling."

King nodded. "We needed some conference room space. The interrogation rooms were just too small."

Whitlowe pointed out the windows. They had a view of the back of Food Town, the local grocery store. "Now you can see the grocery folks taking their smoke breaks."

CHAPTER 3
Take a Walk

After his boss left, Frank went back to the half-finished email. He tried to keep it short and to the point as he updated Tessa Callahan on the case. He'd already emailed her a week ago about the new DNA evidence. The governor would be making the announcement tomorrow, but not release any details. Something like that could influence a future jury. Frank wrapped up the email by mentioning the governor would like her to attend, and Frank included the contact information for the governor's office. Having the last member of the Callahan family there would be a nice touch.

Frank finished up and hit "Send." It was the final to-do item on this case. He glanced at his list and marked off the "Email Tessa" line item, then hit "Save" on the computer files. He sat back from his desk. It felt strange to be done.

Murray looked over. "Now what?"

Frank shook his head. "Not sure," he said, standing and gathering up all the information and reports related to the case. He put them into an expandable file folder for the prosecutor's office.

"Think I'll take a walk, clear my head."

"Hell, take the rest of the day off," Murray said. "You deserve it. Collier won't mind."

Frank thought about it and smiled. "I'm just going to grab some coffee. Want some?"

Murray shook his head, and Frank walked to the elevator, taking the bulging file folder with him. He hit the Down button and opened the folder again, rearranging the contents to make them more compact. He closed it and stretched the attached brown rubber band around the files.

Frank was an ex-cop and still managed to look like one, somehow avoiding the "donut thirty" that sidetracked many aging cops' careers. He was sinewy, wiry, and had been working out regularly over the past month or two. Since he'd taken back control of his life, things were looking up. Not long ago, his life had spiraled completely out of control. Frank had gotten caught up in a web of pills and booze that nearly cost him his life. But through a series of bizarre circumstances, he had clawed his way back to sobriety.

While most of his aging compatriots had died or retired or found alternate employment, Frank Harper was still parked at a desk, still trying to catch the bad guys. It was in his blood, even if it meant closing investigations that no one else remembered.

The elevator doors opened, and he got on, pushing "Lobby." The doors closed, and the car moved lower, opening on the main floor. Frank used to only take the stairs, but recently, enclosed spaces like elevators didn't bother him as much as they used to.

Exiting the elevator, Frank nodded at the security guard and handed him the package.

"The prosecutor's office is on their way over for those," Frank said.

The guard smiled and set it in a tray. "Gotcha."

Frank turned and made his way out onto the streets of downtown Birmingham.

It was the middle of June and everything was green, or as green as it could get in a concrete downtown. He walked in the direction of the closest Starbucks, pondering the last few weeks since his brush with death at the hands of a street gang.

Frank felt like he'd finally gotten his shit together.

In many ways, his life was firing on all cylinders. Equating his life to an old car felt right. Sometimes he felt good, like now, and other times he felt like his old rusty Camaro, puttering around, searching for the good old days. Days that seemed to have slipped into some forgotten rearview mirror. Lately, his days had been better than they had been in a long time.

Frank could be meticulous, especially when he was sober. Six weeks ago, after returning from Ohio, he dove into the cold cases that had stymied him and others, hoping to make a real difference.

He started by going back and reorganizing all the cases, prioritizing those that seemed they might have a chance of being solved. He'd determined which would benefit from new technologies or more interviews, but in most cases, the victims and any suspects had all passed away.

His and Murray's review of the cases led to fifty-one of them being officially "retired," meaning no one was actively working them anymore. They stayed in the computer filing system, of course, and would be flagged if anything surfaced related to the case. After Collier approved, the actual files and evidence boxes on those cases were shipped to the state police archives in Montgomery. Frank had put a note on each computer file to revisit the cold case in five years. New scientific techniques might be invented in the intervening time that could affect the cases, much like DNA profiling had burst on the scene and closed so many cases in recent years.

After those fifty-one cases had been "retired," Frank organized the department's remaining twenty-seven cases. These looked like they might be solved someday, if enough investigative muscle were applied. He set about closing as many as he could. He and Murray hunkered down, poring through the remaining cases, looking for one they could break. They looked for DNA angles or new investigative techniques. They compared each case with the "rumor mill" coming out of the local and state prison systems. They ran background on every major individual involved in each case—criminals, witnesses, victims, even the investigatory staff and beat cops involved in gathering evidence—through the Combined DNA Index system, known as CODIS, and NCIC, the National Crime Information Center.

And then they finally found a case they could close.

It was just there, the piece of information they needed. And, like that, a case was solved. Finished and filed away. There were no charges involved. The perpetrator and everyone else involved in the case had long since passed away. But the case was solved.

And then they closed another case. Then another, and then another. Solid police work, concentration, and a thousand Google searches brought new details to light, facts and clues that others had missed or never thought to investigate in the first place.

Now, several weeks later, the Callahan murders would be the fifth case Frank had solved. Murray had also closed three, bringing their total to eight.

It was unheard of.

But something was nagging him. Things were going so well for him now at work, but it felt strangely empty. Solving cold cases was great, but it left him wanting more.

CHAPTER 4
Case Files

Chief King, Prosecutor Whitlowe and Detective Barnes chatted for a few minutes, mostly about the weather, before Whitlowe leaned forward and put his arms on the table, grasping his hands together.

"So, what do you have for me? We're itching to get started with Hathaway. He was arrested back in April, so we're under the gun. We have 90 days to bring him to trial, or we have to release him."

"Well, you know the broad strokes, I'm sure," Barnes said.

"I've been through all your preliminary reports," Whitlowe said, sitting back. "Seems best to start with the three attempteds and get him locked up. Those charges are much easier to prove."

"These are the final files on the three attempteds. Deputy Peters and the other victim will testify, and Frank Harper would need to fly in from Birmingham," Barnes said. "Obviously, he can testify to the chase and subsequent accident where Hathaway was injured."

King thought about Frank Harper, an ex-cop who had been in town visiting his estranged daughter. The grizzled veteran cop had helped with a few local cases, nearly getting killed for his trouble. But Harper was a wild card, the opposite of meticulous Barnes. Things got messy whenever Harper was around.

Whitlowe looked at the final case files on the table between them. "Anything new in here?"

"More forensics, especially from the car," Barnes said. Hathaway's car was nearly destroyed in the accident. He'd tried to outrace a local freight train and lost. "We recovered the long-range rifle and shell casings from the interior. The vehicle went to the crime lab downtown, where they recovered ample DNA evidence that puts him in the car and in the trunk." Barnes slid a photo of the trunk of a wrecked car across the table. There was a notched hole at the top of the trunk, near the license plate holder. "The hole in the trunk survived the accident as well. He was shooting through it, like the DC snipers. There are matching scrapes and paint transfer near the end of the rifle barrel. With those and the casings, we can tie him to all three of the attempted murders."

Whitlowe nodded. "Good. Expended bullets?"

"Recovered from the ice surface," Barnes said, passing over four bagged shell casings. "We had people out there for days, walking the ice. Found four bullets—one had traveled another half mile. Chain of evidence is solid on those. They were only opened once, at the county crime lab."

"Four? I was hoping for more."

"That's all we got," Barnes said. "There were nine casings in the trunk, so he took at least that many shots. But the lake thawed in April, so anything else went to the bottom."

"Is it enough?" King asked, leaning forward. "I want this guy locked up for life."

Whitlowe nodded. "Yep, easy peasy. I'm not worried about it. Our problem is the defendant—he's still in intensive care." Whitlowe looked at a calendar on the wall. "It's June 18—doctors said he won't be ambulatory until early July. Even then, he'll be in a wheelchair," Whitlowe said, biting his lip. "Jury might sympathize with him."

"Can you get a trial date?"

"Yes," Whitlowe said. "Judge Wilson wants this on the docket as soon as possible. But no jury or anything until Hathaway can get around in a wheelchair."

"Makes sense," Barnes said.

"There is plenty we can do ahead of that," Whitlowe said. "We can set the trial date, take the pleas, read out the charges. Maybe even do preliminary arguments. Jury selection, stuff like that. But he has to be able to participate in his own defense."

King leaned forward. "So, early July?"

"Yeah, no problem. Does this wrap up your investigation?"

Barnes nodded. "Yes, this is everything."

"Good, good." Whitlowe stacked the folders. "I approve the charges—three cases of attempted murder. You can formally charge Hathaway tomorrow and file your complaint with the Court. I'll get started on the pre-arraignment, and we'll do that tomorrow or Wednesday right in his hospital room, as long as Wilson signs off. Finally get this ball rolling, right?"

Barnes nodded, smiling.

Whitlowe smiled and smacked the table. "Come on, men, get excited! Right? This guy is gonna fry. Okay, what about the two murders? Anything definitive on those yet?"

"Murder," Barnes corrected him. "The girl's death happened in Indiana."

"Right," Whitlowe said, remembering. "They'll have to prosecute."

Barnes changed gears. "Hathaway covered his tracks well with Tom Mercato," Barnes said, flipping open another thick folder. "We've been through Hathaway's house several times but didn't find much—no blood, no DNA. We think he wiped the house down."

"We have reports of him holding parties—not normal for him," King added. "We think he cleaned up after the murder, which probably happened in the basement. Replaced everything, the furniture and carpets, had it painted, and then invited groups of people over."

Whitlowe looked at the file. "Guy thinks he's clever. Clean up, paint, then bring in lots of people to muddy the crime scene. So, the only definitive DNA was in the freezer?"

"Yup," Barnes said. "Lots of Mercato in there."

"Jesus," Whitlowe said, looking at the photos of the freezer unit stored in Hathaway's garage. "Was the guy dead when he went in?"

"Long dead," King said. "Bled out somewhere else. But Hathaway kept his body anyway. Not sure why."

"Maybe a prize," Whitlowe said. "A trophy? Some killers liked to keep parts of the victim—or the whole victim, in this case—as proof of their deeds."

"Maybe," Barnes said. "Another weird thing— we found was a chess set nearby. It looked like he'd been playing it a lot."

"With Mercato? Like, Joe was pretending they were playing?"

Barnes shrugged. "Who knows. Maybe. People are weird."

"No kidding," Whitlowe said.

"Hathaway was...is a chess prodigy," Barnes added. "He was always begging people to play, according to that coffee klatch he was in with Mercato."

"Maybe he finally found a really quiet partner," King said with a smile.

Barnes chuckled. "Do you think Hathaway let him win once in a while?"

Whitlowe smiled.

"Don't you just love the crazy ones?" Whitlowe asked, shaking his head. "What about your other witness? Is she coming forward?"

Barnes glanced at King. "She's...she's considering it. She's very reluctant to testify. We want to keep her off the books for now. But I think we can get her to show up for the Mercato case."

Whitlowe nodded. "Okay. On the other murder, we're pretty sure it happened in Indiana?"

"Yeah, car accident," Barnes said. "Died at the scene."

"So, we helping them?"

"Interviews with our locals, stuff like that."

"Okay," Whitlowe said. "If they charge him, we'll extradite, so let's get our cases through first. Assuming we'll have enough to take him to trial for Mercato's murder once these other cases are done."

Barnes nodded. "No problem," he said.

"Good," Whitlowe said with a smile that should have been infectious except for the sudden chill in the room. "We're gonna nail this idiot, and then Indiana can nail him again. Perfect."

King wasn't smiling. "When we extradite, it'll be for a double murder."

"Why?"

"She was pregnant."

"Oh," Whitlowe said, and the room got quieter. King could hear the murmur of conversations out in the bullpen, beyond the glass. Whitlowe's jovial mood had evaporated in a heartbeat.

"Okay," Whitlowe said, closing the folder with a frown. "I'll get started and talk to Judge Wilson."

CHAPTER 5
Coffee Break

Frank Harper found the Starbucks on 20th Street in Birmingham nearly empty, just the way he liked it. Their particular brand of soft jazz, which he didn't altogether hate, drifted quietly from hidden speakers.

He ordered his coffee, a big Americano with a splash of cream. He liked his coffee very strong, and this was as close as the folks at Starbucks got. But he refused to say "venti" or whatever other bullshit Italian words they had invented for their drink sizes. He just gestured with his hands and said, "the biggest you've got."

When they finished making his drink and called his name, Frank found an empty barstool near the windows and sat, sipping and watching the people walk by outside. It was nice to be still for a while and not do anything.

In New Orleans, he had always loved people watching. He liked to guess what people were up to. The Cafe du Monde in downtown "Nawlins" was the best spot to watch people come and go. When he'd been a beat cop in the city, he'd always requested the French Quarter. Some cops hated walking patrol, but he'd always loved walking among the tourists and residents and chasing down an occasional shoplifter.

Frank always found an excuse to linger at the du Monde and enjoy a cup of coffee and a sit in the outdoor seats. The cafe was located on Decatur Street, steps from the Mississippi River. The cafe sat catty-corner from Jackson Square, an expanse of green grass flanked by the impressive St. Louis Cathedral on the west edge. The park was always filled with tourists and locals, and often artists and their paintings lined the sidewalks. On the grass, performers sang and played their accordions for tips. Directly across the street from the cafe was Monty's on the Square, with its red brick walls and wide balconies and ornate metal railings. And behind the cafe, the lazy ships floated by on a flat Mississippi river that stretched away, like a sheet of muddied glass, toward the old abandoned sugar mills over on Algiers Point.

There was something so relaxing about people watching in the bustling French Quarter. Or maybe it was just the coffee and beignets.

The view from the Birmingham Starbucks wasn't nearly as interesting. A few business people walked by, hurrying back from lunch. A nice-looking couple was arguing over something, and Frank saw the young lady shout at the man and then walk away, spinning and flipping him off with a smile. Maybe it wasn't a fight—maybe it was one of those good-natured verbal tussles couples always got into. He and Trudy had been like that, a thousand years ago. They'd gotten along like peas and carrots, back when he'd been a New Orleans Police Department (NOPD) detective and she'd been home with baby Laura.

That was before things had gotten ugly. Trudy hadn't left him yet, taking Laura with her. Katrina hadn't hit yet, killing so many people and upending the town he loved. And the hospital at St. Bart's hadn't been flooded yet, leading to the chilling incidents that had haunted him for years.

But now, things were looking up for Frank. Several weeks on the wagon had made things markedly better. He'd always had a problem with alcohol, but recent revelations—and a few trips to the union-provided shrink—had helped Frank clear up some things in his mind. St. Bart's no longer haunted him the way it used to. He'd told his daughter Laura what happened, and he'd managed to tell the cop shrink most of the story as well. It did make him feel better, talking about it.

Frank sat for a while at the Starbucks, missing New Orleans. Sometimes, he thought about moving back, or moving closer to Laura and Jackson. She lived in a little town near Dayton, Ohio, carving out a nice life for herself and her son Jackson in a charming little suburb north of the city. He'd been up to visit a few times and managed to make some friends while getting pulled into a few police investigations.

The last visit had been the most eye-opening. He was investigating the death of a family. Frank had stuck his nose into their confrontation with a local street gang on an earlier visit, and after he left, the gang had burned down the family's home. As crazy as it sounded, he'd ended up being kidnapped by the gang and tortured nearly to death. After he escaped, the local police raided the gang's headquarters, shutting them down. CNN had even covered the aftermath, tying it into the spike in opioid deaths. It was weird, being involved in something that people were talking about across the country.

Frank would never forget the waterboarding or his harrowing escape. But, in some strange way, the gangbangers had done him a favor. They'd gotten him off the Oxy, and the ten days he'd been held without alcohol had sobered him up. Now, whenever he thought about drinking, or visiting his old Oxy dealer out by the Costco on Tomany Street, his skin would start to crawl.

He missed Ohio, especially Laura and Jackson. And, if he was being honest with himself, Frank missed working on active cases. The cases he'd been solving were interesting, but they could never hold a candle to live police work. Up in Ohio he'd been shot at, chased, nearly drowned, and abducted in the middle of the night. He'd even been left for dead in a burning field.

Thinking about it now, by the windows in the Starbucks, Frank couldn't help but smile. Of course, it was all awful and horrific, but it also had made him feel more alive than he'd felt in years.

CHAPTER 6
Joe in Hospital

Joe Hathaway hated this hospital room.

He was surrounded by medical equipment, beeping and clicking and gurgling, all working to keep him alive. But Joe was tired of all of it.

Sometimes, he felt like he was stuck in an episode of *The Twilight Zone*, the one with the coma patient in a hospital, trapped inside his own body. "Breakdown" was the name of the episode, his mind offered up. The man in the TV show had no way of letting the "outside" world know he could see—and feel—everything going on around him.

Joe's brain was always offering stuff up like that. Now, stuck in this stupid hospital room, his brain was all Joe had. The most important aspect of him was now stuck inside an injured shell. His mind had nothing to do now but plot and plan and scheme, in between offering him up useless *Twilight Zone* trivia and salient Sun Tzu quotes.

Mostly, his mind planned escape from this room.

It calculated the amount of pain he'd be in if he disconnected himself from the machines and the apparatus that held his bones in place. It also wondered how much stolen morphine it would take to deaden the pain enough for him to slip out of a window and across the parking lot. Joe saw the cars coming and going from the lot and racing past the hospital on the nearby highway. There were trucks he could climb into the back of. He could hop a fence and hitchhike out of the county.

Joe knew how to outsmart people. The brainless beat cops guarding his hospital room would never know he was gone. They'd never expect a gravely-injured man to crawl his way to freedom, would they?

On the TV, the old movie *Bridge on the River Kwai* was playing. Men ran around in the war film, planting charges on the titular bridge. For some reason, this movie was on all the time now, and he'd seen it twice in the last week.

Joe shook his head and looked down at his body. At least now he could communicate with the nurses. Up until last week, he'd been intubated to help him breathe. The rest of his body was healing—he'd broken both arms, both legs and several ribs in the crash, along with injuring his neck and face. While he was intubated, he could only communicate through grunts and small head movements. He'd found the limited communication incredibly frustrating.

The door opened, and Nurse Taylor came in, carrying two more large bouquets of flowers. A young cop held the door open, smiling at her. It was one of the same three or four young cops assigned to guard Joe's room. It was no wonder the cop smiled at her—Nurse Taylor was one of the pretty nurses. Joe considered himself lucky on that count.

"How we doin' today, Joe?" she asked, checking him over. He still had two large casts on his legs, and both arms were suspended from a ceiling-mounted rack system to keep them off his chest and ribs.

"I'm okay," he said, his voice still scratchy.

"That's all you've got to say?" She pulled the curtains open, affording him a better view of the grassy lawn outside and the roaring highway beyond. The hospital was located just north of Troy and situated within spitting distance of I-75.

They chatted while she tended to his equipment and tidied the room, gathering dishes and trash from his earlier meal. She talked the whole time.

The door opened again, and Doctor Wheeler entered, followed by three residents. Joe watched the cop outside check the residents' badges to make sure they were allowed access to the room, but Wheeler never paused and marched right in, crossing to Joe and grabbing the clipboard full of charts that hung from the foot of his bed. Joe had noticed that everywhere Wheeler went, he dragged along a gaggle of residents.

"How we doing, Mr. Hathaway?" Dr. Wheeler was an intense-looking man with the shiniest, baldest head Joe had ever seen. The man must buff it every morning to get it to shine like that.

"He's not talking a lot today," Nurse Taylor said, rearranging the pillows under Joe to help him shift positions a little and elevate his head. "He's happy to not be tubed, I'm sure."

"I'm okay," Joe said again, looking at the residents.

Wheeler ignored Joe and stared at the charts, then turned to his gaggle. "Progress checkup for Mr. Hathaway here," he said, handing the chart to the lead resident. "What should we be looking for, seven weeks post-admission?"

The resident scanned the chart, flipping between pages, and then glanced up at Joe and the apparatus that held his arms immobile. "Arm supports to be removed today. Monitor for swelling and secondary infections from being stationary," the resident said. "Starting today, regular movement and careful examination of all extremities to ward off skin necrosis or soft tissue loss from obstructed circulation. Tissue debridement, if necessary." He handed the chart back to Wheeler with a hint of a smile.

"Good, good," Wheeler said.

"Skin necrosis," Joe asked, speaking up. "You mean gangrene? I thought you guys fixed that back in the Civil War days."

Wheeler turned and smiled at Joe. "Yeah, but we bring back the greatest hits every once in a while. We miss them." He turned back to the gaggle and pointed to a different one. "Too soon to remove the arm supports?"

The resident shook her head. "X-rays show the arms are healed enough to remove the casts today. After that, the supports are no longer needed."

Wheeler nodded, then pointed at a third resident. "Recommended meds?"

"Standard pain management, plus consideration of an anticoagulant such as Apixaban or Rivaroxaban to prevent blood clots in the immobilized legs," the young man said, never taking his eyes off Wheeler.

"Good," Wheeler said, then waved them to the door. "Okay, prep for that back surgery we discussed earlier. Review the patient's file and scrub in." As they filed out of the room, Wheeler turned to Nurse Taylor. "We'll get those casts off later. Will you still be on?"

She nodded. "Until 6."

"Good," the doctor said, then looked at Joe. "Your hearing is tomorrow, probably in here. Looks like you've got a couple big days ahead of you."

Joe nodded, not answering. His lawyer had been by yesterday and walked him through what would happen tomorrow.

"Okay, Nurse, can you help me out?" Together, the doctor and the nurse examined both of his legs, each encased in a thick cast. The doctor felt around inside both ends of each cast. "Good. One more week on these. No necrosis. How's the pain?"

"Awesome," Joe said. "When can I get up and move around?"

"Soon, soon," Wheeler said, feeling his chest. "We can get you into a wheelchair soon. Get you outside for some sun and air. Ribs feel like they're in good shape, and your facial bones are healed," Wheeler said.

Joe nodded, not wanting to say anything that might betray how happy it made him.

"Okay," Wheeler said. "When the judge and counsel arrive tomorrow, I'll brief them. I'll tell them the same thing I just told you. Once you're in the wheelchair, we can get you started on some PT for your arms, get those muscles back to work. You should be able to begin your leg PT by the end of July. Walking by September, hopefully, assuming all goes well. Sound good?"

Joe smiled, his brain off like a shot, doing the math. How long until he could stand? How long until he could walk, or run? Joe planned to pretend his recovery was taking longer than it actually was. He needed the hospital staff to treat him like an invalid for as long as possible. Already, he'd been actively working his wrists and hands to build up their strength. When he "started" his upper body PT, he'd have to remember to go easy and act like it was a strain.

"Nothing? No questions?"

He looked at Wheeler. "No, just glad to hear things are progressing."

Nurse Taylor spoke up with a smile. "Like I said, he's a man of few words."

CHAPTER 7
Back to Work

A half-hour later, Frank left the quiet Starbucks in Birmingham and headed back to his office. He took his time walking back, thinking about the cold cases he'd managed to solve and the ones that remained. He might be able to close them all, or have the cases "retired," by the end of summer.

The weather was pleasant and warm. He regretted having to go back inside. Once he got back to his desk, Frank sat down and shuffled the papers and notes and thick folders on his desk, looking for his yellow pad. He'd taken to writing things down on the small yellow pads favored by friends at the police department up in Ohio. The pads were great, small enough to put in your pocket but big enough to make columned lists.

Frank found the pad he was currently working on and skimmed the list of cases he was in the middle of processing.

Most cases grew "cold" because the investigators in charge gave up. It wasn't nice to say, or politically correct, but that was the truth. Most were investigated fully, every name involved with the case interviewed at least once, and every meaningful piece of evidence was investigated. Cases were deemed cold when they made their way to the bottom of the detective's stack of active cases and stayed there for weeks or even months. At some point, most investigators realize the case is going nowhere. New cases come in all the time, and eventually, you have to move on. The cases weren't abandoned, but detectives had a limited amount of time and energy. A good "close" rate was the sign of a diligent detective, but some cases just couldn't be solved.

In many departments, cases made the rounds, getting reassigned to new detectives every six months or so. Often, a new set of eyes could break a case open. "Fresh eyes," as Frank's old partner Ben Stone would have said. Detectives had different ways of looking at things, different modes of investigation. Some detectives concentrated on witnesses, while others relied more on trace evidence. Some had different connections with the community, or informal contacts or informants that could help shine light on a case.

Most detective bureaus labeled a case cold after a year, or after all probative leads had been exhausted. High-profile cases might be given more time or more resources or rotated through more detectives. But eventually, all unsolved cases get moved to storage and marked for routine "reinvestigation" on a rotating basis.

Often, cold cases went unsolved due to the lack of a body. With no body or physical evidence or a crime scene, there could be no DNA or other physical evidence and no way to tie the body to a particular location or person. In these modern times, DNA solved many cases, but it also could get suspects off the hook. Advances in DNA technology had also reopened—and solved—a sizable number of old cases, especially those in which the investigators had had the foresight to retain important samples of hair, skin, or bodily fluids.

CHAPTER 8
Down to Business

The city of Troy, Ohio, was located twenty minutes north of Dayton and about ten minutes north of Cooper's Mill. Troy was by far the largest town in the prosperous Miami County and served as the county seat. Scores of shops and small restaurants filled Troy's downtown, arrayed around an old-fashioned public square. A unique traffic circle wound its way around the square with a tall fountain at the center. Dedicated on July 4, 1976, the date of America's Bicentennial, the fountain and the traffic circle served as the de facto center of Troy and its downtown.

During the annual Strawberry Festival held every August, the locals dyed the fountain scarlet. Many enjoyed the annual display of strawberry-colored water splashing in the fountain, while others joked darkly that it resembled an otherworldly geyser of blood, a hell-fountain spurting crimson into the sky.

Troy was also the center of Miami County administration, with most of the countywide offices operating downtown. City Hall held the offices of the mayor and city council, while the Municipal court system operated out of the massive County Courthouse Building, located a block west of the traffic circle. The Gothic building, built in 1888 and topped with a copper statue of "Justice," loomed over Troy's downtown.

Next door sat a smaller, more modern building known as the Safety Building, which held the probate and traffic courts. Couples walked in and out of the building all day long to procure marriage licenses, while others came to pay fines and parking tickets, sit on juries, or register their vehicles.

The third floor was home to the public defender and county prosecutor's offices. County Prosecutor Whitlowe and his staff took up a suite of offices on the third floor, with Whitlowe's office being the largest, facing out onto the plaza.

On Tuesday morning, June 19, Whitlowe sat behind his desk, ignoring the view of the fountains outside. His desk was stacked with color-coded manila folders: blue and green cases were active, while those in the yellow jackets were pending. One such case sat open in front of him as Whitlowe discussed it with three members of his staff.

He looked at his secretary, Dorothy. "Anything on the pre-arraignment?"

She shook her head. Dorothy was at least seventy but moved with the quickness of a graceful bird. Sometimes, it seemed she was the person in the office with the most energy.

"Judge Wilson's clerk has approved the pre-arraignment paperwork and the complaint. You and the defense attorney are meeting Judge Wilson in the defendant's hospital room today at 1:00 p.m. We should know more then. Pretrial motions are already in the works."

"Good," Whitlowe said. "The opposing counsel is Tomlinson, from Dayton, right?"

"That's right," she said, making a face. They both remembered Tomlinson. "What about the trial location? Will they hold it at the hospital?"

"No," Whitlowe said. "We have to wait until Hathaway can use a wheelchair. Judge Wilson won't want to prejudice the jury by letting them see him in a hospital bed."

"Could it be means for a mistrial?" Dorothy asked.

"Possibly," Whitlowe said. "Hathaway has to be able to participate in his own defense. But all the preliminary meetings could happen there." It was not unheard of to meet with the defendant and opposing counsel in such an unorthodox location.

Whitlowe turned to Bridget Turner, his assistant prosecutor, and Winn Bartlett, a third-year law student from the University of Dayton. Bridget was tough as nails—he'd seen her argue a case earlier in the year involving a group of white supremacists from a farm in a rural area of the county a dozen miles west of Troy. They were slowly building up their own compound, buying up and stringing together lots and building fortified structures. Now, they were putting up long rows of barbed wire fence. She'd argued the case, which involved some shady firearms sales, and won a judgment against them, sending two of the perpetrators to jail.

"Bridget, you'll be running point on witnesses and evidence. We can't afford a single misstep or a single witness that doesn't come across as a slam dunk," Whitlowe said. "Go through the forensics and get everything tested again by an outside agency if there's time."

"Outside agency?"

"Yes. Not from Ohio," Whitlowe said, thinking. "Anything local, and the defense could argue it was tainted by prior relationships with investigative staff. Get one from the West Coast—that always impresses jurors. Be especially thorough with the ballistics. Have the rifle tested again, and make sure the casings found in his car are a solid match with the slugs found on the lake."

Bridget nodded, taking notes. "I understand, sir. We need to nail them down."

"Yes, we do," he said, smiling. "But we have to do it right. I don't care if it takes all of us working nights and weekends, or personally flying the evidence around the country for testing. We're going to get three convictions out of this. Three. Not one or two. You need to read all the files again and re-interview the principals and verify everything in—"

"I've read the files, sir," she said. "I'll get on the interviews. Most are local, but I'll call the one principal in Alabama and go over his testimony again."

Whitlowe nodded. "Hold off on that one until we know when we're flying him in. No point, unless he can testify. Dorothy, can you get the ball rolling on that? Frank Harper. He'll need a plane ticket and a local hotel. After today, we should know the trial date. Bridget, you can call him then and kill two birds with one stone."

She nodded, and Whitlowe looked at Winn. "Finish the complaint and let me look it over. Dorothy, I'll need five copies by noon. The defense will ask for a delay for the defendant, but I doubt Judge Wilson will go for it, considering we're on the clock and meeting at the hospital."

The three others were taking notes, nodding, and Winn looked up. He was working the summer with the county prosecutor's office to get some real-world experience for his transcripts. "Should we start looking at the voir dire?" He was asking about the selection process for jury members.

"Yes, I'd like you to handle that. And after the pleas are finished, work with Bridget to write up the defense's case." Often, clerks were tasked with playing the devil's advocate, anticipating the most likely strategies and arguments that could be presented by the defense. Also, it would help Whitlowe prepare counter-arguments ahead of time.

Whitlowe looked around at all of them.

"Folks, this is going to be the most high-profile case we conduct this year," Whitlowe said. "I'm not kidding. There will be local press, maybe statewide. And we'll get protests, too. The defendant has grown quite a following online since his accident."

Bridget nodded. "I saw that on Facebook and Instagram."

Whitlowe shook his head. "Mr. Hathaway looks like a delicate old man in his wheelchair, and he will have the jury's sympathy from the start. We will look like the mean old government, picking on a frail old man. Nothing can go wrong, and I mean nothing. Triple-check *everything*. If anything feels off, you bring it to me. Got it?"

The three staff members arrayed around Whitlowe's desk nodded solemnly. The fourth person, an older man seated on a couch on the far side of the office, had yet to speak.

"This should be easy," Whitlowe said. "Three attempted murders, with all the witnesses we could ask for. Let's get to work."

His staff stood and left, discussing the case. Whitlowe followed them, closing the door before turning to the old man, who sitting on the couch, sipping from a glass.

"Sounds like it's yours to lose," the old man finally said, waving the glass at him. "Scotch?"

"It's a little early for that," Whitlowe said, turning to look out the window at the fountains. "And I hate these kinds of cases. They look open and shut, but then something comes out of left field. Any advice?"

The old man stood and walked to Whitlowe's desk.

"I don't think there's anything left for me to teach you. And this office suits you," he said, looking around. "I'm glad you redecorated."

"Yeah. Had to get at least some of your old stuff out of here," Whitlowe said with a smile. "Kept the desk, though."

"It's a classic Jonathan Charles," the older man said, running an appreciative hand along it. He patted Whitlowe on the shoulder, then turned and headed for the door. "You'll be fine. Call me if you need anything."

Whitlowe looked up as the man left. "Thanks, Dad. The case is ours to lose."

"Then don't lose."

Chapter 9
Prepped

After lunch on Tuesday, Nurse Taylor returned to Joe's room to gather his lunch tray and to prep the room for his upcoming meeting. Joe glanced over and saw a different cop working the door this time. Joe was studying them, trying to memorize their shifts and rotations. There were only four of them—with enough observation, he should be able to accurately predict who was on duty and for how long. Having them out in the hallway made it more difficult.

An old black and white movie was playing on the TV. He ignored the remote near his hand and watched the nurse as she moved about the room, tidying up. She straightened his pillows, checked the IV bags and the bag of yellow fluid from his catheter. It was humiliating on one level, having someone take care of everything for you. But on another level, it was like having a personal servant, waiting on you hand and foot. He could get used to that, especially if the women were pretty. Nurse Taylor finished up her check of Joe's room.

"Need anything else?"

"No, I'm good." He wanted to add something more, something along the lines of "yes, please pull down your top so I can finally get a good look at those beautiful breasts," but he couldn't figure out a way to convey that message subtly.

"Okay," she continued. "I'll see you later. Dinner will be around six."

He watched her leave, admiring the fall of her uniform from behind. He blinked and reached for the TV remote. There had to be something good on.

Several of the nurses on staff were cute, but none of them held a candle to May Mercato. Joe knew she was out there, somewhere, and wondered if she missed him and their friendship. He'd hoped to deepen that friendship—they had spent countless conversations discussing her husband's many infidelities. Joe wanted May for himself, and sat patiently while she went on and on, complaining about Tom. Joe had always been a patient listener, especially after Tom had "left town" and abandoned May. But Tom had never appreciated her, not really—Tom had been a well-known philanderer, stepping out on May with a new girl every month. Joe wasn't sorry he'd killed Tom and stuffed his body in a freezer.

There was a knock at the door and Joe's lawyer walked in. Ned Tomlinson was a good lawyer with Reed, Patsing and Tomlinson, an expensive firm out of Dayton. Ned knew the situation and showed his ID to the cop outside before entering and pulling up a chair.

"How we doin' today, Joe?" Tomlinson always spoke that way—maybe he was used to lumping himself in with his client's situation. It was the royal "we," to be sure, but also along the lines of "we're in this together." Technically, this wasn't true, but Joe appreciated the sentiment.

"Good, good."

Tomlinson nodded. "We're going to meet with Doctor Wheeler in a few minutes. He'll update me and the Court on your status. I'll be back after that, along with the judge and the prosecutor, and we'll start the proceedings."

"Here? I figured we'd move to a conference room or something."

Tomlinson shook his head. "No, we can do it here. It's just the pre-arraignment."

"Okay."

"Just stay quiet," Tomlinson said, heading for the door. "I'll handle everything. When the judge reads your rights, just answer him with a 'yes.' If they want to read out the charges or ask us to enter a plea, I'll take care of it."

CHAPTER 10
Doctor Talk

Kevin Whitlowe leaned against the hallway wall of the Miami County Hospital, waiting. Joe Hathaway's lawyer, Ned Tomlinson, was just down the hall, but they hadn't spoken yet. It was customary for attorneys working against each other in a case to avoid talking outside the presence of the Court, but Whitlowe couldn't help himself.

"Tomlinson, what's your guy gonna plead?"

The lawyer looked up from the stack of papers—he was reading through the folder Whitlowe had just handed him with the official criminal complaint. Technically, they were still the "accused" at this point as they hadn't been formally charged yet.

"Not guilty, if we get there," Tomlinson said.

"Oh, we'll get there," Whitlowe said. "The judge is in a hurry."

"The 90-day time line?"

Whitlowe nodded. "We have to be done by then. Wouldn't be surprised if we skipped to the probable cause hearing today. Might even arraign him and take a plea."

Tomlinson shook his head, pointing at the folder. "I hope not. I haven't had time to go through any of this."

Of course, this was bull. Defense attorneys lived to stall. It was their bread and butter—delay, delay, delay.

Whitlowe saw movement at the end of the hallway and Judge Wilson came around the corner, flanked by his people. Wilson was a pudgy fellow with sallow skin that always made Whitlowe wonder if the judge was sick. He had the pallor of someone dealing with a chronic medical condition. The judge was accompanied by a clerk of the court, a court reporter, and his bailiff, Will Duff. Whitlowe knew them all well and nodded as they approached.

Tomlinson didn't notice them until they were nearly stopped in front of him. The attorney straightened himself awkwardly, almost dropping his paperwork.

"Your Honor," Whitlowe said.

"Your Honor," Tomlinson added.

"Good morning," Judge Wilson said, then looked at Whitlowe. "Who are we meeting with?"

Whitlowe pointed at an office three doors down. "Doctor Wheeler."

The judge walked over to the office and knocked, then entered, holding the door open behind him. The judge looked around, said something to someone, and walked back out. "Not enough room in there."

The doctor emerged and led them to a conference room in an adjoining hallway. Whitlowe and Tomlinson sat at one table, and the judge and his court reporter sat at another. They made the introductions, and Judge Wilson began by asking the doctor questions about the accused and his medical condition. The court reporter took notes and the clerk and bailiff sat at the other end of the table.

"Doctor, please give me his current prognosis," the judge began.

Doctor Wheeler shook his head. "He's progressing, Your Honor. That's all I can say. He isn't ready to start his walking physical therapy, that's for certain. But he's recovering from his other injuries. The casts on his arms came off yesterday, and the leg casts should come off next week. He'll be starting his upper body physical therapy this week. It could be months before he can walk, though."

Tomlinson leaned forward. "Forcing him to testify while he's physically unable to stand could prejudice a jury, Your Honor. It could be grounds for a mistrial—"

"We're not discussing a jury trial at this point, Counsel," the judge said curtly. "The Court is simply trying to ascertain the physical condition of the accused." He turned back to the doctor. "After the casts come off, can he be transported by wheelchair?"

"Yes, he'll be moved to the recovery ward and begin his PT."

The judge looked at Whitlowe. "Aren't you concerned you may lose sympathy with the jury by showing him in court in a wheelchair?"

Tomlinson interrupted. "Is this an official motion of the Court?"

Whitlowe rolled his eyes. God, this guy was an idiot.

"Your Honor, we're willing to allow the jury to see him in a wheelchair," Whitlowe said. "Or we can wait until he's fully recovered, if the defense will waive the 90-day time limit."

The judge nodded and looked at Tomlinson. "The Court understands these are unique circumstances due to your client's injury. Do you want to waive the time limit?"

"No, Your Honor."

"Do you object to a jury trial, if it comes to that?"

"We object to this whole situation," Tomlinson said, making sure he was heard by the court reporter, who was tapping away on her machine, taking everything down. "This whole thing is unorthodox."

Whitlowe was really starting to hate this guy. He hated the way he talked, hated the way he dressed. This was going to be a long trial.

"I looked in on him earlier," Whitlowe said. "He looks like any other hospital patient, recovering from injuries. Doctor, the machines around him are monitoring his recovery, not helping him breathe or keep him alive, right?"

The doctor nodded, and Whitlowe began to make a point about the accused when Tomlinson interjected with every argument imaginable. His tone was grating, and his points were annoying and repetitive. He kept bringing up the 90-day window.

Judge Wilson finally put his hand up. "We're not getting anywhere, and we're wasting the doctor's time. Sir, in your opinion, can Mr. Hathaway be transported safely to and from the courthouse for a period of up to ten days?"

The doctor nodded. "Certainly, Your Honor. You'll have no objection from us, other than to keep him hydrated. We can send a nurse along with him daily, if that helps, or the defense could hire a qualified assistant."

"It might be easier to grant him bail, Your Honor," Tomlinson offered.

Whitlowe shook his head. "He tried to kill a police officer, Your Honor. And two civilians. On top of that, we're looking at him for at least two murders, one of a well-known person in Cooper's Mill, and the other a pregnant woman. He's a highly-trained marksman. He's the very definition of a flight risk."

The judge nodded at Whitlowe. "Bail will be denied in this case. And Mr. Whitlowe, be careful. You're making him sound like some kind of evil genius."

Whitlowe shrugged. "If the shoe fits, Your Honor."

CHAPTER 11
Pre-Arraignment

There was a knock at Joe's hospital room door and a flurry of commotion as several people entered. Joe flipped the TV off and relaxed to watch the ensuing commotion.

The first man was a judge, based on his robes, which looked odd and completely out of place in the hospital room. The judge was a portly fellow who looked sickly and constipated. Behind him, two women and a man entered, and they seemed to answer to the judge. The man was a bailiff—armed and wearing a uniform—and Joe was surprised to recognize him. It was Will Duff, a regular member of Joe's old coffee klatch, a daily gathering of older folks at the local McDonald's in Cooper's Mill.

Duff nodded at Joe but said nothing, and Joe got the impression that they weren't supposed to talk. The judge instructed Duff and one of the women to get more chairs from the hallway and arrange them in a particular way.

A second man followed the judge and his people. He was Whitlowe, the county prosecutor, who had visited earlier. Last into the room was Joe's attorney, Ned Tomlinson, who pulled a chair over and sat next to Joe.

Soon things were all arranged to the judge's liking—he and his people sat in chairs along the wall by the window, facing Joe and his lawyer. The prosecutor sat next to Joe's lawyer. The bailiff stood guard by the door even though there was already a police officer outside. It all seemed awkward to Joe, but he wasn't going to say anything. Instead, the following popped into his head: "Pretend inferiority and encourage your opponent's arrogance." There was a Sun Tzu quote for almost any occasion.

"Okay, let's get started," the judge said. "Tomlinson, can you do the introductions?"

Joe's attorney stood and introduced himself, spelling his name. One of the women, the court reporter, had set up recording equipment and a stenography machine and was taking notes. Tomlinson went around and introduced the people in the room: Judge Meyer Wilson, who would oversee the trial; County Prosecutor Kevin Whitlowe; the court reporter and a clerk of court, both of whom worked for Wilson; and finally, the bailiff, Will Duff. Joe's mind wandered during the introductions and remembered that Duff had been a bailiff for nearly a decade, often speaking about his more interesting cases to the coffee klatch.

"Good, thanks," Judge Wilson said. "Clerk?"

The woman clerk stood and spoke. "All come near to this place to hear case number CC 11-5334, State of Ohio versus Joe Hathaway, now called for pre-arraignment. Counsels, state your name for the record."

Tomlinson stood and said his name. He also gave the name of his firm and the mailing address. Joe saw the court reporter typing it all down.

"Good afternoon," Judge Wilson said. "I am informed that charges have been formally filed against Mr. Hathaway. Mr. Whitlowe, is this true?"

Whitlowe nodded. "Yes, Your Honor."

Judge Wilson looked at Joe and Tomlinson. "Was Mr. Hathaway informed of his rights at the time of his arrest?"

"Yes, Your Honor," Tomlinson answered. Joe kept his mouth shut. Technically, they read him his rights after he woke up from his surgery.

"Okay, well just for the record, let's go through them again." Judge Wilson read Joe his rights—the right to remain silent, that any statement he made could be used against him, blah-blah-blah. Anyone who had seen a cop show in the last thirty years knew the Miranda warning by heart.

"Do you understand your rights as the Court has presented them to you?"

"Yes, we understand," Tomlinson said for them both.

Judge Wilson looked at Joe. "Mr. Hathaway?"

Joe spoke up, his voice a croak. "Yes, Your Honor. I understand."

"Good," Judge Wilson said, glancing at Whitlowe. "Are we ready with charges?"

"Yes, Your Honor," Whitlowe said, standing. "I sent the final charges over this morning."

The clerk turned and handed a folder to the judge, who opened it and scanned the contents while waving Whitlowe back down into his plastic seat.

"No need to stand, Counsel. There's not enough room in here for you and Ned to be popping up all the time." The judge looked at Joe's lawyer. "Mr. Tomlinson? Are you prepared to waive the probable cause hearing in this instance?"

"No, sir, we will not waive the hearing. We've only just received the indictment this morning and haven't had time to review—"

"All right," the judge said, sighing and putting up his hand. "We can fix that. Mr. Whitlowe, your indictment indicates that you have probable cause to go to trial. Is this true?"

"Yes, Your Honor."

The judge waited for more information, looking at Whitlowe expectantly. "Well? Let's begin the probable cause hearing. Present your evidence."

"I object, Your Honor," Tomlinson said, standing suddenly. Joe had no idea what was happening. "We're not prepared for a preliminary hearing or to make a plea in this case."

The judge nodded. "I understand, Counselor, but we need to move things along. The county is under the obligation to either charge Mr. Hathaway with a crime and begin a trial or set him free."

Tomlinson waved around at the hospital room. "We understand, Your Honor, but shouldn't proceedings be held in an official courtroom? We don't have room for additional counsel, or to call character wit—"

"There will be time for that at trial," Judge Wilson said. "Due to his injuries, these proceedings cannot yet be held in a courtroom. The pre-arraignment has ended, and the Court sees no reason why it can't move on to arraignment. Your objection is noted," he said, nodding at the court reporter, then back to Joe's counsel. "Anything else?"

Tomlinson shook his head and glanced at Joe. "No, Your Honor."

The judge pointed at Whitlowe. "Proceed."

"Yes, Your Honor." Whitlowe cleared his throat, flipped open a folder, and began reading. "We have what we consider to be probable cause in this matter. At the time of his arrest and detainment, the accused was found in possession of the instrument of violence outlined in the charges. Several witnesses encountered him after the attempted crimes and will come forward to testify, including those he tried to harm. And he was arrested upon his extrication from the vehicle. He was gravely wounded and has been in this hospital since the accident. He also has been under arrest by a police officer at all times. The county is ready and prepared to move to trial."

Joe could see Judge Wilson reading along with the paperwork. Clearly this was all already written down somewhere. Joe looked at Tomlinson, who was reading his own copy. At the top of the page, it read "Criminal Court Complaint," and it listed the items Whitlowe was covering.

The judge turned to Tomlinson. "Counsel, your response?"

Tomlinson stood. "We object to this proceeding and move for an official probable cause hearing. We would need to call witnesses to refute the accusations and to question the chain of evidence..."

The judge put his hand up. "Okay, Mr. Tomlinson, I understand. But that's what we're doing right now, seeing if the prosecution has probable cause. Do you have any comments?"

"No, Your Honor."

"Then I am ruling that the prosecution has probable cause and can move to officially charging the accused."

"Your Honor, I'd like to object again," Tomlinson said.

"Noted," the judge replied with a smile. "Prosecutor, what are the official charges in the indictment?"

Whitlowe stood and read. "The charges listed in the complaint are three counts of attempted murder, carried out by Mr. Hathaway, on or about April 27 of this year, upon three persons of good health located in greater Miami County in the state of Ohio."

The judge waited for the court reporter to finish typing, then looked at Tomlinson.

"How does the accused plead?"

"The defense would like to delay asserting a plea until the Court can convene proceedings in a proper venue."

Judge Wilson looked at him. "So, no plea is to be entered? Is that what you're saying?"

"Yes, Your Honor," Tomlinson said. "Or the Court may enter a plea on the defendant's behalf. But we aren't interested in moving forward without the county meeting the lowest standard of proof. Without a proper probable cause hearing, which allows for testimony, we cannot enter a plea."

Judge Wilson sat back in his plastic hospital chair and shook his head.

"It is the Court's opinion that the prosecution has shown probable cause to warrant a trial. The Court enters a plea of 'not guilty' on behalf of the defendant in all three counts." He flipped through a small calendar among his papers. "The trial will commence on Monday, July 2, in the Court's chambers in Troy, Ohio, at 9:00 a.m." Judge Wilson looked up at both attorneys. "Any objections?"

Tomlinson started to say something else, but Joe gently grabbed his arm. "You've made your point," he whispered.

"Let the record show that the prosecution and defense agreed to the date and location," the judge said. "Pretrial conference will be held on June 26 at a time and location of the defendant's choosing. Will that work?"

Again, only silent nods from the two lawyers. Joe had no idea about the different stages of the trial, but it all seemed to be moving very quickly. Without more information, he wouldn't be able to be much help in his defense.

"Okay, then the Court stands adjourned."

The judge and his people stood, and the bailiff held the door open for them as they exited. Will Duff walked over and helped Whitlowe carry the plastic chairs back out into the hallway. The last person to leave was the court reporter, who spent a few minutes packing up her stenography machine and the tape recorder. She nodded at Tomlinson as she exited.

"Okay, that went fast," he said, turning to Joe. "Judge Wilson is obviously in a hurry."

Joe nodded. "I figured that out. What was all that 'pre-arraignment' and 'probable cause' stuff?"

"Usually the pretrial stuff is spread out over a week or so, and the prosecution has to prove they have enough evidence to go to trial. Sometimes it's like a minitrial, with witnesses and everything. Afterward, the judge decides if there is probable cause. Then the indictment comes down and we enter a plea. Judge Wilson wanted to do it all today."

"Is that bad?"

"No, not really. He just wants to get us onto the docket ASAP. Before we came in, Judge Wilson was grilling your doctor about your physical condition and if you were fit to stand trial."

Joe nodded. "Can't come soon enough, I'm telling you. But I'm going to need help. Can you hire me a personal assistant? I need a nurse or someone to help me get around."

"Yes, absolutely," Tomlinson said. "Dr. Wheeler suggested a trained EMT, and the Court approved. They can also monitor your medical condition when you're away from the hospital."

Joe nodded. "Great. I need someone to fetch stuff for me—newspapers, books. And I don't want cops pushing my wheelchair or 'escorting' me to physical therapy."

Tomlinson nodded. "We'll get you someone."

"Female. Young, with lots of energy," Joe said. "She's going to be running all over the place. What about transportation to and from the courtroom?"

"The county will handle that. There is no way they're letting you out of their sight. Sorry."

Joe nodded. It had been too much to hope for. But he could work with it. Joe already had one helper lined up, someone Tomlinson and the others didn't know about. A young man named Trapper had helped Joe out in the past, and they had been communicating anonymously over social media, setting things up. But over the course of the trial, there would be lots of coming and going, and Trapper would be too conspicuous. Joe needed a minder to get him around and to fetch things for him. She would come in very handy, especially if she were easy on the eyes.

Joe considered the possibilities and smiled. "That will be fine."

CHAPTER 12
Caught Up

Twenty-four hours later and Frank's mood had not improved a whit.

It was late on Tuesday afternoon and he was back at his desk again, nearly ready to knock off for the day. Frank was bored and tired.

He was digging into an old cold case, a double murder from the late 1980s. It had also taken place in extreme southern Alabama, near the border with Florida. It had gone unsolved, obviously, and everyone involved with the case had shuffled off this mortal coil. No one cared whether or not this case was solved except for Frank, and even he didn't think he'd be able to move the case forward. At least someone was trying, right? He'd been revisiting this case off and on for the last month, researching and requesting obscure reports or pieces of information. So far, he'd found nothing.

Frank's latest theory was a huge stretch, but he was willing to look anywhere. He was trying to connect the murders to the infamous Jack Terrington. The dates didn't line up at all, but Frank kept checking anyway.

Everyone involved in law enforcement in the U.S. in the last twenty years knew about Terrington. He was one of the most famous serial killers in American history, right up there with John Wayne Gacy and The Zodiac Killer. Everyone in the country had probably heard of Jack Terrington, the mysterious killer who wandered the country in the eighties and nineties in his white van, maiming and torturing and killing scores of victims.

Terrington's case was now studied at police academies across the country—and around the world—as a textbook example of how investigators in separate jurisdictions can fail to put clues together. It was often used as a prime lesson in the importance of interagency communication.

It had taken a strange confluence of unconnected events—a massive hurricane, a breakthrough in computer technology at the FBI, and a town full of curious folks—to finally catch Terrington.

After the case had been broken, the lead FBI agent on the case, Julie Noble, had spent the next four years gathering and publishing information on the case and the notorious killer. She reconstructed his "tour of death" using eyewitness accounts and early surveillance, along with the most disturbing part of the story: the man's "trophies." Terrington was a twisted creature, for certain, and went out of his way to collect and preserve portions of many of his victims. And, while gruesome, those trophies ended up serving a truly useful, albeit unintended, purpose: DNA testing positively identified many of the victims, closing scores of missing persons and murder cases across the country. Twenty years later, nearly every date of Terrington's "tour" was accounted for, enabling law enforcement to verify nearly every part of his travels and tie dozens of missing person's cases back to him.

Frank had the textbook of Terrington's career propped open on his desk in front of him, trying to line up the dates with the double homicide in 1987. But the dates just didn't work—Terrington was supposedly in Seattle between 1982 and 1990. It was the time of the famous Green River killings, either the work of Terrington or an accomplice, who later went to jail for the crimes. But it didn't look like Terrington was anywhere near Alabama during that stretch of years.

Finding nothing helpful in the textbook, Frank skimmed Agent Julie Noble's famous book on the case, *Angel of Death*, published a few years after the investigation. It recounted her story. Frank searched for instances when Terrington had traveled outside of his kill zones, even for short periods of time. Noble had most of the dates accounted for, especially those when Terrington was in Seattle. Frank jotted dates down, calculating travel times, but couldn't figure out how to make it work. He couldn't place Terrington in the area, and unless something else popped up in his research, Frank would be able to officially eliminate Terrington as a suspect in the case.

He was typing up his notes when his cell phone rang. Frank set the books aside and pulled the phone out of his pocket, answering it before looking at the display.

"Hello?"

"Hi, I'm looking for Mr. Frank Harper?"

"You've got him."

"Hi, Mr. Harper. I'm Bridget Turner with the Miami County Prosecutors Office. I understand that we reached out to you a few weeks ago about the upcoming trial for Mr. Hathaway. Is that right?"

Frank sat back. "Yes, I got the postcard. Is it going to trial? I thought he was too injured."

"It looks like we're prepping to get started, sir," the young woman said. "Hathaway has recovered enough for Judge Wilson to set the trial date, July 2. I'd like to check your availability." She also went on to explain that the case should take four or five business days and he would need to remain in Troy and available, in case of any redirect or further questions. In addition, court would not be held on July 4 because it was a holiday.

Frank looked at his calendar. Nothing on this end but dusty file folders and meals alone in his small apartment without even a cold beer to keep him company.

"Mr. Harper, are you there?"

"Oh, sorry. Yes, that works. Do I arrange for a hotel?"

"Oh, we'll do all that. Dorothy from this office will coordinate that— the county will cover the cost, of course."

"I'm happy to drive."

"Oh, no, that's okay. We'll fly you in. I'll also have her fax over the summons for your records. Can I get that number?"

He gave her the number, smiling at the notion. Did anyone other than the government still use fax machines?

"One other thing—I'm assisting County Prosecutor Whitlowe on the case, and he's asked me to go over each witnesses' testimony. When would be a good time for me to call? We need about a half hour."

"Any time is good," Frank said. "After work hours, if that's okay. Tonight or tomorrow night works."

The young woman thanked him and ended the call. Frank went back to flipping through the Terrington books. They included maps, victim accounts, and a full chapter on the end of the case, when Agent Noble and a group of civilians managed to track Terrington down, and a civilian finally cornered and killed him in a local shopping mall.

Detective Murray turned from his desk and looked over at Frank. "Anything?"

Frank shook his head and pointed at the book. "No, but I always check. What about you? Any progress?"

Murray held up the folder he was working on. "This is one I keep coming back to. You have those, too? This one feels like it's one phone call away from being solved."

"Yeah, I have those," Frank nodded. "I think we all do."

CHAPTER 13
The Hive

"Careful."

Tyler Danvers looked up at his father. Tyler could barely see the man's eyes in the heavy white mask that covered his entire head, but the boy could see his father nodding. His dad was holding up a thin wooden frame covered with bees and a thick layer of honeycombs that hung from it. He also held the smoker, a small metal pot that gave off smoke, waving it around to get the bees to relax and move away from both of their protective suits. The smoker calmed the bees, scattering them, or they would have likely swarmed while the man and boy extracted the honeycomb from the hive.

"There," his father Jim said. "You've got it."

The young boy, using the wide tongs designed for just such a task, broke away a three-inch piece of the honey-drenched comb. The tongs were difficult to manage in his gloved hands, but Tyler had done this before. In fact, he'd even practiced at home, using kitchen tongs and oven mitts to pick items up off the floor.

"Good," Jim said. "Careful."

The boy lifted the broken comb and smiled. His father stepped in, holding out an empty glass jar with his own gloved hands. The young boy turned the comb and lowered it into the jar, two dozen bees still swarming over the gooey mass, which dripped with honey. The boy opened the tongs, letting go, and stepped back.

Jim waited, moving the glass jar around to shake the bees out while replacing the wooden rack, sliding it back down into the hive. When the bees were gone, he reached over to the top of the hive and picked up a round metal lid, screwing it onto the jar.

"Great job, Tyler. Great job."

Tyler nodded, happy. It was a rare chance to spend time with his father. Since the divorce, he'd been seeing less and less of him. His father rarely let him help with the bees and had never let him gather the honeycombs.

Mr. Danvers set the jar down into a basket filled with other similar jars, counting them. "That's it for now. Close up the hive and we'll get out of here."

Tyler turned and used his gloved hands to pick up the cover and lay it across the top of the hive, sealing it. Honey-producing beehives were artificially designed to replicate a real bee hive, while at the same time, making it easier to extract the honey-filled combs. Most man-made beehives used a series of racks that hung from a frame to do this while also giving the bees a place to live and grow.

The pair walked away from the hives and crossed the wide field, heading back to their truck. Behind them, the cluster of white wooden hives stood near a rotten tree that pointed at the sky like a broken spear. This grassy field stretched from the river to another yard next door. Tyler had often been curious about the neighboring property. It was an abandoned farmhouse with a back yard ringed with a tall, foreboding wooden fence that his father never allowed him to explore.

"Be careful, son," his father said, pointing at the ground. "Step where I step. Avoid the holes."

Tyler nodded and followed closely, treading in the footsteps of his father.

"Why does the smoke relax them?" Tyler asked as they walked.

"Not sure," his father said. "It just does."

"People like the honeycombs?"

"They do," his father said. "It's not where most of the honey comes from, though. But people like to buy the combs in glass jars. Later, in the fall, all the hives will be emptied of combs and the honey extracted off-site. If you don't, the bees will get angry and swarm."

They walked to the truck and Tyler waited for his father to take off his head covering, called a veil, before he removed his own. It was hot and sweaty in the veils, but they were better than being stung. The kids at his school knew that he gathered honey with his father and that was always the first question they asked: how often do you get stung?

Rarely, he told them. You had to wear light colored shirts, like white or tan. Black clothes made the bees mad, so they wore white, long-sleeved shirts and jeans. Gathering honey was more exciting than it sounded.

With his veil off, Tyler looked around at the hives behind them, six of them on stands in the middle of the field by the broken tree. His father rented the field from a local farmer who was letting it go fallow. Between this field and others, his father operated several hives in the rural parts of Miami County, many in low fields near the river.

"How many hives do you have now?"

His father looked up at the sky and counted as he set the basket of honeycomb jars in the back. Once they were cleaned and labeled, they'd be ready for sale at local farmers' markets. "Twenty-four, six at each field. Wish I had more, but the hives are expensive. And I've lost some hives—the bees aren't doing as well as they have in year's past. Something is bothering them."

"Disease?"

"Maybe. It's been hot, so maybe they're sluggish." His father folded his veil, and Tyler did the same.

"You mind if I run down to the river?"

"No, not today," his father said, climbing into his truck. Tyler got in too. "The yellow jackets are out in full. This field, especially," he said, pointing at the holes in the peaceful looking stretch of grass.

Tyler looked. "They live in the ground?"

Jim nodded. "I counted six holes. They build their nests in fields like this, but always underground. You don't want to step in one of those. And the nests are hard to get rid of—I have to burn them out."

"What?"

"It's dangerous, but it kills them in the ground. Last year, I got called to a construction site up in Troy. Massive nest in the ground. They kept burying it, and the yellow jackets would just dig their way out. They called me in to get rid of it." Tyler knew his father was considered a local expert and was often hired by people in the area to remove bees or wasps. Mr. Danvers had a standing contract with animal control departments in several area towns for similar situations.

Jim looked up through the truck windows at the sky—there was a line of dark clouds coming in. "Got time for one more? I want to be stocked up for the market Saturday in Cooper's Mill."

Tyler nodded, happy for the time with his father. Tyler's mother was always saying mean things about his father, but Tyler wasn't sure they were true.

"Sounds good."

CHAPTER 14
A New Direction

Frank Harper was back at work at his desk, referencing his handwritten case list. He was working on nineteen cases right now, listed in two columns on his yellow pad. The first column read "Work On," his list of the twelve cases that looked like they might go somewhere. Some were old enough that the "new" DNA techniques might make a difference. The 1987 double murder was at the top of that list, along with the case that Murray apparently couldn't let go of.

The second column read "Close Out," a list of seven cases that couldn't be moved forward. He and Murray had looked into each of them and found no way of moving them forward. Frank had marked the cases for "retirement" and prepared the batch of folders to go to storage—but Collier had to sign off first. With a sigh, he stood and picked up the stack of folders and walked reluctantly to Collier's office, knocking on the closed door.

"Come on in," the voice inside said.

Frank pushed the door open and entered the small office. It was decorated with pictures on the walls of famous people from the Birmingham area. His boss, Tim Collier, was a hometown boy, born and bred, and took pride in his "local-ness." Front and center was a photo of Collier with the current governor of Alabama.

"Sir, here is that stack I talked about," Frank said, placing the pile of folders on Collier's desk. "These seven can go to Montgomery, then come back out in two years and get looked at again." All the retired cold cases were on a regular "review" schedule. Each jacket was marked with a date in the future for it to be retrieved and assigned to a detective for follow-up. Every time Frank marked a case with a "revisit" date in the future, he wondered if he'd still be working at the ABI when the cases came back up.

Collier picked up the stack and flicked through it. "Okay, Frank. Thanks."

"One other thing sir—I got that summons. They just called."

Collier nodded again. "What's the date?"

"Two weeks out. They need me up there July 2. They said the trial should only take four or five days, but it'll be split over the holiday."

Collier moved his computer mouse and checked his screen, probably looking at the department calendar. Frank had already added his days out. "That should work. Should be a slow week, with the Fourth on Wednesday."

"Okay, thanks. And thanks for understanding." Frank turned to leave.

"Hold up a second. Have a seat," Collier said, pointing at the chair in front of his desk.

Reluctantly, Frank sat. It was never good when Collier wanted to talk. It used to be that Collier wanted to rip him a new one for not keeping on top of his caseload. Or for coming in drunk. Frank had done that more times than he'd like to admit. But over the past few weeks, Collier had started complimenting him. Complimenting might be too strong of a word, but Collier had noted Frank's work progress and dedication.

Frank hadn't mentioned how bored he was, or how he (and every other government employee) was counting the number of days until retirement. A few people on other floors had their number written on a post-it note on their computer. The really excited ones wrote it on their calendars, counting backwards until the end.

But since Frank had cleaned up his act, he and Murray had been closing or "retiring" cases at a fast pace, and Collier was happy.

"So, after these seven," Collier pointed at the stack of cold cases as Frank sat, "my count says you've got twelve left."

It seemed crazy, but it was true. Actively deciding to "retire" the majority of their cold cases that couldn't be helped by modern investigative techniques had made a serious dent in the total number of cold cases. Frank realized they might have them all done in the next month or two. Done, as in solved or retired.

Like, nothing else to work on.

Frank nodded. "Of the twelve current cases, we're waiting on DNA on seven. The state lab is backed up. Some of that is our fault," Frank said with half a smile.

"That's a great problem to have," Collier said, straightening the keyboard on his desk.

"If you want, I could send a couple to the big forensics lab in Atlanta. They can turn stuff around a lot faster, but it's an outside expense," Frank said. Collier would know what that meant—any work that stayed in Alabama was charged against the state budget, and sometimes the in-state work was done gratis as a sign of cooperation between agencies. Outside agencies or states cost actual money. "It's your call, of course."

"And after those cases?"

Frank shrugged. "Well, the next set of reviews won't come around until January 2013, six months from now. I guess I can start looking at those again, once our caseload is gone." He didn't sound thrilled about it and realized how uninterested he must have sounded.

Collier didn't say anything. Instead, he stared at the pile of folders that Frank had brought in.

"Frank," Collier began, then looked up. "Are you happy here? I mean, are you happier than the last time we had this exact conversation?"

Not the question Frank was expecting.

"Yeah, I'm enjoying getting us all caught up," Frank said. "It's like a game. And I've been sober now for a while and able to focus."

"I can tell," Collier said, nodding at the folders. "But that's not what I asked. Once you're caught up, are you really going to feel like going back and reopening the same cases, over and over? Even with the 'new' cold cases we get monthly, it seems like you're going to be bored."

Frank didn't know what to say. Clean and sober was hard for him, but he was hanging in there. For his daughter Laura and her son Jackson. And for himself, to a lesser degree. He remembered that feeling of floating. Would he ever forget that feeling, the bourbon and Oxycontin combination, that made him feel like the king of the world? Like he was on the front of the Titanic. Sometimes he missed that feeling of infallibility, of floating along, moving through life without a care. Even with people shooting at you.

Frank wasn't sure of anything anymore. Once he'd gotten off the pills, and the need for alcohol had faded, Frank didn't want any more painkillers. Ever. It was a weight that had been lifted from his shoulders, a doorway through which he could walk and find escape.

After a few seconds, Frank nodded. "Yeah, I am bored," he said. "The cold cases are interesting, but they're nothing like active cases."

"Like up in Ohio?"

"Yeah," Frank said, looking at Collier. "Those were exhilarating. Felt like I was alive again."

Collier turned and organized the folders and other papers on his desk, thinking. Frank waited, unsure of what else to say. He felt like a Catholic in confession. An awkward silence hung between them for a long time.

"You might think you're a cypher, difficult to read," Collier said finally. "But you're not that deep, Frank. It's obvious you hate it here. These cases aren't for you," he said, nodding at the stack of folders on the desk between them. "Sober, you can do these in your sleep, right?"

Frank nodded slowly, unsure of what to say. "Maybe it was being back out in the field, working active cases, chasing the bad guys," he said with a half-smile. "Literally. But I thought I was done with all of that, especially after Katrina."

Collier turned and picked up a different folder, this one green in color. Frank noticed it had Frank's name on the label. "I did a little research. Your four-year anniversary here with the ABI is coming up next month."

"Really?"

Collier nodded. "Before that, you did twenty-one years with the NOPD."

Frank shook his head. "Yeah, but we...we didn't part on the best of terms," he said.

"The few years you were a detective?"

Frank nodded. He was unsure where Collier was going.

"How did things end?"

"Badly," Frank said. "After Katrina, I was having a lot of trouble dealing with things."

"But things are better?"

Frank nodded. "Getting there."

"I don't think you should be working cold cases anymore," Collier said matter-of-factly. "I hope you can appreciate how hard that is for me to say, considering your stellar close rate over the last few weeks. God knows it's making me look good. But it's not worth you being miserable."

Frank's mind raced. Was he getting fired? Was he being let go, or transferred?

"You want me...to be a cop again?"

Collier shrugged. "Is that what you want? I can talk to the B-ham PD and see if we get you back on active duty."

"I don't know."

"You'd probably have to start as a junior detective, work the grunt work. No one wants a know-it-all to come in and upset the apple cart."

Frank nodded, lost in thought. The last few minutes of conversation whirled in his head.

"Of course, there are other options," Collier said, tapping on the green folder.

Frank looked up at him. "What do you mean?"

"You parted dishonorably from NOPD. What happened?"

"Alcohol on the job. Other things."

"Sounds familiar. You only had a few years left before you would have earned a full pension."

Frank shook his head. He remembered a similar conversation with Chief King up in Cooper's Mill, but he had been mistaken on some of the details of Frank's ill-fated career.

"When the writing on the wall was clear, I 'retired' from the NOPD. I left with no retirement or pension. Got a few weeks of severance, but that was it. Money was tight. I applied around to a few places in the south, and the ABI was kind enough to hire me."

"Well, I had a talk with them. Did you know your old boss is still there?"

"Peterson?"

"Yup," Collier said. "He was happy to hear how you were doing."

Frank thought about his final months with the NOPD. They had put up with him for as long as they could, until he'd become a liability.

"I just assumed that retirement or a pension was off the table forever."

"Nothing's forever," Collier said. "You should have figured that out by now. Peterson had great things to say about your early career, and he was happy to hear you were back up to full speed."

"Took long enough," Frank said.

"Doesn't matter now. He wasn't surprised at all by your closure rate. Peterson said you were a top-notch detective during the brief windows of time where you...hang on, let me quote him." Collier flipped open the green folder and read from notes he must have taken during his call with Peterson. "'Frank knew what he was doing, that was for damn sure,' and he was a great asset to the detective's division 'in those rare moments when he gave half a shit,'" Collier said with a smile. "Colorful."

"You have no idea," Frank said. "He cursed me out like no one else ever had. Before or since."

"We talked about how you left that position and the union rules related to that. I think we worked out a way to restore your pension and retirement. Not all of it, but half. Still, the money's not too shabby, almost what you make here."

Frank felt a weird sensation crawl up the back of his neck. That part of his life, all those years with the NOPD, they were a distant, weird memory.

"Wow," Frank said. "I don't know what to say. But I thought you were talking about going back on active duty. You want me to retire? And what about you and Murray?"

"Don't say anything," Collier said. "It's still all coming together— Peterson needed to pull your file and review it with the union reps. But, if you're interested, it looks like you might be able to retire. Sergeant Peterson agreed to 'update' your file to an honorable separation from the NOPD due to the work you've done lately, both here and up in Ohio."

"Ohio?"

"Oh, I also spoke to Chief King. He had some very nice things to say about you. King agreed to write two letters of commendation to Sergeant Peterson on your behalf. For your NOPD files. Between that and your work here over the last four years, and especially these last two months, it's all good." Collier set the folder aside. "As soon as it's all final, I'll let you know. Of course, you're welcome to stay as long as you like," he said. "But I think we both know you'd rather be somewhere else."

Frank wasn't sure what to say. "I feel weird. Like I'm being let go again."

Collier shook his head and moved some pens around on his desk. "No, it's nothing like that. I've been looking for a change. Murray too. At his last review, he said he wanted to move. Florida, I think."

Frank didn't know any of this.

"Oh, don't worry about it," Collier said. "I can tell you're surprised. But I've been wanting to leave for a while," he said, glancing at the pictures on the wall of local luminaries. "I'm actually thinking of running for office. Maybe city council, or a ward seat on the mayor's advisory board. So, if you decide to leave, you won't be upsetting the apple cart. With all the cases you and Murray are closing, I've been talking to the higher-ups. Might be able to mothball this division entirely," he said with a smile. "They would love that, and it would look great on my resume. Closing this division, saving the government money, all that."

Frank nodded.

Collier continued. "Frank, you've been happier in these past few weeks than I've ever seen you. And your visits to Ohio are the reason, I think. You're better for them. And so are a bunch of other people, including those two girls you managed to find."

Frank sat quietly, his mind racing.

Collier looked at him. Finally, he leaned forward and put both hands on his desk. "If I were you, I'd retire on half-pension. Take the money and move up to Ohio. You'll be happier."

It was a string of words that Frank was scared to even consider. And Collier made it sound so simple. Just move. Pack up and leave. But it wasn't that easy, was it? His whole life was here: his job, his home, his life since leaving New Orleans.

Frank stood and thanked him, heading back to his desk. Murray was gone—probably stepped out for a coffee. Frank had the outer offices to himself and sat back at his desk. He looked at the few remaining cases sitting in a pile in the middle of his desk, but he didn't reach for them.

Retirement? Like actual retirement? And a half pension out of nowhere? He had no idea it was even an option. But the money wasn't the whole story—an official retirement from the NOPD meant he hadn't left in disgrace. Just the idea of not having that dark cloud hanging over him made Frank giddy. And he was the kind of person who was rarely giddy.

Questions swirled in his mind. Did he belong here or up in Ohio with his daughter and grandson? Could he get work with Chief King, or maybe talk to Sergeant Roget with the Dayton PD? Or could he freelance and become a private detective? Or should he move back to New Orleans and pick up where he left off?

Frank shook his head. Too much to think about, too many notions to keep in his head at once. He turned and found his yellow pad. He flipped to a blank sheet and grabbed a pen. He needed to make a new list.

Frank had a lot to think about.

Chapter 15
Driving

It was early on Friday morning, June 22, and Monty Robinson was driving west on Main Street, heading for McDonald's. He was coming straight from work and was tired, but he didn't feel like going home yet. A few cups of coffee and some breakfast would really hit the spot. At least he was guaranteed some lively conversation.

Monty liked his peace and quiet, but he also liked chatting with people. His job didn't really afford him much socializing. He was a night guard at a local construction site. Every night, Monty was mostly alone with his magazines and a television. And almost no one ever visited—he'd had one guy come by last fall, and that guy had gotten jumped in the parking lot and abducted. Monty had gotten questioned by the police and written up by his bosses for not paying attention.

Work wasn't that bad—at least he got to watch TV. He loved the old movies, the classic black and whites from the forties and fifties. Sometimes he could get into modern films—that one Batman movie with Heath Ledger was a favorite. But Monty preferred the old films. Fewer explosions, better writing.

Most people didn't know old movies well. If he did the standard "quote a movie line" thing in casual conversation, few people recognized anything before 1970. And he missed most of the pop culture references to current films. It made him feel like Captain America in that one Avengers movie. At one point in the film, someone referenced something from *The Wizard of Oz*, and Captain America had smiled, saying "I got that reference!"

Working the night shift gave Monty unlimited access to the classics, unspooled all night every night on channels like TCM and AMC. The good ones, like *Rio Bravo* or *Bridge on the River Kwai* or *Citizen Kane*. Good films filled with sparkling dialog and great actors and great locations. And exactly zero computer-animated robots.

Monty changed lanes and slowed to make the turn onto Garber Drive, seeing the McDonald's sign off to his left. He met a group of locals at McDonald's most mornings for coffee. It didn't bother him that he was the only black person in the coffee klatch. Hell, half the time, he was the only black person in the whole town.

Cooper's Mill was pretty white. It was just something you got used to. He loved it when the conversation turned to something race-related and everyone looked at him like they were asking permission. For a while, whenever anyone said anything about President Obama, or any black person for that matter, they would glance at Monty and say "sorry." He'd put a stop to that a long time ago with a lengthy diatribe about the president and how Monty personally felt about the man.

To be sure, it was a good thing that a black man had finally been elected president. A great thing. And the white people he knew mostly agreed. Hell, a bunch of them must have voted for the man. But, as the first term passed, and Obama seemed to get less and less done, Monty grew frustrated. Black or white, it didn't matter. Obama had come into his office with a historic mandate for change, and he was in the unique position to fundamentally improve race relations for every person in the country.

Instead, the president was the guy who had invented the whole absurd concept of "leading from behind." Was that even physically possible? Monty had hoped he would make things better in America, starting with race relations. If anything, they'd gotten worse. Monty wanted to see things improve, especially for black America. Lower the unemployment rate, improve the schools. To Monty, "improvement" didn't mean tripling the number of black people on food stamps. It meant raising up the black community, improving the standard of living, bringing in jobs, and instilling in the community and the police a sense of mutual respect.

Monty shook his head and turned into the McDonald's parking lot and parked. He slid across the bench seat and climbed out of the passenger side, because the driver's side door didn't work anymore.

A few more months of saving and he could afford a new car, Monty hoped. The old Mercury Montego was on its last legs, and the caved-in driver's door only made it more frustrating. It was white and huge, and the front hood went on forever. Sometimes, he imagined small planes landing on it like an aircraft carrier. The Montego was one of those cars that looked like it was having trouble staying in one piece—as if it wasn't really a car but just a collection of car parts, all moving in the same direction at the same time.

Inside, he ordered his food and coffee and made his way over to the coffee klatch, where his friends sat, discussing the news of the world and politics. They greeted him warmly. They were discussing the upcoming trial of Joe Hathaway. Several expressed their surprise at how quickly the trial was coming together.

Will Duff, a bailiff for the courts, leaned in to comment. "They're on a ninety-day clock."

"What's that mean?" Monty asked. "And are you allowed to talk about the case?"

"Yeah, I'm not telling you anything that isn't public knowledge," Duff said. "They have 90 days from the day they arrested him to go to trial, or they have to free him."

"I'm surprised they're starting with the attempted murders and not with Tom's case," Murphy Collins said. Murphy had been a local letter carrier until he retired three years ago. He always wore the same blue windbreaker and sat where Tom Mercato used to sit.

The table grew quiet. Tom Mercato had been the group's de facto leader up until he'd apparently "run off" with his girlfriend to Chicago. Turned out he hadn't been living the high life in the Windy City. Instead, another member of the klatch, Joe Hathaway, had killed him. The whole thing was too bizarre to even contemplate.

Monty shook his head and went back to his Egg McMuffin.

"I still can't believe Joe did it," Will said. "I mean, Tom was always riding him, picking on Joe. But killing him? That's crazy."

Monty nodded. "I knew they didn't get along, but damn."

Janette Duff spoke up. Will Duff's wife was a portly woman and was usually much more talkative. Something must be bothering her. "What if...what if Joe didn't kill Tom?"

Monty and the others looked at her.

"I mean, we know they found his DNA in Joe's freezer," she continued. "But that stuff can get planted, right? Joe disliked Tom, we all knew that. But I can't believe he'd kill him. And keep him in his freezer. And then drive him out to Tom's ice shanty and drop his body into the lake. It's too crazy. Plus, Joe's an old man—how'd he drag Tom all the way across the lake? So many things about the case just don't add up."

This was a replay of yesterday's discussion, and the day before that. Most of the people at the table were sure Joe had killed Tom, but the whole story was so bizarre and convoluted that it was easy to pick it apart.

"Joe crashed his car after running away from the lake," Darren Vallone added, speaking up. Darren was thin, quiet man and a retired cabinet maker. "That ex-cop, the one that interviewed us? Harper. He was looking for Tom. Joe must have got spooked and moved the body."

Jeannette shook her head but didn't say anything.

"And there was a sled for carrying heavy stuff across the ice," Vallone added. "Right there at the camp. Wouldn't be too hard to drag it across the ice."

The discussion continued for another hour as they debated the ins and outs of the case. Apparently, the prosecutors were going to go for the attempted murder cases first because they were easier to prove. If convicted, they could lock up Joe and take their time working on Tom's murder. After that, Joe would be tried for the murder of Tom's young girlfriend. She'd been pregnant and died over near Indianapolis, so the state of Indiana would prosecute that case.

Monty refilled his coffee twice and skimmed the papers while the others talked. He liked these people, liked being around them. And they valued his opinion. It was another half hour before the group started to break up. Even retired people had things to do. But not Monty. He was the last one to leave and wasn't in any hurry to get home. Usually, shooting the breeze here at McDonald's was the best part of his day.

CHAPTER 16
Trial Prep

On Friday morning, Whitlowe held a meeting on the Hathaway case, which included his staff and Detective Barnes up from Cooper's Mill. Whitlowe liked to go around the room—it was usually the easiest way to get everyone up to speed. Dorothy took notes.

"Bridget, why don't you go first?" Whitlowe asked.

"Okay," the young woman said. "I spoke to Frank Harper twice—he's all lined up, and we went over his testimony. It's by the book. You can tell he used to be a cop."

"That's true," Detective Barnes added.

"He knows all the dates and times," Bridget continued. "His description of the chase was harrowing. The jury will love it." She went on to say she'd interviewed all the primary witnesses again and explained what they would be covering in their testimony. She warned the witnesses about potential cross-examination questions and reminded them to stay on subject when they were on the stand.

Bridget also updated them on the forensic retesting. It was being carried out by a lab in El Segundo, California. The lab was expediting their samples and results—so far, everything had matched up with the Ohio forensics lab's results.

"Good," Whitlowe said. "That's good to hear. I wasn't looking forward to asking Judge Wilson for a continuation if our forensics got delayed. Okay, the pretrial conference is this afternoon. Winn, what do you have on Tomlinson and the defense?" Winn Bartlett had been assigned to play the devil's advocate, so to speak, and come up with information on the defense team and their likely arguments.

"Tomlinson has a good record," Bartlett said, looking at his notes. "He usually goes after the evidence—in five of his last seven cases, he worked hard to get some of the forensics tossed. He's also big on chain of evidence, calling into question every transfer and lab test. But we're good on all that," Bartlett said with a nod to Detective Barnes.

"Nothing went anywhere without a triple-check," Barnes said.

"Good," Whitlowe added. "Can't be too careful."

"He's likely to argue the tests were rushed," Bartlett continued. "Or that they were tampered with. I've gone ahead and pulled some precedents on multiple forensics tests on the same samples. The case law is pretty clear on the legality of that."

Whitlowe nodded. "And their defense?"

"Evidence tampering and bad science, probably," Bartlett continued. "But we can place Hathaway at the lake, and we have the weapon and the shell casings. It's pretty cut-and-dried. I think he'll go for the ballistics and play up the jury's sympathy for Joe's injuries. He'll trot Hathaway out, let him testify and make him the victim, or at least try."

Whitlowe was jotting down notes, not that it was really necessary: Winn Bartlett would be providing him with a written strategy before the case went to trial, with the major defense arguments and pre-written passages Whitlowe could use to counter them.

"Okay, what about jury selection?"

Bartlett switched to another piece of paper. "We're ready. The Court's jury pool is full, so it could happen as early as Monday morning. Should take less than an hour. Opening statements would be Monday after lunch. Judge Wilson is notorious about speed—I've been looking through his pretrial procedures in past cases. He won't tolerate Tomlinson delaying things."

"Are you ready for voir dire?"

Bartlett nodded. "I am."

"Good," Whitlowe said. "Dorothy?"

"Everything is on schedule, Mr. Whitlowe. All the relevant papers and files are copied and ready. Mr. Harper's arrangements are set up. When we're done here, I'll set this room up for this afternoon's pretrial conference."

"Good, good," Whitlowe said. "When Tomlinson gets here, we'll cover discovery, motions, and his plea options."

"Maybe he'll plea out," Bridget spoke up.

"Doubtful," Winn said. "Based on his past cases, that's not Tomlinson's style. Do we have an offer for them?"

Whitlowe thought about it for a moment. "I haven't decided. He's charged with two cases of attempted homicide and one case of aggravated attempted homicide."

"Because Deputy Peters was law enforcement," Barnes asked.

"Right. Bridget?"

She leaned forward, jotting down numbers on a pad in front of her. "So, one first- and two second-degree felonies. Based on Wilson's last few guilty verdicts, the max for all three convictions is forty years."

Whitlowe nodded. "If Tomlinson wants to plead them all out, he might take third-degree on all three. I would be satisfied with that, as long as he got significant time. What do we offer?"

"Four years each," Bridget said, doing the math. "You could offer him that. Twelve years. With good behavior, he'd be out in eight."

"Eight years?" Barnes asked. "That's a joke."

Whitlowe leaned forward. "Yes, it is. For three attempted murders, it's not enough. But remember, this is just the appetizer. We want him locked up so we can move on to the murder trials. We're sure he killed Tom Mercato, and I'd say there's a 99% chance he killed that girl over in Indiana, right?"

Detective Barnes nodded.

"That's the death penalty," Whitlowe added. "No getting around that."

"It's true," Barnes added. "Planned it, lured him to his house, killed him, kept the body in the freezer for several weeks.

"A jury won't like that," Whitlowe said.

"Nope," Bartlett spoke up. "I read the file—Hathaway made the wife think Tom had left town. Shows premeditation, so it would be aggravated murder."

Whitlowe nodded. "And the other case is even worse. The young woman was pregnant," Whitlowe said quietly. "That's a double murder. Indiana has the death penalty as well, and they have an aggravated murder statute just like Ohio for killing a pregnant woman. He could be looking at three convictions where the punishment is death."

Barnes nodded and sat back. "I just don't like the idea of the guy pleading down like that."

"I know, I know," Whitlowe said. "But he's clever. I wouldn't be surprised if he had a plan to get away somehow. We need to keep our eye on him, and on the big picture. We want him locked up."

CHAPTER 17
Frustration

Frank sat at the small dining room table in his apartment. It had been three days since his surprising discussion with Collier, and today Collier had passed along the related paperwork. He had also poured himself a glass of bourbon. It sat next to the paperwork, untouched. Frank was excited by much of the stuff he and Collier had talked about.

According to the paperwork, Frank's twenty-one years with the NOPD and four with the ABI qualified him for a full pension, but being let go under "circumstances" knocked the full pension down to half. He could live with that. Half a pension, which came to a little over $28,000 a year, was a lot better than nothing.

But moving? That was scary. Exhilarating and frightening at the same time. Here in Birmingham, things were a known quantity. He got up, went to work, came home, went to bed. Back in the day, there would have been a few, or a dozen, drinks sprinkled in there somewhere.

Frank looked at the bourbon and felt the distant tug of camaraderie. It was like an old friend had called him up out of the blue. Just a buddy, passing through town, wanting to catch up on old times.

He picked up the tumbler and sniffed at it. The glass was clean, as were the table and the apartment, a far cry from his crackhead living conditions a few months ago.

Frank looked at the retirement paperwork and finally took a tiny sip of the bourbon. It burned its way down the back of his throat. He needed to learn how to handle his drink. He'd been a social drinker all his life. If he could get back to just drinking once in a while, he could get a handle on it.

He set the glass down and went back to the folder of papers. The half-pension was 28K. He made 33K now. Interestingly, Collier was wrong on one count—when Sergeant Peterson called back after discussing it with the policeman's union, the option for going back on active duty presented a wrinkle. Frank could take the pension and retire, or he could seek employment with any police department or detective division. But if he went on active duty, any pension would have to be deferred. Of course, there was some upside—more years on the force would increase the base pension.

It was a lot to think about. If he left the ABI, Frank had two choices. Return to the Crescent City and his old haunts. Frank had spoken to Peterson yesterday, the first time in years. Peterson had mentioned an available entry-level detective position at the NOPD. Frank could settle right back in. His heart did loops, thinking about being back in New Orleans. Back to the French Quarter and the Cafe du Monde and the sticky, sweaty summers of his youth.

Or he could move to Ohio.

Honestly, the second option scared the shit out of him. One option was a return to his youth. But the second one felt like growing up, moving on. He could settle into Cooper's Mill, maybe take a job with the local police department—Frank had worked with them in the past and got along with them well. Or he could set up shop on his own. Spend some time with Laura and Jackson, make some friends, solve some crimes.

It all sounded too easy.

He picked up the bourbon and took another sip. There was no way he was moving to Ohio without getting Laura on board. Frank knew he'd be heading up to Ohio in a week and a half to testify at the trial, but he needed to call Laura first. They had a lot to talk about.

CHAPTER 18
Pretrial Conference

The conference room door opened, and Whitlowe looked up from his phone.

"It's right through here, Mr. Tomlinson," Dorothy said, holding the door open for the defense attorney.

Whitlowe stood and walked over, greeting him. "Hello again," Whitlowe said, pointing at the conference room table. "Have a seat."

"Thanks." Tomlinson sat his bulging briefcase down and took off his coat, shaking it. Drops of water went everywhere. He apologized and hung it over the back of a chair.

"Too late for coffee?"

Tomlinson smiled. "Never."

"Dorothy, can you rustle up some? Maybe Toffee's from down the street?"

She nodded and pulled the door shut as she left.

Whitlowe smiled and went around and sat back down on the other side of the conference room table. His phone was waiting there, along with the notes from the rest of his team. The notes were covered with another folder, just in case. No need for Tomlinson to see what Whitlowe would be discussing or what he might be offering. At one end of the table, there were several large boxes stacked up, each numbered and marked "Discovery."

"Coming down out there?"

"Yeah, the highway's a mess," Tomlinson said, digging into his briefcase. "Some wreck on I-75. Sorry I'm late."

"It's fine. I love the last appointment of the day." Whitlowe launched into small talk while Tomlinson got out his papers and arranged them on the table. They talked about the weather and the recent heat wave. The power grid in southwestern Ohio was so overloaded—too many air conditioners running nonstop—the local power utilities had started rolling brownouts to cut down on power consumption.

After a few minutes, Tomlinson looked up from his papers. "Okay, I'm good. Should we get started?"

"Yes, let's. I have a list, and then we'll go through yours, okay?"

"Sounds fine."

"Okay," Whitlowe said, looking at his top sheet, a list of discussion topics they needed to cover. Dorothy had typed it up, as she always did, but he'd been doing this so long he knew it by heart. "Let's see. Witness lists." He took another sheet from a folder and handed it over. "No surprises here, I'm sure."

Tomlinson scanned it and seemed satisfied. "Here's my list. Mostly character witnesses."

Whitlowe took the paper and studied the short list of names with interest. Whitlowe wasn't worried about character references. The defendant had tried to kill three people, including a cop, right after he'd rigged a small building to sink into a frozen lake. Character witnesses. Right.

While he was reviewing the list, Dorothy entered with coffee. "Thanks, Dorothy," Whitlowe said. When she was gone, he pointed at Tomlinson's list. "Looks fine."

"And if you add anyone, I need to know forty-eight hours ahead of time," Tomlinson said.

"I know," Whitlowe replied. "We'll keep you posted. I'm guessing people will come out of the woodwork to testify against Hathaway. Right now, the whole 'freezer' thing is just rumor. The press is going to have a field day with that."

"Hmm."

Whitlowe counted that as a win. Half the time, these pretrial conferences were just jousting matches, or fishing expeditions, to see what the other side knew or how they might approach the case. "Okay, next on my list is discovery. We've boxed it all up for you," Whitlowe said, indicating the boxes on the table. "You have everything we know, and everything's been tested. We got it back, and it's all been logged."

"Okay," Tomlinson said, standing. He opened the boxes and glanced through them. "Any new evidence we need to know about?"

Whitlowe shook his head. "Nope." He checked his phone, giving Tomlinson time to check the box contents against a list he'd brought with him. After a few minutes, Whitlowe set his phone down. "So, any motions or pleas?"

Tomlinson sat down. "No motions, not yet. Are you offering a plea?"

Whitlowe shrugged. "I'm always happy to plead something out. Save the taxpayers money, get on to the next case. The complaint lists three attempted murders, one of them aggravated. Judge Wilson usually throws the book at people, gives them the maximum. You had him before?"

Tomlinson shook his head.

"If convicted, your client's looking at forty years minimum," Whitlowe said, taking a second to let it sink in. "We might take three guilty pleas of third-degree murder. At five years each, he's looking at fifteen."

Whitlowe wasn't sure what reaction he was expecting, but Tomlinson's face betrayed nothing. "I'll take it to my client."

"Okay," Whitlowe said. He looked at his list. "That's all I've got. Do you have anything?"

They talked for another ten minutes, covering minutia related to the logistics of the case—how the accused would be transferred to court, how often they would take breaks, and how the accused would appear in court. Whitlowe got what he wanted—Hathaway would not appear unless he was in a wheelchair. For that concession, Whitlowe was willing to negotiate on the transportation and other logistics.

"Oh, one last thing," Tomlinson said as he was packing up. "Hathaway wants a helper, someone not on your staff."

"Like an assistant?"

"Yup, someone under our employ to help him get to and from the courthouse, fetch his papers, make sure he's got his meds. We found a freelance EMT who would qualify."

Whitlowe thought about it for a second, then nodded. "We'll have to approve them, of course, with a background check."

"Already done," he said, passing over a copy of the person's information and background check. "But feel free to check it again. She's an EMT with the Dayton Fire Department."

"That's fine."

Tomlinson shrugged. "Well, I think that's it."

Whitlowe stood and shook his hand. "Excellent. I'll see you in there."

Tomlinson nodded and found his way out. Whitlowe sat, jotting down notes and his thoughts about the conversation. Outside, a heavy rain fell on the windows, causing thick rivulets of water to run down the wide glass panes.

CHAPTER 19
Market

It was Saturday morning and, as usual, Laura Powell was struggling to get out the door. She had her bags and purse ready and now was standing by the door, waiting. It felt like what she did with most of her life, lately.

"Come on Jackson. We gotta go! Socks and shoes!"

"Coming, Mommy!" he called from his room. "I need socks."

"We're gonna be late." She pawed through a basket by the door of her apartment, looking for something. Laura was a pretty brunette in her late thirties and wore her hair up in a tight bun. She finally found what she was looking for—a pair of Spider-Man socks. "Found them!"

A little boy emerged from the hallway. Jackson, her five-year-old son, ran toward her. "Oh, thank you!" He took the socks and plopped down on the floor to pull them on.

"Are you bringing money?"

Jackson pointed. "Oh, I forgot. My money is on my bed."

Laura smiled and walked back across the dining room/living room combination of her small apartment and turned, heading into his small bedroom. On his unmade bed, she found a wallet with "JACKSON" written across it in blue crayon. The room was a mess—clothes everywhere, a pile of toys by the open closet door. The blinds hung at an angle, half of them bent in a weird way from Jackson pulling on them to look outside.

She walked back into the living room as he was pulling on his shoes. "You have to clean that room before you have any more guests over," she said. "It's stinky."

"That's the dinosaurs."

Jackson was obsessed with dinosaurs now—everything was T. rex this and brontosaurus that. He'd been really into them since last fall, when Laura's father had visited. Frank had been out of her life for a long time, and it was nice to be reconnecting, even if the guy was a wagon full of trouble sometimes. But Frank had made quite an impression on Jackson, the grandson he'd never met until last fall.

It was good for him—Jackson didn't have many male figures in his life. And although Frank didn't have all his ducks in a row—that much was certain—at least he'd been nice to Jackson. Thoughtful and pleasant. Really, what else can you ask for in a grandfather? Frank had been back for two more visits. Each time, he brought Jackson plastic packs of dinosaurs from the local toy store.

Laura stood and watched Jackson struggle with his shoes and resisted the temptation to bend down and help. She always struggled with this. How much help should she give? She was torn between doing everything for him, which was always faster and less frustrating, or waiting for him to do it himself. How much was being helpful versus making him dependent on her? She needed Jackson to be normal when he grew up— for some reason, she was obsessed with that word. Despite her problems and the divorce, he needed to turn out normal, as if nothing bad had happened.

Jackson finally got his shoes on and stood up, smiling.

"Okay, here we go." Laura opened the front door, and they were blasted with warm air—even early, it was already warm. She followed Jackson to the car and got him strapped into the car seat she had up front. She knew he was supposed to ride in the back, but her car was a two door, and it was a pain to push the passenger seat up and back every time Jackson got in or out. Laura wondered if the cops could pull her over for it. Technically, she was breaking the law. Sometimes, when she passed a cop car, she had Jackson duck down like a common criminal. She wasn't proud of it, but there it was.

Laura went around and got in the driver's side, starting up the car and cranking the AC.

"Ready, Freddie?"

"Ready," he said. "And my name's not Freddie."

"You sure?" It was their little ritual every morning in the car. Sometimes she did this thing where she pretended she was an Uber driver and "Freddie" was her passenger and Jackson had somehow gotten into the wrong car. He usually laughed his head off, but they were in a hurry today.

Laura pulled the car out of the driveway and headed downtown. She was glad they had little rituals like that. Jackson needed them. All of that mess with her dirtbag ex-husband had been crazy enough for her to leave and strike out on her own with Jackson in tow. That was late 2007, five years ago this December. Had it really been that long?

Laura drove, glancing over at Jackson. He had been less than a year old and didn't remember any of it, of course, but growing up without a father wasn't ideal. Sometimes, Laura thought it made Jackson weak. He was quick to cry and whine, but maybe that was the way it was with every kid.

She pulled into the parking lot of the Cooper's Mill Methodist Church. Jackson's preschool was in the basement.

Across the lot, she could see the stalls of the Cooper's Mill Farmers' Market, located on Third Street between Main and Dow. The road was barricaded at both ends and the market sprawled in the middle, rows of vendors on either side. The booths and tents on the east side of the street backed against several buildings, which included the local newspaper, a lawyer's office, the chamber of commerce, and a small salon.

Laura and Jackson made their way across the lot and into the market, greeting friends and acquaintances. This was one of her favorite parts of living in Cooper's Mill. People were so friendly. She didn't even live in the downtown or see these folks often, but nearly all of them greeted her warmly and asked about Jackson and her father, who was somewhat of a local celebrity.

"Deputy Peters?"

He turned around quickly—too quickly, it turned out, and knocked over a stack of tomatoes. The tomatoes rolled off the table and bounced to the pavement, scattering in all directions. Two of them split open. The deputy scrambled to grab them, and Laura bent to help, along with the vendor and other customers. Jackson chased one tomato, which rolled nearly twenty feet and came to rest in the booth of a handmade jewelry vendor.

Finally, all the tomatoes were retrieved. Deputy Peters took out his wallet and paid for the broken ones. "Sorry about that," he said. "I'm always doing stuff like that."

"It's fine, Deputy Peters."

"Please call me Floyd, ma'am."

"Okay, Floyd. How are things?"

"Good, good," he said, resting his hand on the butt of his gun. She was pretty sure he wasn't supposed to do that. It looked like he was getting ready to draw. "How are you guys doing? Any word from Mr. Harper?"

"Not for a couple weeks," she said. "He's staying sober, I think. That time with the gang really scared him."

"That was pretty bad," Peters said, looking around. "So, what are you guys up to?"

She waved her bag. "Fruits and vegetables. In that order."

"Wow, that's very specific."

"It is," she said. "You guarding the vendors from some evil criminal?"

Peters glanced around. "Actually, we try to have someone here each week. Public outreach. Mostly, I answer questions, like 'what should I do about my neighbor's fence,' that kind of stuff."

She nodded. "Mind if I shop while we talk?"

"No, that's fine," he said, following her to a honey vendor. The rugged-looking owner, Mr. Danvers, looked like he spent a lot of time in the sun. Laura bought a jar as she and Peters chatted. Laura also bought fruits and vegetables from the Muddy Boot Farms. Peters chatted away, talking about the upcoming Hathaway case and his testimony.

"Are you nervous?"

He smiled at the ground. "A bit. I just get so tongue-tied, you know?"

An old woman stopped Deputy Peters and engaged him in a conversation about a house near hers with a long grassy lawn that needed tending. She wondered if the city could step in. Peters made a face at Laura. She smiled and mouthed the words "good luck" before waving goodbye.

Laura and Jackson investigated the other booths: food vendors, people selling crafts, a guy selling chili peppers, and a woman selling dog treats that she'd made herself. One booth was a local writer, selling and signing copies of his books. The man's daughter, Katie Greene, was hanging out at the booth. Jackson knew her—they'd gone to preschool together. The two of them chatted for a minute while Laura looked through the author's stack of books. He had apparently written a series of mysteries set in Cooper's Mill, although he had changed the name of the town.

Near the southern end of the market, a man was playing a guitar. Laura and Jackson wandered down and listened for a few minutes. Jackson bent and put fifty cents of his own money in the man's open guitar case. For a moment, Laura couldn't help but feel like the perfect parent.

"Jackson!"

They turned to see one of the booths set up at the market was for the Tiny Tots Preschool, where Jackson had gone last year. Two of the teachers were sitting in the booth, handing out fliers and signing up students for the fall semester. One of the teacher stood and walked over.

"Jackson, you're getting so big!"

"Thanks, Mrs. Wendy."

Mrs. Wendy looked at Laura. "It's only been a few months—he's so much bigger! Is he looking forward to kindergarten?"

"He's so excited," Laura said. She loved Tiny Tots, but she was glad he was out of preschool and enrolled in the Cooper's Mill public schools. For one thing, it would save her a lot of money.

"Where's he going?"

"Broadway."

"Oh, that's nice. That's close to you, right?"

"Sort of. It will be a nice walk every morning until it gets cold."

Mrs. Wendy nodded. "Well, don't get used to it—I heard they're changing up the schools soon to save money. Busing all the kids out to Nevin Coppick for kindergarten and first."

"Really? That's a bummer."

"Yup, Broadway will be just for second and third, I think. Don't hold me to it. Supposed to save them money, I heard."

"It better save them a lot. Sure is inconvenient for people who live near Broadway."

An older woman walked over and joined them. It was May Mercato, the administrator for the preschool. "Hello, Ms. Powell. Hi, Jackson."

They greeted her with smiles, and they talked for a few minutes before Jackson got bored and started asking to visit the cookie and cake vendor. Laura gestured toward the vendor and smiled.

"You two have fun, okay?" Mrs. Mercato said.

Laura and Jackson said their goodbyes and went back to their shopping. It was terrible what had happened to May Mercato. Her husband had been killed, murdered by a man who lived here in town. It was the first murder in Cooper's Mills in years. Frank had helped out with the investigation.

Jackson sampled a cookie while Laura bought one of the vendor's banana nut loaves.

"Okay, you ready? I'm dropping you at Allison's before I head to the restaurant," Laura said as they headed back to the car. Laura had taken another part-time job, this one as a waitress in a local restaurant, the Drunken Noodle, an Asian fusion restaurant near the highway. Laura was working two jobs now, but in the fall, she'd be taking advantage of Jackson being back in school and adding a third job. She worked a good number of shifts at the restaurant. She was also still cutting hair and doing the accounting at A Cut Above, a local downtown salon.

But between the two jobs and taking care of Jackson and studying for her degree in accounting, Laura was getting burned out. She was looking forward to next spring and her final semester of school, along with the CPA exam. After that, her options would improve and she could get one good job instead of three bad ones.

"I like Allison. She gives me snacks."

Laura wasn't happy about that, but she didn't say anything. At this point, she needed Allison more than Allison needed Laura's money.

CHAPTER 20
Phone Chat

Frank spent most of Saturday running errands. He'd been burning the candle at both ends at work and was exhausted, but he had a long to-do list.

First up was his car. It had been making a cacophony of weird sounds lately, and he'd been putting off getting the old Camaro looked at. He took it to a local service station and dropped it off for an oil change and to see if they could figure out what the rattle was about. He crossed the street and had a late breakfast at the IHOP. Mid-breakfast, the service station called with an update—it was a muffler issue, and Frank authorized them to fix it.

After breakfast, he walked back over and waited another half hour for the car to be done. While he waited, he checked the *Dayton Daily News* website on his phone and read about the upcoming Joe Hathaway trial. They were charging him with three counts of attempted murder, one each for Frank, Peters, and that dorky Derek kid. The trial was expected to take four days, with a break over the Fourth of July holiday. Opening statements would be on Monday, and it was speculated that Frank, mentioned by name in the article, would also testify.

It was weird, seeing his name on the newspaper website. He wasn't used to even that tiny bit of notoriety. That reminded him—he navigated to Google on his phone and set up a Google Alert for his name. Now, if he was ever mentioned online again, he'd get an email from Google and a link to the article.

When the car was done, Frank paid and drove to the Eastern Birmingham Mall and got a new wallet and a new case for his phone. Several weeks ago, he'd lost most of his personal affects, and he'd replaced most of them by now. But the cheap wallet he'd gotten was already falling apart, so he got a new one. Frank also picked up a few other things at the mall, including a new suitcase and a nice jacket for the trial.

Walking back to his car in the blazing heat, Frank decided to throw caution to the wind and really live it up. He locked his new purchases in the car and went back inside and splurged on a middle-of-the-day movie. It was something he never did, but he settled into the cool seat and enjoyed a cop movie and a large soda and some real, old-fashioned movie popcorn. It was nice to relax.

On the way home, he resisted the temptation to drop by Tammy's Liquor and pick up more bourbon. He was feeling good and doing a great job of managing his drinking. He had a few glasses here and there, but nothing like the old days. In fact, he still had half a bottle left.

It was after dark when he got home, and he texted Laura to see if she was around. They had lots to talk about. She texted back that she was home, and Frank called her as he hung up his new sport coat in the closet.

"Hello?"

"What?" Frank asked. "It's Saturday night. Not out on a hot date?"

Laura laughed. "Nope, just me and Jackson, who just went to bed. What's up?"

"Oh, got some news. Though you might've already heard."

"I heard you're coming to town," she said, mentioning she'd heard about the trial. "When is it?"

"Week after next," Frank said, glancing at the calendar on the wall in his kitchen. "I'll be flying up for the trial on Monday, July 2. I testify on July 3."

"Flying? Fancy."

"Nothing but the best. Actually, I offered to drive, but the prosecutor's office insisted. I need to be 'fresh,' they said."

"Where are you staying?" Laura asked.

"Not sure," he said, going to the counter and leafing through his papers from work to find the fax from the prosecutor's office. He read off the name of a hotel in Troy. "Is that near the downtown?"

"No, it's out by the highway."

"They rented me a car, too."

They chatted for a few minutes about his trip. She invited him over for dinner on the nights he was in town.

"How long are you staying?"

"I'm heading back on Wednesday."

"Hmm, that's too bad. You should stay for the fireworks."

They talked for a few minutes before Frank got around to the real point of the phone call. "So, I wanted to ask you something, and I want your real answer. Not what you think I want to hear."

"Oh," Laura said. "The conversation just got interesting."

"Well, you know I've been working on cold cases here for a while," he said, explaining how the cold case division worked. He mentioned how he'd been closing a lot of cases—so many that, ironically, he might be running out of things to work on.

"That's good, right?"

"Yes, it is, actually. We can give closure to a lot of people. But it's been making me think about where I want to go from here. What I want to do."

It felt weird, talking about himself.

"What do you mean?"

"I really enjoyed helping out with those cases up in Cooper's Mill—too much, I guess," he said. "Now that I'm back here, working on these stacks of dusty old cases, it's just not that exciting."

He felt like he was in a confessional, baring his soul to her. He thought about things a lot, like everyone else, but Frank rarely took the time to say what he felt out loud.

"Well, for me, I'm glad to hear it," she said. "You need to take stock, just like anyone else. Figure out what you want to do—and where you want to do it."

"Well, I'm thinking about leaving Birmingham," he said quietly. There, it was out. He waited a second, then plowed on. "I'm done here, I think. I moved here because they were the only law enforcement agency who would hire me when I got let go in New Orleans."

"What's changed?"

"My boss, actually. He's been talking to my old boss down in NOLA, asking about my service record. Collier, my boss, thinks I've strung enough years together in different agencies to possibly qualify for half-pension if I retire."

"Hmm, that's interesting. I thought you were going to say they were letting you go."

Frank nodded even though he was on the phone. "Yeah, after that whole thing in the spring, I thought so, too. Turns out he's happy with my work lately. Very happy."

"Wow, that does sound good," she said. "Is the money good?"

"About what I'm making now, actually. Weird, getting paid not to work. But I'd have to retire. Or I could work somewhere else and increase the pension for when I do retire. My old boss in New Orleans actually offered me a position there, with the detective's division."

"Congrats! That must feel good. After they let you go, now they want you back. Why?"

"My cases down here. I've been closing a bunch of them. And helping out with those Ohio cases. I guess I impressed some people down in New Orleans."

"Impressed a few people up here, too," she said, her voice proud and sad at the same time. "It's weird to hear your name on the news or get asked about you at the farmers' market. So, you're moving back to the Crescent City? I'd love to come visit."

He looked at the stack of papers on his desk, rearranging the same papers over and over. "Actually, I wanted to talk to you about another option. What about Cooper's Mill?"

"You want to move up here?"

"I was thinking about it, but I don't want to intrude, so to speak," he said. "You've got friends, and you started a new life—"

"Well, let me tell you, we would love it," she said without hesitation. "Jackson would love to have you around more, and I'm liking getting to know you again," she said, cutting through the bullshit. Trudy had been the same way sometimes. When you got her talking, she just told you what she thought. It could be refreshing, but other times, like during a divorce, it was pretty painful.

"Really? I figured you liked having your own life to yourself."

"Nah," she said with a laugh. "It's really not that exciting. Though you would need your own place eventually. It would really cramp my dating to have my father crashing on the couch."

He smiled. "I get that. And yup, I'd want my own place anyway. But seriously, what do you think?"

"I think it would be great. What about work?"

"Maybe I'll talk to Chief King when I'm up there. Put off the pension for now. I'm sure there's a local PD who could use an old codger like me. I can still sprint around like one of the young folk."

"They'd be lucky to have you."

"Or, and this is just a thought, I could freelance. Private investigations, security, that kind of stuff. The pay is better if you can stay busy. Plus, I'd get to draw my half-pension."

"Interesting," she said. "Well, I support you in whatever you want to do. New Orleans sounds fine if you like a big stinky city. Or you could come to Ohio and hang with your family. No pressure or anything, but what kind of idiot wouldn't want to see his grandson on a daily basis?"

He laughed again. She was good—no pressure, but making it clear what she preferred. What if she was just saying that to be polite?

"Well, let me think about it," he said. "We can talk some more when I'm up there. It's just nice to have options."

"Preach it, sir," she said, laughing. "I'd love to be in your shoes: 'Here's a bunch of free money. Okay, now what do you want to do all day?' Sounds good to me."

"Yeah. I'll text you when I get to Troy. You and Jackson are invited up if you want to meet for dinner Monday night."

"Cool. Talk to you soon."

"Okay, love you."

If she was okay with him moving to Cooper's Mill, then his choice was an easy one. But what if moving to town changed things between them? She was working hard, building her own life in a new town. What right did he have to intrude on that?

CHAPTER 21
Pretrial Motions

The week of June 25 was a busy one. Prosecutor Whitlowe and his office scrambled to pull together everything they needed to go to trial on July 2. There had already been several proceedings, including three meetings with the defense attorney and the Court to coordinate evidentiary issues. Whitlowe also had three other cases on his plate, all in various stages of completion, but the case with Joe Hathaway had the highest profile. His office was already fielding questions and interview requests from the press.

On Wednesday morning, Whitlowe was hunched over his desk, prepping for his opening statement while the rest of his team raced around getting ready. Winn Bartlett, his third-year associate, had already submitted his "version" of what he thought the defense's case would be. Whitlowe was working from that report, along with a draft opening statement Bridget had written. Whitlowe was blending all the elements and his own thoughts, crafting an opening statement that, he hoped, would get the jury on his side from the get-go.

Bartlett had mentioned how Hathaway had used his notoriety to grow quite a following online. Bartlett quoted some sizable social media stats and suggested Whitlowe try to work something about them into his opening statement.

Bridget was handling the witnesses and had spoken to each of them about what they would be discussing—and not discussing. The hardest part of calling witnesses was they had a nasty tendency to just keep talking. It was up to the prosecution to rein them in—keeping the witnesses "on message" was crucial. And it was just as important what they didn't say. An errant comment or a bit of "additional information" from a witness could introduce new evidence, hearsay, or even open up a whole new line of questioning that the prosecution wasn't prepared to deal with.

Dorothy was coordinating the on-the-ground logistics, including the hotel and flights for Frank Harper, who was coming in from Alabama, as well as the testimony schedules with the Dayton Crime Lab and several other people. She was also setting up the police transport for Hathaway to and from the courtroom every day, and arranging for the salient information to be transported down to the courtroom on the second floor, along with a dozen other things Whitlowe would never even know about. She was his rock and made his job a thousand times easier.

When Whitlowe was finished with the opening statement, he grabbed Bartlett's prep for the voir dire and reviewed it. Jury selection would take place on Thursday and Friday, the first actual courtroom pieces of the trial. Judge Wilson always insisted on having twelve jurors, plus another six alternates, who heard testimony during the trial via a closed-circuit television hookup with the courtroom. If one of the primary jurors had to be dropped off, any of the alternates could step in without any delay. The forty-four potential juror first names and short biographies had already been sent over, and Bartlett had gone through the list, ranking which jurors they would like to keep and who they needed to dismiss. All of Bartlett's reports and suggestions were good, thorough, and Whitlowe would have no problem giving him a letter of recommendation when his summer was over. His work was top-notch.

By the end of the day on Friday, they would have a full jury of twelve, plus six backups, all picked out. Judge Wilson was usually very kind to the jury. Based on Whitlowe's experience, Wilson would likely let them spend the weekend with their families before sequestering them starting on Monday night.

CHAPTER 22
Voir Dire

Joe Hathaway sat in his wheelchair in the courtroom on Thursday morning, itching. Everything hurt, and it seemed like every part of his body was sore. Transitioning to the wheelchair had not been fun, and now it seemed like he was in it twenty-four hours a day.

He was also working out as much as he could in private. His hands and arms were sore, but he could feel his upper body getting stronger. And he was keeping his mind alert as well, plotting and planning. He had been in contact with Trapper, who was now busy working on several items.

One good thing had already happened this morning—he'd met his new assistant. His law firm had found a young woman that fulfilled his requirements: thin, pretty, under thirty. Fiona McGinty was a firefighter and trained EMT from Dayton. The law firm had convinced her to take a leave of absence. For what they were paying her, she had apparently jumped at the chance.

Joe looked over at his new assistant. She was attractive and moved like an athlete, her red hair bouncing. Maybe this situation would turn out even better than he had planned. If he could just get her horizontal... but getting an assistant was a crucial part of his plan. Joe's brain was always working, reviewing the plans in his mind and looking for any problem areas that needed to be addressed.

"I'm sorry again for being late this morning, Mr. Hathaway," Fiona said. "The dry cleaners weren't open yet, and I had to call them and get them out of bed to open up for me."

"It wasn't a problem," he said.

Joe looked around the courtroom, suddenly bored. He thought it would be exciting and had been looking forward to the relief from the hospital monotony. But the trial itself didn't start until Monday, and today they were just picking a jury. He found the whole voir dire process incredibly tiring. No one was allowed in the gallery, so the courtroom was deathly silent. Joe knew that the right to a trial by a "jury of one's peers" was enshrined in the Constitution. But getting from a group of random people down to a jury of twelve and six alternates was incredibly dull. Maybe it was because the people who showed up for jury duty had nothing better to do. Literally. These were the folks who weren't smart or desperate enough to weasel their way out of performing their "sacred" public duty.

The jury pool started with forty-four people, and Judge Wilson described before the first group of twelve came in how things would work. He would instruct the bailiff to bring in the potential jury members, and then the prosecution and defense would take turns asking short questions of particular jurors.

Once the first group was brought in, the prosecutor got up and started talking. Joe noticed a few specific things. Most often, when the jurors were listening to the prosecutor or defense team talk, they often looked bored. They rarely made eye contact.

Joe listened to the first few jurors, his mind racing ahead to figure out if they would help him or hurt him, but after a time he tuned them out. It wasn't up to him. Tomlinson's team of attorneys had pre-ranked the jurors, which meant they had gone through the basic biographies provided and picked out the ones they wanted to keep. It was a little bit like chess, planning your moves ahead of time.

There were two assistants at the prosecutors table, and Joe could see that one of them was writing everything down, including the names of the jurors and their seat location. The other person was a very attractive young woman. She seemed more thoughtful, staring at each juror and looking for clues as to how they might react during the trial.

The prosecution and defense teams took turns making statements and asking questions and then talked quietly at each table, announcing which jurors they wanted dismissed. After four hours, the process was over. They had selected eighteen total jurors, twelve main and six alternates. When it was all over, Joe's attorney turned and patted him on the arm.

"We got some good ones," he said. "Not all our favorites, but most of them. It could help."

Judge Wilson announced that the jury selection had gone more quickly than he'd anticipated and there would be no court proceedings on Friday. The trial would begin on Monday, July 2.

Great, Joe thought as McGinty rolled him out of the courtroom. More time to think about things he couldn't control. At least Joe had his pretty new assistant to fetch him papers and things. And Trapper was hard at work.

CHAPTER 23
Dispatch

Lola got to her desk at the Cooper's Mill Police Department around 6:00 a.m. on Monday morning. Her first task, as always, was to start the coffee maker. If the coffee wasn't ready when the first shift of deputies arrived, the rest of the staff would be cross all day.

Once the pots were brewing in the break room, she went back to the reception desk and started unpacking her bag. At the same time, she dialed the phone on the desk and put it on speaker.

"Miami County Dispatch," the voice came back. That was Trina, a dispatcher up at the Troy office.

"Morning. It's Lola."

"Morning," the woman's voice came back, cheery. "Getting in late today?"

"Yup," Lola said, glancing at the clock on the wall. 6:14 a.m. She took her lunch and a stack of newspapers and magazines out of her bag and laid them on the desk. "Overslept. Anything going on?"

Lola could hear typing. "Nothing much. A fire over in Darke County late last night pulled in some mutual aid from nearby departments, but it's out now and everyone's back home. A few DUIs overnight. Oh, and there was a giant car chase and shoot-out on I-75."

"What?"

"Just kidding," Trina answered. "It's been a while since we had anything that exciting around here. So, you ready?"

Lola nodded and took the call off speaker, pulling on a wireless headset. "Yes, you can transfer local 911 service for Cooper's Mill to me until 2:00 p.m.," she said in an official voice. She knew it was being recorded, and the 911 transcripts occasionally made it into criminal cases, so she always tried to sound good when she knew she was being recorded.

"Thanks, Lola. Have a good shift."

Lola waited for the series of tones that signified her phone was accepting calls from the emergency system, and then Trina said goodbye and hung up.

Lola quickly settled into her routine. She had three lines to take care of: the 911 line forwarded from the county switchboard and the two local numbers for the PD, one for non-emergencies and one for the staff. The local phones kept her busier than the occasional 911 call. If she got too busy, she could just redirect the 911 calls back to the county switchboard. There were multiple people on staff there at all times, folks like Trina who worked out of the Miami County Communication Center up in Troy, near the Outback Steakhouse.

Over the next three hours, Lola took the occasional call, got caught up on her email, and then read her newspapers and magazines. She liked to stay current on entertainment news, along with politics and other news. She had plenty of time to read between calls and the chief didn't mind. He was always asking her questions about the news and other topics.

Heavy rain began to fall outside, and she checked the weather, which sometimes changed the volume and nature of the 911 calls. It looked like it would be raining off and on all day—a welcome break from the oppressive heat. Rain pounded on the roof, and thunder rattled the doors.

Around 9:00 a.m., Deputy Peters and Chief King entered the station, stomping their feet loudly and remarking about the rain outside. Peters somehow got his feet tangled in the door and the rug and took a spill, dropping his papers and his cup of Speedway coffee.

"Wow, you really know how to go ass over teakettle," Lola said, getting up to help. They kept a mop and paper towels near the front door for just such cleanups, half of which seemed to be caused by Peters.

"Oh, man, my coffee," Peters said as Chief King helped his cousin back to his feet.

The chief smiled. "You okay?"

"Yeah, the floor was slippery, I guess," Peters said, brushing off his now-soiled uniform. "Good thing there was a rug there."

Lola handed paper towels to Peters, who dabbed at his uniform. The chief shot her a smile—everyone knew about Peters' clumsiness. It was legendary around the office. She and the chief knelt and gathered up the papers, and Jeff shot her a quick wink and mouthed the words "thank you." She and the chief had been dating off and on for the last three years, and no one knew about it yet. It was also completely against the rules.

They stood, and Lola helped Peters through the doors that led back to the offices of the police station. The chief lingered and waited for the doors to close behind his cousin, then looked at her.

"Thanks for coming over last night," he said. "It was nice."

She nodded. "Thank you for letting me talk. You'd think I'd be used to it by now, right?"

"It's okay," Jeff said, smiling. "I feel the same way. It's weird, not being able to tell anyone."

"Yes," she agreed, keeping her voice down. "But it was different when we were just dating. We didn't know where it was going. But now, you know..."

"Yeah, I know," he said, looking at her. He brushed a hand against her shoulder. "I love you," he said quietly.

She looked up at him. "I know. Me too. That's what makes this so difficult."

They were silent for a moment. "Well, there's really only one thing we can do," he said.

She looked at him, trying to figure out where he was going.

"We talked about so many options last night. I don't even remember where we ended up."

Jeff looked at the door and then back at her.

"There's only one option, Lola," he said sadly. Then he smiled at his joke. "We tell everyone."

"You serious?"

Jeff nodded. "Yup. Now we just have to figure out what you're gonna say."

"Me? But you'll get in so much trouble..."

"I'm not worried about that. It's one thing for us to be dating—it's another thing if we're making a commitment. And that's what I want to do, if you're ready. Either way, we'll figure it out."

She glanced at the closed doors to the office area, then at the other doors leading out into the parking lot. The rain was falling hard outside. She took a chance and threw her arms around Jeff, kissing him.

CHAPTER 24
Laps

Joe started the day with an assessment of what he had and what he needed. It was going to be a long, stressful day that might even hold a few surprises. But he would handle it, just like he'd handled every other day that came before today and would handle every other day that came after. He'd been knocking around this pitiful planet for a long time, and he wasn't about to give up yet.

The first thing he assessed after waking up was his body. The nurses had awakened him with breakfast just before 6:00 a.m. and he ate alone, thinking. Sometimes, he enjoyed the company of the nurses, especially the attractive ones. But today, he needed to be alone with his thoughts as he ate the bland-tasting eggs and turkey sausage. Did they manually extract all the taste out of the food here at the hospital, or did it come that way?

Back on track. Body. His legs had mended to the point where he'd started therapy to learn how to walk again. The physical therapist would report that he was taking a few ginger steps and would be back to walking in a few weeks.

That wasn't exactly true.

He finished his meal and looked around the room, admiring all the flowers and cards lined up on the tables and along the window. He'd been getting so many that the nurses had brought in three extra folding tables to hold them all. His fans loved him. There were so many, the extras were now going to other patients.

This new room was smaller, but it had a better view of the highway. He spent a lot of time staring at the cars passing. There was also far less medical equipment then the room he'd been in—in fact, all of his instruments were attached to a single metal pole on wheels.

Joe swung his legs over the side of the bed and stood, swaying. It felt good to stand. He reached over and grabbed the pole and pulled it behind him as he staggered to the window. The pole moved easily with him. If someone walked in on him, he'd just collapse to the ground and blame it on "ambition."

But no one did.

Joe walked to the window, looking out at the pouring rain. He turned and walked past his bed to the door, glancing out into the hall. One of the young cops was seated in the hallway, asleep. Joe brushed his fingers on the door and walked back to the window, counting each circuit. Yesterday, he'd made fourteen trips before he got tired. Today, he did twenty, then settled back into his bed. He remembered to place the pole back where it had been and to loop the tubes and wires across his bed in such a way as to suggest he'd never gotten up.

He was thinking about his day when the nurse came in.

"Hey there, old dog," Tammy said with a smile. She called him old dog when she was in a good mood. "You ready for today? It's got the whole hospital talking."

She was always pleasant. She had nice breasts and wasn't too smart—she hadn't figured out that his penchant for dropping things around her was his way of getting a peak down her shirt. Or maybe she'd figured it out long ago and was just doing the old man a favor.

Plus, he was famous, right? Tammy and the other nurses were well aware of his following online, along with the group of young people that gathered outside of Joe's hospital every day. Hell, they'd helped recruit them. He'd hit 14,000 followers on Twitter, even though he barely knew how to tweet. Young kids, mostly, and women, all drawn to him for some reason after he'd started telling his story online.

"Yeah, not excited about it," he lied. "How are the crowds today?"

She smiled. "Bigger than usual."

He nodded, sneaking another look down her loose top as she gathered up the remnants of his breakfast.

Joe had started out borrowing the nurse's laptops, dictating to them what to type. This was before he could use his hands, and the nurses posted for him. It was something that felt natural at the time, complaining to anyone who would listen. He'd done a lot of posting in those first few weeks, and people had really responded to his stories about being injured and being railroaded by the police.

He'd also run a lot of Facebook ads to get people to "like" his page. For some reason, none of his financial accounts had been frozen, so he ran ads twenty-four/seven and the "likes" poured in. Soon, people were responding to his posts and debating how the cops were treating him. He'd get twenty or thirty new likes a day, along with dozens of messages of support—even a few marriage proposals. Joe had stopped looking at Facebook weeks ago after the sudden surge in followers. And then, two weeks ago, the cops had returned his cell phone to him. It had been in the wreck with him and was a little worse for wear, but now he could post whenever he wanted. Of course, he assumed his communications were being monitored, so he never used his personal cell for anything surreptitious.

He didn't understand it, the sudden following. But then, he barely understood most people. They were content to just pass through this world, never leaving their mark and eating and humping and farting their way to the grave. Why didn't people try harder? Why did people act like sheep, believing whatever they were told?

"Guess all those posts you had me type up did the trick, huh? You're more famous than anyone else in the county." She looked around. "Your assistant ain't here yet?"

Joe shook his head. "Nope," he said.

"Okay, I'll send her in when she gets here. Need anything else?"

Joe pulled back the sheet with a smile. "I need a little company—you should lock that door and climb in here with me."

"You *are* an old dog!" She laughed and turned, leaving. Joe always flirted with her and the other cute nurses—what could it hurt? He wouldn't mind a roll in the hay with her or any of the others. In his experience with women, it never hurt to ask. Let them know you were attracted to them, play the percentages.

He wanted to flip on the TV—he was feeling anxious about the morning and wanted to zone out—but forced himself to review the day instead. The trial was pointless. He'd shot at those men across the lake, and the police had all the evidence they would ever need to put him away. He'd been careless and hadn't managed to drown those two cops from Cooper's Mill. The case seemed open and shut to Joe—in fact, if he hadn't been grievously injured in the wreck, he'd probably already be sitting in a jail cell. His injuries had delayed his prosecution, and that delay would be the key to his escape.

Only time would tell. Chess moves—planning and failing and planning some more. It was the only way to be ready. And fortune always favors the prepared.

CHAPTER 25
Monty Finds a Seat

The first problem Monty Robinson encountered on Monday morning was parking. Monty had been in downtown Troy more times than he could count, and it was rare that you couldn't find parking near the circle. He'd been down there for the Strawberry Festival and other events a hundred times and never had trouble finding a spot either on the circle or a street or two over. Even in the pouring rain, he figured something must be going on. He couldn't find any spots big enough for the Montego. Eventually, he found a spot three streets over, and parked.

He walked up the tidy residential street to Main, gusts of wind pulling at his umbrella. The rain came down in sheets. At Main Street, he turned east and headed for the massive courthouse building and the fountains that surrounded it. People sure loved to decorate their towns. Monty could appreciate that. People liked to live where things were nice. But it seemed there had to be better ways to spend money than to have a half-dozen fountains pumping water into the sky day and night. That had to cost a pretty penny.

Monty grew confused as he approached the courthouse and saw what looked like a crowd of people around the door, some holding picket signs in the rain. He was here to see the trial—what were these people here for? Monty walked up to the doors, assuming he could go around and get inside for the trial, but a cop stopped him.

"Hey, buddy, there's a line," he said, pointing at the crowd.

Monty nodded. "Not sure what thems folks are here for. I'm here for the Hathaway trial."

"Like I said, get in line. There's another cop over there handing out numbers. Only the first thirty people are getting in," the cop said before walking away.

Monty turned and really studied the crowd for the first time. It was mostly kids, all dressed in ratty clothes. Every one of them looked like they had escaped from Woodstock and needed a shower, even drenched in the rain. Several of them held up signs, smeared and handwritten: "FREE JOE HATHAWAY" or "HE DIDN'T DO IT" and one that just read "FREEDOM." Another read "KEEPER OF TRUTH" and had a picture of Joe on it.

"Sir," Monty said, waving the cop back over. "Seriously, what are all these kids here for? It can't be Joe's trial, is it?"

The cop shrugged and pulled his hat down to block the rain. "What can I say? I guess the guy is famous," he said, looking at the protesters. "Though how a killer gets famous is beyond me. You local?"

Monty nodded. "Yeah, Cooper's Mill. Joe...well, we were acquaintances. He killed a friend of ours, Tom Mercato."

"Oh, I read about that. You a witness?"

"No, but they interviewed me. I know Will Duff."

"The bailiff?" The cop glanced around. "I can get you in, if you want."

Monty looked at the crowd and nodded. "That'd be great." The cop lifted up the police tape surrounding the entrance and walked Monty to the front doors and inside the building. "This guy is F and F," the cop said, letting the guard know he was friend of the bailiff. "Monty Robinson. Knows Duff."

The guard asked for ID, and Monty got out his driver's license and showed it to the guard, who called in and verified Monty's address in Cooper's Mill. "Okay, follow me," the guard said. Monty turned and thanked the cop, then followed the guard to the elevator. They climbed on and the guard pushed "2."

"Friends and family get priority seating over observers," the guard said when Monty started to ask.

"Why are they here?"

The guard shook his head. "Who knows why people do things. I guess he's got a following online. They call themselves the 'Keepers of Truth,' whatever that means. Will Duff said Hathaway was pleading his case online, and it got mentioned by someone in the press. Things just took off. Now he's got supporters, here and at the hospital. People, right?"

Monty nodded as the elevator doors opened and the guard walked him over to the courtroom. There were many people in the hallway knotted around the doors of Courtroom 3. Monty saw several lawyers and other people in suits, preparing to go in. There were at least three members of the local media, including Tina Armstrong, the lady who ran and wrote for the *Cooper's Mill Gazette*. She was a strange one—even now, inside, she was wearing sunglasses. Folks said there was something wrong with her eyes.

There were also folks from the Dayton TV stations and a man with a lanyard that read "Cincinnati Daily Reader." There was also a small group of protesters down the hallway, three young men and two women chanting something about freedom and peace.

"I figured I'd be the only one here," Monty said, half to himself.

"Nope," the guard said, then stopped to talk to the bailiff, who recognized Monty immediately. "He's F and F."

Duff nodded and shook Monty's hand. "Hey, man," he said, pulling the door open and walking Monty in. "Okay, it's like an f'ed-up wedding in here. Prosecution is on the right, nearest the jury box. Defense is on the left. Grab a seat."

Monty thanked him and searched for a spot on one of the wooden benches. It was a small courtroom, much smaller than the ones on TV. These seats would only accommodate probably twenty people on each side. Monty found a seat and waited for the show to begin.

Chapter 26
Courtroom

Whitlowe took the elevator down from his office, straightening his tie. It was pouring outside, thunder rattling the windows of his office. He was glad his offices and the courtrooms were located in the same building. He carried only a banged-up briefcase—Dorothy had made sure the rest of the papers were already down in the courtroom. Whitlowe waited for the doors to open and walked off the elevator.

The hallway was crowded, much busier than it should have been. A guard saw him and walked over.

"What's all this?" Whitlowe asked. "Who the hell are all these people?"

The guard only shook his head and led the prosecutor through the crowd to the courtroom, shooing people out of the way. At the doors, the guard grunted and pulled them open, holding them for Whitlowe.

Inside, the courtroom was just as busy. People were jostling for seats in the gallery, and the defense's side was already full. The bailiff and guards had started seating defense spectators on the prosecution side, which required interjecting themselves between groups to keep them from pushing each other and bickering.

Whitlowe walked to the front and through the low swinging doors. He set his ratty briefcase on the prosecution's table and turned to the assistant county prosecutor. "Who are all these people?"

Bridget stood and nodded. "I knew he had a following online, but this is crazy."

"Yeah."

She held up her phone. "He's been posting hourly on Facebook and Twitter all weekend, calling his 'people' to come out and protest the 'injustice.' Looks like it worked. The bailiff said three people have already been removed after they refused to sit down."

"Wilson won't like it," Whitlowe said. "He hates distractions."

"Good," she said. "He'll kick them out."

Whitlowe shook his head. "So, we ready?"

Bridget nodded and glanced at Winn Bartlett, seated at the prosecution table. Dorothy was in the front row, in case she was needed, along with

Chief King and Deputy Peters from the CMPD. Whitlowe walked over and nodded at Dorothy, then shook the policemen's hands. "Thanks for coming," he said. "Deputy, we'll get you on the stand soon, okay?"

"Yes, sir."

"Have either of you seen Derek Vole?"

Chief King nodded. "He's here—went to get some water. Have you heard from Harper?"

Whitlowe nodded. "Dorothy is coordinating with him," he said, introducing his secretary. "Dorothy, can you chat with Chief King?" Whitlowe excused himself and went to find the bailiff, who was out in the hallway. He was in a heated discussion with a protester, trying to get him to settle down.

"Get him out of here," Duff finally said, pushing the protester toward another guard, who started leading the man outside. "Oh, hello, Mr. Whitlowe."

"Any problems, other than the crowd?"

"No, not yet," Duff said, lowering his voice. "Though that's been nuts. And they all need a shower. Bunch of freeloaders. We drew numbers to see who made it into the gallery. There's another thirty or forty out by the fountains. We'll rotate them in over the course of the trial. How many days you think?"

"Five," Whitlowe said. "Maybe six. Depends. You need MCSO here?" he asked, referring to the Miami County Sheriff's Office.

The radio on Duff's shoulder buzzed. Duff shook his head as he picked up the call. "No, we're good for now. Duff here."

"Defendant's coming in," someone on the radio said.

"Roger," Duff said, then hung his radio up and looked at Whitlowe. "Here we go."

The bailiff excused himself, and Whitlowe went back into the courtroom, which was starting to quiet down. Whitlowe took a seat at his table and retrieved a few things from his briefcase before setting it on the floor beside him. It didn't look like much, but it was his lucky briefcase, the one that had seen him through law school and passing the bar. He'd used it while working his way up in the Miami County Prosecutor's Office. It wasn't a sure thing—he'd lost a few cases with it—but it never hurt to have a little luck on your side.

The doors at the back of the room opened, and Joe Hathaway entered, his wheelchair pushed by a young woman. The courtroom erupted in cheers, and Hathaway seemed genuinely surprised, putting up his hands to high five the two rows of people cheering as he passed them.

The whole thing felt like a circus.

Whitlowe stepped over and held the swinging doors open for

Hathaway and the group of lawyers following his wheelchair.

"Mr. Hathaway," Whitlowe said.

Hathaway only nodded, a scowl on his face. The young woman smiled and thanked Whitlowe for holding the door. Whitlowe greeted Tomlinson and the rest of the defense team, shaking hands. It was always better to be friendly. These were good men, good lawyers, and they deserved his respect.

It wasn't their fault that they were defending a psychopath.

CHAPTER 27
Wheelchair

Joe Hathaway was stunned. He never thought the county would allow any of his "fans" into the actual courtroom. He'd seen them at the hospital, of course, and waved at them during his few "walks" outside, pushed by McGinty or his physical therapists. They sent him gifts and flowers and clothes and cards, all dutifully inspected by the cops before turning them over. Joe had hoped that some of the more "faithful" would be grouped outside the courthouse. Maybe the judge or jury would see them and take pity on Joe.

But Joe hadn't guessed that any members of his fan club would be allowed inside the actual courtroom. Hey, every little bit helped. Maybe people were sympathetic to him, because he was injured and under arrest. Many people, despite the preponderance of evidence, seemed to think he was innocent.

It hadn't started out as much of anything until Tammy suggested they start an account to take donations to help with his recovery. He'd resisted the idea at first, but she had told him that everyone was doing it. People set up "Go Fund Me" pages for accidents or to raise money for trips or just about anything. Tammy even showed Joe how several young women were using the internet to raise money for breast enlargement surgeries. It was crazy.

But Joe allowed it, and the money and the "likes" and "re-tweets" started trickling in. He didn't care about the money—he had plenty—and wasn't spending any of it lying in the hospital. But he couldn't get over how people he didn't know had rallied around him.

At some point, he'd started mentioning something to Tammy about him being a "keeper of the truth." It was silly, pointless claptrap, much like another saying that had become popular lately, "speaking truth to power." These trite, oversimplified phrases sounded like brainless bumper-sticker slogans to him, but the "keeper of truth" saying took off, and people began repeating it online. They created something called a "hashtag" around the saying and appended it to posts and messages, making it popular. "Trending," Tammy had called it.

Joe looked around the packed courtroom and smiled. It must be working.

"You need anything?"

He turned and looked at McGinty. She looked nice today, dressed up. He'd never seen her in anything other than her EMT uniform or casual clothes. "No, just admiring the crowd. Nice to see my supporters showing up."

She smiled and sat down in the front row.

Joe turned to his lawyers. "We ready?"

Tomlinson nodded. "Yes."

"Opening statements from both sides today, right?" Joe asked. "Anything else?"

"If we get through those, the prosecution will start their case. Call their first witnesses."

Joe scanned the prosecution side and saw Deputy Peters and Chief King. They were looking at him as well, but he didn't nod or acknowledge them. Joe turned back to Tomlinson. "Where's Frank Harper?"

Tomlinson looked at a sheet in front of him showing the witnesses the prosecution was planning to call. "Not listed until tomorrow," Tomlinson said. "Probably flying tonight or tomorrow. Don't worry—he's their star witness. He'll be here."

Joe nodded, wondering if it was good or bad the ex-cop wasn't here for the opening statements.

There was movement near the front of the courtroom and the bailiff came out of a door near the witness box. "All rise for his honorable Judge Wilson," he said.

Everyone stood except for Joe. He smiled at the irony of that. Joe could have stood, if he wanted to, but then his secret would be out.

Judge Wilson walked in and climbed up to his seat above the courtroom.

"Thank you, ladies and gentlemen of the Court. You may be seated. Are we ready to proceed?"

Whitlowe nodded. "We are, Your Honor."

Wilson looked at Joe and the defense lawyers next to him.

Tomlinson stood. "We're ready to begin."

Wilson nodded and looked down at the clerk. "Good. Clerk, please read off the charges."

Chapter 28
Prosecution Opening

Judge Wilson asked the bailiff to bring in the jury. There was some commotion as they filed into the room and were seated for the first time in the jury box. Once they were settled and sworn in by the bailiff, the judge turned to Whitlowe and nodded.

"You may begin."

Whitlowe stood.

"Thank you, Your Honor," he said as he walked to the center of the room and spoke directly to the jury. "Thank you for coming today. Several months ago, three members of our community were nearly murdered. This man, Mr. Joe Hathaway, tried to kill them, one of whom is a member of our local law enforcement."

He paused, letting that information sink in before continuing.

"Two of the men were actively investigating Mr. Hathaway in connection with a local double homicide. As part of their duties, they investigated Trapper's Lake, a nearby location probably known to every person in this room," he continued. "On this cold, white expanse of ice, these two men, one of whom is a Cooper's Mill police officer, were fired upon by Hathaway with a long-range rifle. The bullets ricocheted nearby, striking ice shanties around them before hitting a third man. The prosecution will show beyond a reasonable doubt that Mr. Hathaway attempted to kill our three victims."

Whitlowe paused for a moment and looked over at the defendant before turning back to the jury.

"Members of the jury, the Court has put a solemn oath before you," he continued. "Today, we will begin to lay out our case against Mr. Hathaway. You will learn the great lengths he went to set up the situation in an attempt to kill Deputy Floyd Peters of the Cooper's Mill Police Department, Mr. Frank Harper of the Alabama Bureau of Investigation, and Derek Vole, a local resident."

Whitlowe paused again, letting the preliminary evidence sink in. It usually made sense to hit the high points of the prosecution's case during the opening statement before the defense got a chance to mention and refute it.

"Thankfully, each man survived, and you will hear from each of them. You will hear how these attempts on their lives has affected them. We will show you all of the evidence," Whitlowe continued. "And we will make it quick. We don't want to waste your time on a lot of boring testimony. This is a simple case that is easy to understand. We will show how Mr. Hathaway tried to kill these men to cover up other crimes, and when that didn't work, how he fired his weapon at the men. We will also show that Mr. Hathaway fled the scene, was involved in an accident, and was taken to the hospital, where he has been in police custody ever since. The gun and matching bullet casings were recovered from Mr. Hathaway's vehicle at the crash site, and these were an exact match for the bullet removed from one of our victims."

Whitlowe walked toward the jury box, stopping and placing a fist on the wooden railing in front of them.

"If Hathaway's plan had worked, these three men would be dead," he continued, his voice lower, conversational. With this, he slammed his hand on the wooden railing four times in quick succession. On one finger, he wore a thick metal ring, and it CRACKED loudly against the wood with each slam. "Four shots," he said, stepping away. "Followed by eight more. Aimed at the men on the ice. He was trying to kill them."

Whitlowe walked away and stopped in the middle of the courtroom, turning to look back at the jury. "At the end of this trial, I expect you to find him guilty of the charges before him: three cases of attempted murder. Our evidence will show beyond a reasonable doubt that Mr. Hathaway carried out these crimes, and that he should be punished to the fullest extent of the law. Thank you, members of the jury."

Chapter 29
Defense Opening

After Whitlowe sat down, Joe glanced at the judge, who was moving papers around on his desk at the front of the room. Once the courtroom was quiet, Judge Wilson nodded at Joe's defense team.

"Defense, you may begin."

Tomlinson stood and turned, patting Joe on the shoulder, a move that made Joe angry. Joe wasn't interested in people—or the jury—feeling sorry for him. He wasn't some child who needed to be comforted by his own paid employee.

Tomlinson turned to the jury.

"Members of the jury, thank you for being here today. I also want to thank everyone in the gallery for joining us to be witnesses. As you can see, the gallery is packed, and I think it's safe to say that most of the people attending today are here to make sure my friend, Mr. Joe Hathaway, gets a fair trial. There are crowds of people standing in the rain outside, as well, who share their interest. In fact, many people around the world have been drawn to Mr. Hathaway's riveting story, which he has been sharing over social media as he underwent the painful process of recovery. Now that he has started to regain the use of his arms and legs, we can proceed with this trial, and Mr. Hathaway can finally get his day in court. Mr. Hathaway is being railroaded by a prosecution determined to make a case. The prosecution has waited until the last possible minute to bring my client to trial, and now it looks like their entire case is built on what they found in a car accident."

Tomlinson walked closer to the jury. "Well, I don't know about you folks, but I've seen a few car accidents, and who knows what ends up in those vehicles? I once saw a car with an entire deer stuck in the backseat. During any car accident, the contents inside the car can get thrown out, and items that were not originally in the car can end up inside. It just happens. I hope their whole case isn't predicated on what they found in the car, right?" He smiled and shrugged. "Doesn't sound very air tight to me. Who can say how items ended up in a wrecked vehicle?"

He turned and pointed at Joe. "Mr. Hathaway is an upstanding citizen and is well-known locally as somewhat of a minor celebrity. He's lived in and around Ohio for most of his life and is active in the community, enjoying the friendships of many. Up until his accident, he shared coffee regularly with a group of friends every morning at a local fast-food restaurant, where they discussed politics and the news of the day. Mr. Hathaway has never had any trouble with the law. In fact, he's never had so much as a speeding ticket! How could he go from humble community member to a mass murderer, you ask? Well, we're asking the same question, along with the people gathered outside. It is true, Mr. Hathaway is an expert marksman. In fact, he has competed in local shooting matches at ranges for years. He has won trophies and accolades from his fellow sportsmen. Yet the prosecution says that he fired multiple times at these so-called 'victims' and missed? Why would an expert marksman miss on purpose if he were trying to kill them?"

Tomlinson paused, letting his point sink in with the jury. After a moment, he continued.

"The prosecution has a long way to go to prove beyond a reasonable doubt that my client, Mr. Hathaway, tried and failed to shoot these men. We'll also go over this suggestion that Mr. Hathaway was being investigated for murder. It is true that, during an investigation for a local disappearance, Mr. Hathaway's name came up as a person of interest. Mr. Hathaway and Mr. Tom Mercato, the deceased, were close friends. Tom and Joe often got into discussions over politics. But does that mean Joe killed him? Or somehow 'arranged' for Tom's disappearance? Absolutely not."

He paused, then continued.

"During this investigation, many people were questioned. That is the nature of a police inquiry. They want to get to the bottom of the case and figure out what happened, so it makes sense they would talk to Tom's closest friends, including Joe."

"In the end, we'll show you a few things about this man, Mr. Joe Hathaway. We'll show you that he's well-known and well-liked in the community, with many friends who will vouch for him. We'll show that despite what the evidence supposedly shows, the prosecution cannot prove its case. The items recovered at the accident do not prove anything. And let me remind you fine gentlemen and ladies: the prosecution must prove beyond ALL reasonable doubt that my client deliberately tried to kill these three men. We are confident that, at the end, after you've seen all the evidence for yourself, you will agree with me and find the defendant innocent of all charges. Thank you."

Tomlinson smiled at the jury and crossed to his seat.

Judge Wilson glanced up at the clock on the wall, which read 11:18 a.m. "Very well, Counselors. Are you ready to proceed after a brief recess?"

"We are, Your Honor," Whitlowe said. Tomlinson nodded in agreement.

"Okay, let's stop for lunch and begin at 1:00 p.m. Everyone please be on time."

CHAPTER 30
First Witnesses

After lunch, people returned to the courtroom and began talking amongst themselves. At precisely 1:00 p.m., the bailiff appeared and called everyone to order. As the courtroom quieted down, the judge entered, taking his seat behind the bench.

Deputy Peters thought it all seemed kind of silly, all the pomp and circumstance. It was like going to one of those Catholic weddings where everything was in Latin, and they gave you communion and you couldn't understand anything they were saying.

The judge began with some announcements about the gallery and how visitors would be chosen each day via a random lottery. He read more court instructions to the prosecution and defense teams, mostly about not sharing information about the trial with the press, and then asked the bailiff to bring in and seat the jury.

While the jury was filing in, Whitlowe leaned over the railing that separated the prosecutor's table from the front row of the gallery. He turned to where Peters was seated and whispered. "You ready?"

Peters swallowed. "Yup."

In truth, he was far from ready. This was the thing he was dreading the most. He tried to stop thinking about how nervous he was or what might happen when he got up on the stand. He'd been having dreams lately, ones where he was testifying and couldn't remember any of the relevant facts in the case. He would stutter and stammer, and then the judge would ask him to stand, and everyone would see that Peters had somehow forgotten to wear his pants.

Whitlowe whispered. "Don't worry. You'll do fine," he said, turning back to the courtroom. Peters wondered how he could be sure. It was the kind of thing you told a child before they got on an airplane.

The judge reminded the jury of their "somber duty" and reminded those in the courtroom that this was a serious matter and that he expected everyone to act accordingly. Then he asked the prosecutor to call his first witness.

Peters gulped and got ready to stand. But, to his great surprise and relief, he wasn't the first witness called. Instead, it was the ballistics expert from the Montgomery County Crime Lab down in Dayton. Peters sat back and relaxed and realized his hands were shaking.

The way it had been explained to Peters, there were four phases during witness testimony.

During the "direct" phase, the prosecution asked the witness questions, and then next, the defense got their chance to "cross-examine" them. If clarification was needed, the prosecution could then "re-direct" questions from the witness, followed by a "re-cross" if necessary. Peters hoped they kept it to a minimum.

The ballistics expert, a Dr. Bledsoe, discussed the weapons found in Hathaway's vehicle, along with the bullets and slugs found with them. He also talked about the bullet casings found on the surface of Trapper's Lake before the ice melted. Peters thought back to those freezing days, searching the ice.

Prosecutor Whitlowe walked Bledsoe through the discussion, making sure to tie the bullets and the slugs to the weapon—they all matched. Dr. Bledsoe then shared how he had categorized the slugs and bullet fragments, including the one removed from Derek Vole, and how he'd test-fired the rifle at the crime lab to create matching slugs.

When Whitlowe was done, Tomlinson stood and did his cross-examination. It was pretty routine and followed much of what Peters had seen in previous cases and on TV. It was Tomlinson's job to poke holes in the prosecution's case, but Dr. Bledsoe kept calm and addressed all of Tomlinson's questions.

When they were finished with Bledsoe, the judge dismissed him, and Peters started to get nervous again, but it was for nothing—Whitlowe called another person from the crime lab. This woman testified about the chain of evidence, sharing with the jury how a paper trail ensures the weapons and other evidence traveled from a crime scene through the hands of the authorities to a lab or other testing facilities without being tampered with or altered in any way. The crime lab technician, whose name Peter's missed, testified how the evidence bags all arrived at the lab sealed and initialed.

Whitlowe wheeled out a monitor, and they showed a short video of the evidence bags being opened and processed. It all seemed cut and dried to Peters. When Whitlowe was finished and Tomlinson was allowed to cross-examine, he only clarified a couple of points and verified the time line for the evidence arrival.

When the technician was done, Peters was startled when his name was called. He stood and made his way through the low swinging doors, tripping over Whitlowe's briefcase, which was leaning against the prosecution's table leg. Peters composed himself and walked to the witness box, where he was sworn in.

Once he was settled in and sworn in, Peters looked at Whitlowe and tried to ignore all the faces in the gallery.

"Thank you. Deputy, can you state your name and service record briefly for the Court?"

Peters began speaking, giving his name and quickly summarizing his career with the Cooper's Mill Police Department. Despite his best effort, his nerves got the better of him and his voice started to fade. The judge asked Peters to speak up, and Peters did so, ending with a summary of his investigation of the Mercato death.

"Thank you, Deputy. So, you were investigating the death of Tom Mercato, and you and a Mr. Frank Harper were investigating the defendant, Joe Hathaway, and his involvement, if any, in Mr. Mercato's death. Is that correct?"

"That's correct."

"Who is Frank Harper, and what is his involvement with the CMPD?"

Peters quickly sketched out Mr. Harper's background, his visits to Cooper's Mill, and his involvement in the Martin kidnapping case last fall.

"He was instrumental in catching the kidnappers?"

"Yes, he and I tracked them to a local farmhouse. We were both shot during the raid, but the girls were recovered alive and most of the kidnappers were killed. One escaped."

"One got away?"

Peters nodded. "Yes, the fourth member of the team. He got away while Mr. Harper and I were injured."

"Okay. So why were you investigating Hathaway?"

"We weren't, actually. We were going over the coroner's reports, and I was working from a theory that Tom Mercato's death wasn't accidental. Due to the amount of air in the lungs, I thought that he might not have drowned."

"Okay, so it's safe to say the investigation was ongoing?"

"Yes."

"And you were investigating?"

"Yes."

"And Mr. Harper?"

"He didn't think there was anything there. He thought the coroner was right in her report, which theorized the man fell and died from a blunt trauma, then ended up in the lake later."

"Okay. So, what happened next?"

Peters quickly covered the events that occurred that day on the frozen lake—the 911 call about someone breaking into Tom Mercato's abandoned ice shanty; Peters' arrival to investigate, followed by Harper; the ragged open hole in the middle of the floor of the shanty, combined with the heater going full blast; falling into the water and nearly drowning before being pulled out by Derek and Harper; and then someone shooting at them from far away. He ended with seeing Harper running toward a shooter in the nearby parking lot.

Whitlowe stopped the deputy several times for clarification, but by now Peters' nerves were calm. He clarified a few points and Whitlowe wrapped up his questions.

On the cross-examination, things went more smoothly than Peters could have imagined.

Tomlinson was thorough, of course, and asked some of the same questions again to make sure he got the same answers. He poked and prodded around Peters' suggestion that Hathaway wasn't being investigated at the time for Tom Mercato's murder, but Peters told him the truth—there was nothing to tie him to the death at that point.

When the defense was done, Whitlowe got up to clarify a few points. Peters answered two more questions, both about his time on the frozen lake and whether or not he could identify Hathaway from that distance.

After answering these final questions, Peters was excused. He walked carefully back to his seat with a sigh.

Whitlowe called his next witness, Derek Vole. The young man, dressed nicer than Peters had ever seen him, walked up to the witness stand and was sworn in. His testimony went even faster, as Derek had seen much less on the ice that day. Derek spoke about sleeping in his cabin and hearing people crying for help. He'd helped Frank Harper pull Peters to safety and then heard gunshots before being struck.

The cross-examination of this witness also went quickly. Tomlinson didn't refute anything in Derek's testimony. He only asked a couple questions about the time line and whether or not he could identify who had shot him. Derek answered "no" to the last question, and Tomlinson excused him.

At that point, it was nearly 4:00 p.m. and Judge Wilson called it a day. He instructed the jury to return to the local hotel, where they were sequestered, and reminded them they were not to discuss the case with anyone, read the newspapers, or watch the news. They were also told to avoid using social media for the remainder of the trial.

With that, he dismissed the jury, then called both attorneys up to the front of the courtroom. They conferenced for a minute or two, and then the judge put the court in recess. The bailiff asked everyone to stand as the judge exited, and then the bailiff told the courtroom full of people they were free to leave.

Whitlowe chatted with his team for a minute while he gathered his things. They seemed pleased with the day's efforts. When he was finished, he approached Peters.

"Great job, Deputy. You stuck to the script. And you stayed calm. Good job."

"Thanks."

Chief King slapped his cousin on the back. "Great job, Floyd. Just be happy you didn't puke," he said with a smile.

"Felt like I would," Peters said. He rubbed his palms on his pants. "But you're right. It could have gone a lot worse."

CHAPTER 31
Winging In

Frank's flight from Birmingham, to Dayton, on Monday evening proved uneventful. It had been years since he'd last flown anywhere—Frank preferred to drive, especially if he could travel in an old car with some Coltrane or Benny Golson to keep him company. Frank told himself that he liked the simple things, and that there was too much hustle—and hassle—with airline travel. In reality, he had always felt trapped in a metal tube, a victim of his claustrophobia. But cruising along the dark highways, enjoying old jazz? That was more his speed.

But there wasn't time for him to drive on this trip. He'd offered, but the woman from the prosecutor's office had insisted he fly. And now he was sitting in coach, waiting for the plane to land.

He'd figured out how to subscribe to a music service called Spotify on his last visit to Ohio. Laura had gotten him set up with an account, and he'd been impressed with the depth of their jazz and blues selections. Frank also liked how you could save music to your phone. He couldn't believe kids nowadays were listening to Sonny Stitt. There must be other old-timers subscribed to the service.

As Frank looked out the windows at the dark night below, he was listening to "We'll Be Together Again," a bluesy piece by Eddie "Lockjaw" Davis. It was one of those jazzy blues numbers that made you feel like you were sitting in a dark, fashionable bar, sipping bourbon with friends while a quartet played quietly up on the stage. The piano melody elegantly traded places with the saxophone, while the slow drum and bass cruised along in the background. In Frank's mind, it was the perfect song.

He smiled at the thought of seeing Laura and Jackson again. As the plane turned, he could see an airport below. The plane was on final approach into Dayton and leveled out as the stewardess came on to remind them about their seats and tray tables and asked everyone to turn off their electronics. Frank took his headphones out and tucked them into his shirt pocket along with his phone. The plane was sparsely filled, and he had the row to himself.

In a few minutes, they were on the ground and taxiing to the gate. He put headphones back in and gathered his items. With this new phone and Spotify, there was a danger he would turn into one of these modern teenagers with their headphones in all the time, listening to music wherever they went and shutting out the world.

When the plane stopped and the "Fasten Seat Belts" sign went off, Frank stood and reclaimed his one piece of luggage, the new suitcase he'd bought for the trip. The pilot and flight crew smiled as Frank deplaned.

Apparently, Dayton was a small airport. He walked out of the gate area and followed the other passengers, passing closed restaurants and a darkened Starbucks. It seemed like most of the airport was already shut down for the night.

Everywhere he looked, there were reminders of Frank and Orville Wright and their discovery: Dayton seemed very proud of its "Legacy of Flight."

Frank made his way to the central hub of the airport—there were only two "corridors" of gates that branched off in opposite directions. He was passing through the "Exit Only" security checkpoint when someone yelled his name. He took out his headphones and looked ahead and saw Laura and Jackson, who was literally jumping up and down and waving at him.

"GRANDPA!"

Frank smiled and walked faster, pocketing his phone. Jackson ran up to him and threw his arms around Frank, who squatted down to hug him. "Hey, champ! How are you doing?"

Jackson gave him a big hug. "This place is awesome! They have an *actual* plane hanging up," he said, pointing over the main entrance. "Did you see it?"

Frank stood and walked with him toward Laura. Above the entrance was what looked like a full-size replica of the Wright Flyer, the original canvas and wood plane built by the Wright Brothers.

Jackson pointed, holding Frank's hand. "Did they fly it up there?"

Frank smiled. "Maybe," he said as he approached Laura.

"Hi, Dad. Good flight?"

Frank hugged her. "Yeah, but you didn't need to come out to see me."

"Don't worry about it," she said, pulling away. "This little one is never out of the house at night, so he's loving it."

"It's past my bedtime," Jackson said with a smile. "We're not even in our house!"

"That's true," Laura said. "Why are you still up?"

Jackson shook his head. "We have to get Grandpa!"

"Actually, I have to get my rental car," Frank said, frowning. "I hate to see you and run."

"Oh, no, that's okay," Laura said. "We just wanted to see you and welcome you to town. Do you have any more bags?" she asked, pointing at the baggage claim area.

"Nope, this is it," he said, hoisting his bag. "You want to get something to eat?"

"Yes! Let's get donuts," Jackson said, hopping up and down again. "Tim's Donuts! We passed it on the way here!"

Laura shook her head. "No donuts," she said to Jackson, then looked at Frank. "It's okay, I need to get him home. You sure you don't want to stay with us?"

"Free hotel room," he said. "Can't pass that up, right?"

"Can we come over in the morning?" Jackson asked. "Do they have free breakfast? Some hotels have free waffles in the mornings."

"Jackson, no," she said.

"I don't know about the breakfast," Frank said. "I have to be in court early." He looked at Laura. "Dinner tomorrow night?"

She nodded. "Yes, and then come over and hang out. And on Wednesday is the fireworks. When are you flying back?"

"Not sure yet."

They walked to the kiosk for Frank's rental car company and followed the signs to the shuttle.

"Looks like you're headed outside. We'll walk with you," Laura said.

He nodded and they left through the main entrance. Four empty lanes butted up against the sidewalk in front of the airport. "You're over there," Laura said, pointing at an idling van with the name of his rental car company on the side. "Better hurry—no telling how long you'll have to wait for the next one."

Frank nodded and hugged them both. "Thank you for coming, and I'll see you tomorrow." He gave Laura a peck on the cheek before hurrying off.

"Take care, Grandpa!"

He waved and climbed aboard the van as Laura and Jackson walked to a nearby parking structure.

The rest of his night was pretty uneventful. Once he got his rental car, Frank followed directions from the Waze app on his phone to the hotel, located just off the highway in Troy. He passed the exit for Cooper's Mill on the way north and felt a pang of sadness—he wouldn't be staying there on this visit. He saw the neon signs for the Vacation Inn and the Tip Top Diner and other places he recognized as he sped past the exit and continued north.

He found the hotel in Troy with no trouble and in ten minutes was parked and checked in and unlocking the hotel room door. He'd thought about a quick visit to the hotel bar, but decided against it.

The room was nice and the shower huge, one of those walk-in showers he coveted. He went about settling in and unpacking, then texted the assistant prosecutor to let her know he'd arrived. She wrote back and asked him to be at the courthouse at 8:30 a.m. and included directions. With all the logistics handled, Frank took a shower and fell asleep within minutes of hitting the pillow.

CHAPTER 32
Spectator

Early on Tuesday morning, July 3, Monty Robinson was catching the rest of the coffee klatch up on the trial, which started at 9:00 a.m. They peppered him with questions, mostly about Joe Hathaway and how he looked. He hadn't been seen in public for a while and Monty was the first of their group to get a look at their former member. Monty passed along his impressions, including the fact that Hathaway was stuck in a wheelchair. Apparently, his defense attorneys had hired a young woman to assist Hathaway in getting around, and she pushed his chair and got him food.

When the questions about Hathaway were done, they wanted to know about the trial. Will Duff, the bailiff in this and other trials, wasn't at the klatch. His shift started early on trial days, but he'd passed along some stories, so most of the people around the table knew what a normal trial looked like. Monty also mentioned the protesters gathered to support Hathaway.

"What a bunch of bunk," Murphy Collier said with a huff. "Joe was always clever—he had us all fooled. But then to get a bunch of random people online to follow you and send you money and speak up for you? That's just crazy."

"I guess," Monty said. "He does look pretty sad sitting there in his chair."

Janette Duff looked at him. "You're not feeling sorry for him, are you? I always knew there was something wrong with him."

Monty let that one go—Hathaway had fooled them all, especially Janette. But they said hindsight was twenty/twenty. "No. It's just...I can see why people who don't know him might sympathize for him."

The last of the questions trickled in, and then the conversation turned to politics again, at which point Monty stood and excused himself. "We getting together tomorrow?"

"Nope, this place is closed for the Fourth," Collier said, pointing around them. "Thursday?"

"I'll try to make it." Monty nodded at everyone and went to refill his coffee, then headed out. It was already getting warm outside, and it was barely 8:00 a.m. He didn't mind the heat, but when the humidity kicked in, Monty missed winter. Of course, when it was snowing and his boat of a car was sliding all over the road, he would miss summer again.

He walked to his Montego and climbed in the passenger side, slamming the door with a very satisfying thud. The door weighed like thirty pounds, and getting it open and closed was a workout. Monty slid across the bench seat and started the car, pulling out of the McDonald's parking lot. He turned left, making his way to the on-ramp onto I-75 north toward Troy. He needed to hurry if he was going to get a seat.

CHAPTER 33
Frank on the Stand

Tuesday morning, Frank was up early. He showered and enjoyed the free breakfast bar at his hotel before heading out. It was already getting warm as he crossed the parking lot.

Frank drove his rental car downtown, and circled the courthouse a few times before he found a spot. Downtown Troy was nice, although not as nice as Cooper's Mill.

He locked the car and walked to the courthouse. It took him a minute to finally realize why parking was at such a premium—there were protesters all around the courthouse. He saw two TV trucks parked nearby, with their long antennae sticking in the air. Next to one truck, an attractive woman reporter was doing a live shot, talking into a camera and pointing over her shoulder at the courthouse behind her.

As he got closer, Frank read the protesters' signs and realized with a jolt that they were Hathaway supporters. The people were chanting Joe's name and holding up pictures of the old man. One of the signs even read "I named my baby JOE." Somehow, the man had grown quite a following. Hathaway must have hired a PR firm or something.

Frank circled the protesters and spoke to a guard at the front of the courthouse. He explained who he was and was allowed inside, where he made his way up to the courtroom. In the hallway, he spotted Chief King and Deputy Peters and walked over to say hello.

"Frank, good to see you," King said, shaking Frank's hand and smiling. "Thanks for coming all the way up to testify. Hope it didn't put too much of a damper on your week."

"Not a problem," Frank said. "Happy to do it, actually. They flew me up and got me a nice room."

"Good," King said.

"Oh, and thank you for those letters you sent," Frank said to King. "They went a long way toward smoothing things over. You didn't have to do that."

"My pleasure. It was Peters' idea. Your boss said you might be retiring?"

"Thinking about it. Actually, I'm pondering a move. North, maybe."

"Cooper's Mill?" Deputy Peters said, surprised. "That would be great." Peters shook Frank's hand with a wide grin on his face.

Frank looked around at the hallway—it was full of people, including another reporter who was talking into a camera. "So, this is all insane. How is it going?"

"Good, we think," King said. "The prosecutor seems confident."

"They always do," Frank answered.

"I testified yesterday," Peters said. "You missed me tripping and almost falling on my face."

King and Frank laughed. "You know, Lola has a name for that," Chief King said. "Whenever Floyd almost kills himself, she says that he's falling 'ass over teakettle.'"

Peters made a face while they laughed. "I don't know why she can't just say 'bottom over teakettle.'"

"Because the cursing makes it funnier, Peters," Frank explained.

Two other people walked up to their group, and King introduced Kevin Whitlowe, the county prosecutor, and the assistant prosecutor, Bridget Turner. Frank shook their hands, and Bridget asked about his flight and the hotel.

"Thank you, the flight was great. And the hotel is very nice," Frank said.

Whitlowe lowered his voice. "Bridget covered with you what we'll be discussing?"

Frank nodded. "A quick run through the events of the date in question. No elaborating."

"Right," Whitlowe said. "Deputy Peters gave most of the details yesterday, so you'll be filling a few holes today. Mostly, you're here to talk about the chase and the wreck."

Frank glanced at King. "How much are we talking about Tom Mercato?" Frank fell quickly back into cop lingo. The question was obvious, but it actually was meant to find out if they were discussing the details of that murder investigation in open court. Policemen and prosecution often carefully planned out ahead of time what topics they were keeping off the table. In many cases, other investigations were still ongoing and couldn't be discussed, or a case was still being built. Or topics were explicitly avoided so the defense couldn't use them to introduce reasonable doubt.

"Not much, really," Whitlowe answered for King. "They know the CMPD was looking into it," talking about the jury. "We only discussed it to show motive."

Frank nodded. "Makes sense."

They discussed the case for a few more minutes, keeping their voices down. They were joined by another assistant, a law student named Winn Bartlett, who was carrying a stack of files.

The doors to the courtroom opened and the bailiff, a large man in a brown uniform, held the doors open. Frank recognized him—the guy was one of the old-timers from the McDonald's coffee klatch Frank had interviewed. "You all can go on in. Judge Wilson will call to order at 9:00 a.m."

Frank looked at his watch. "Do I have time to run and get a coffee?"

Whitlowe shook his head. "Not really, but I'll have one of my guys get you one. Bartlett?" Bartlett got Frank's coffee order and scurried off.

"How did your testimony go?" Frank asked as he and Peters headed into the courtroom.

"Good, good," he said. The place was filling up fast. The bailiff and other guards were letting a few protesters into the gallery, choosing them with some kind of lottery. "I didn't like the cross examination, but it went fine. They also covered all the ballistics yesterday."

Frank nodded. He'd testified in court more times than he could count, but it had been a while. He had been instrumental in solving many cases in the past, but the actual prosecution always fell to other people. Frank sat with Peters and King, and they chatted for a few minutes. It was friendly and casual and more pleasant than Frank could have imagined. It was nice to have friends, nice to be appreciated.

Bartlett returned with Frank's coffee while he and King and Peters talked about the closing down of the Dayton Area Heroin Task Force and the apparent demise of the Northsiders, a local street gang. Frank was sad to hear about the task force. The gang had attacked off-duty members of the task force in their own homes.

Just before 9:00 a.m., Joe Hathaway was wheeled in and pushed to the defense table. He looked better than the last time he'd seen him, mangled in the car accident. Hathaway gave Frank a look of pure evil, but Frank only smiled.

"I don't think he likes you much," Chief King said with a grin.

"The feeling's mutual," Frank said.

The bailiff called the room to order and everyone rose as the judge entered. Frank was surprised to recognize Judge Wilson. Frank had met him in the winter when he and King and Peters had been investigating Tom Mercato's disappearance. When Tom's frozen body was recovered from the lake, Frank had toured the ice shanty village. Judge Wilson's ice shanty had been the fanciest by far. He guessed it was one of those small-town things, where everyone knows everyone.

"All right, all right," Judge Wilson said, sitting down. "Clerk, read off the case."

The clerk stood and read off the case number and a few other salient points, then sat down. The court reporter started typing on her stenography machine. Frank noticed she also started a digital recorder.

"Mr. Whitlowe, you may begin."

The county prosecutor stood. "Thank you, Your Honor. We'd like to call Mr. Frank Harper."

There was a low murmur in the courtroom as Frank stood and made his way to the witness stand, where the bailiff swore him in. Whitlowe followed him.

"Good morning, Mr. Harper. Were you in the courtroom yesterday?"

"No, I was traveling here."

"You've flown up from Birmingham, Alabama, to testify today?"

"I have."

"Well, thank you for taking the time away from your work as an investigator for the Alabama Bureau of Investigation," he said loudly and slowly. He was obviously playing up Frank's credentials for the jury. "Can you tell us a little about yourself?"

Frank gave a quick overview, starting with his years in the military and his time as a beat cop for the NOPD. He talked about graduating to detective, then leaving the force and finding work in Alabama with the ABI, working cold cases.

"And you're still working there?"

Frank nodded. "Yes."

"Thank you," Whitlowe said. "So, you don't work for the Cooper's Mill Police Department?"

"No. I assisted on the Martin kidnapping case last fall, at the request of Chief King," Frank said, glancing at King. "I wasn't compensated for that, but I did share in a monetary reward after the victims were successfully recovered."

"That was last year, 2011. And this year?"

"I was in town on two occasions and helped a few people," he said, leaving it at that.

"How? Are you a licensed private investigator?"

Frank shook his head. "No. One woman hired me to deliver some divorce papers, and another man asked me to look into a situation with one of his tenants. They were being harassed."

"I see. So, were you assisting the CMPD with their investigation of the Tom Mercato disappearance?"

"Yes, unofficially. Mrs. Mercato asked me to deliver her papers and I learned he had disappeared. Until that time, everyone thought he had relocated to either Indianapolis or Chicago."

"At the time you were working with..."

"Deputy Peters, mostly. And Chief King, of course."

"Good, thank you," Whitlowe said. "Okay, in your own words, take us through the events of April 27, please."

Frank nodded and began describing that winter day months ago, starting with breakfast with his daughter and then a call to assist Deputy Peters at Trapper's Lake. Someone had reported a break-in at Tom Mercato's abandoned ice shanty. Frank covered all the highlights, only adding details when asked by Whitlowe.

Frank identified Joe Hathaway and pointed at him—the prosecutors always asked for that. Juries loved it, apparently. He wrapped up with his description of the frantic car chase and Hathaway's ill-fated encounter with the train. Frank did not mention what the CMPD found in the car or during their searches of Hathaway's property. Frank wasn't there to see them and didn't want to speak to the chain of custody or anything like that.

Whitlowe asked for minor clarification on a few things, such as Chief King talking Frank through the directions during the chase. Frank didn't know the area well enough and King had been on Frank's phone speaker, telling him where to turn.

When Whitlowe was done, a rat-faced man with the defense team stood and did the cross. Frank kept his answers short and didn't let the man bait him down any other lines of questioning. The defense attorney tried to get Frank to talk more about the Tom Mercato investigation, but Frank stuck to the task at hand. It wrapped up faster than Frank had expected. There were very few objections. The cross-examination went quickly, and Frank was soon seated back in the gallery.

Whitlowe raced through five more witnesses in the next two hours: the surgeon who cared for Derek Vole and his gunshot wound; two men who owned other ice shanties in the on-ice "village" of squat cabins; and an expert who testified on Tom Mercato's ice shanty and how it had been rigged to melt through the ice and sink to the bottom.

The fifth witness was CMPD's Detective Barnes, who reiterated the salient points of the prosecution's case and tied everything up in a nice bow for the jury. Whitlowe was clearly hurrying to finish his case before the judge broke for lunch. Just before noon, right as people were starting to get restless, Whitlowe wrapped up.

"The prosecution rests, Your Honor."

Judge Wilson smiled and looked at the clock on the wall. "Good. Let's break for lunch and reconvene at 1:30 p.m."

The bailiff led the jury out, followed by the judge, and then the courtroom was excused. Whitlowe came over to the gallery railing.

"Thanks, Mr. Harper. Great job."

Frank nodded. "You raced through those witnesses."

Whitlowe nodded and leaned in. "A trick I learned years ago. Keep it short and sweet, of course, but also make the defense present their case after lunch, if possible. Everyone is tired. Sometimes you can see the jury members falling asleep."

Frank smiled. "You need me to stay in town?"

Whitlowe glanced at Bridget, who had joined them. "Not sure yet. Let's see how the defense kicks off today. Would you mind staying through Thursday? We should know by that morning if we need to put you back on the stand or not. Barring any big surprises, you should be able to fly out Thursday evening. Closing arguments should start on Friday—we won't need you for those. Then it will go to the jury over the weekend."

Frank nodded. "No problem."

CHAPTER 34
Concentrating

Joe watched Frank Harper and the other members of the prosecution chat for a few minutes after the jury left. They all looked like chums, pals. He was certain they were talking about him. Joe tried not to stare, but he couldn't help it. Whitlowe was an animated speaker, waving his arms around as he spoke.

Joe was also thinking. Right now, he was concerned with pondering all the ways he could make that man's life miserable. What did Frank truly love? Who did he love? Joe knew he had a daughter, and a grandson—

"Do you need anything tonight or tomorrow?"

Joe turned to Tomlinson.

"No," Joe said, watching Harper and the two cops, including the retarded klutz, finally leave. "Just line up some good witnesses. I'm paying you guys a fortune."

Not taking the bait, Tomlinson only nodded. "We'll be in the office tomorrow anyway, preparing for our direct and closing."

Joe started to say something snarky, but McGinty joined them at the table, smiling. She was always so damned pleasant. "We ready?"

Joe scowled. "Yes, get me out of here."

McGinty pushed him out through the doors, where they were joined by their police escort, two junior Troy PD cops. They couldn't come in the courtroom, but they went everywhere else with him, even to the bathroom.

The whole thing was humiliating. He was the smartest person in the state, and he needed a woman's help to get onto the toilet. All while a cop stood in the corner in case Joe tried to escape.

Escape. They probably weren't *actually* thinking he could escape—as far as they knew, he was still crippled. He was making "some progress" with his physical therapy, but if anyone asked or checked in on him, they'd see he was still apparently dependent on the chair. They had no idea. Every night, when he was alone, Joe stood from the hospital bed and walked, pacing back and forth across his room, wearing out a path between the bed and the door and the windows that looked out over the humming highway.

He saw some of his followers in the hallway. Actually, they saw him first and let out a loud cheer, rushing toward him. The cops held them back, but Joe leaned over and signed a few autographs before the cops could stop him.

Joe saw a face in the crowd and nodded, recognizing him. Trapper always looked high as a kite. He stepped forward, nervous.

"Can you sign this, man?"

Joe nodded and smiled. He opened the brown autograph book and flipped to the first blank page, signing it. As he did, Joe felt a rectangular object beneath the book. He dropped it into his other hand and tucked it under his leg as he handed the book back to Trapper with a nod.

The kid took the book back. "Thank you, sir."

One of the cops came over. "Okay, move along," he said to Joe, then looked at Trapper. "Let me see that book." The cop flipped it open and checked for a signature, then handed it back, satisfied.

"You have a problem with my fans, Deputy?"

"Officer," the cop said. "You know that. Let's move along, people."

They got to the elevator and got on, and the cop pushed the button. They rode down in silence, the two cops, Joe and McGinty. Joe ignored the object under his leg.

When the elevator doors opened, the cops made a path from the back doors to the parking lot. Another group of fans swarmed around Joe, but he barked at McGinty to push him on. The cops held the back doors open and got Joe to the police van. The driver had the wheelchair lift already down and waiting, so he was wheeled right onto the small platform.

"Thank you! Thank you for coming!"

Joe waved at the crowd around him as he was slowly lifted up. He looked at the waving signs and the small crowd and smiled as he disappeared back into the white police van. These stupid sheep adored him. It was transcendent.

A few minutes later, they were on their way to the hospital. The Troy Police Department was escorting the van, a car in front and a car behind.

Joe watched them all through the windows, trying to get a sense of the scope of this operation. Was it a major focus for the Troy Police Department (TPD), or were they just escorting a prisoner from jail and back? Joe got the sense the TPD wasn't as hell-bent on prosecuting Joe as the Miami County Prosecutor's office or the cops in Cooper's Mill. As far as Joe could tell, this was just another job for them. Escort, watch over, make sure nothing untoward happened, guard the courthouse, and manage Joe's throng of fans.

But Joe had a few advantages to calculate into the percentages: his hidden ability to walk, his growing throng of fans, the untraceable cell phone he'd acquired only minutes ago, two loyal sidekicks (or loyal to a point, at least), and expert-level marksmanship. How could he use these things to his advantage, to turn the tide?

Joe thought about Tomlinson and the team of lawyers. It didn't look like they were going to be very useful. Joe knew he looked guilty. Could his lawyer throw up enough distractions and doubt to make at least one of the jury members reconsider?

Joe also watched the route—he'd already memorized the three different routes they took, seemingly at random. Today, the police van traveled through northern Troy, passing the Miami County Fairgrounds on the left. It was the land of county fairs and pig races and 4H clubs—thankfully, Joe had never been. It all sounded like a stinky mess.

This road paralleled the highway for a mile or two and then they arrived at the hospital, turning into the entrance and stopping in front. They reversed the loading process, extending the wheelchair loader and lowering Joe to the ground.

Another group of fans gathered around the hospital doors. They were not allowed inside or around the back of the hospital, where they might group around his windows to look into his room.

Joe nodded at them, noticing several attractive women in the group. If he were a rock star, he could have one of his "people" go out to the groupies and pick out a few young ladies for him to entertain. Unfortunately, he neither had the time, nor the privacy—nor the "people"—to make that happen. Instead, he waved as he and McGinty and the two cops headed inside.

Back in his room, Joe let out a sigh as McGinty tidied up. She reorganized the vases of flowers and threw out a few that were wilting or starting to brown.

"You okay?" she asked.

He nodded. "Yes, I just wish this thing would go faster. I hate waiting."

"I was sitting in the back of the courtroom," she said, her back to him. "Don't you feel bad about any of the things you've done?"

"Quiet, Missy. I don't need your judgment."

She said nothing. He knew she needed the job, and she was being paid handsomely, too handsomely to give him sass. She shuffled around the room for another minute, cleaning and tidying, then turned to him. "I'm off tomorrow for the holiday, but I'll be back on Thursday morning to get you ready and transported," she sassed.

"Are you mad at me now?"

"A little," she said. "Clearly you tried to kill those men. Was it to end the other investigation?"

He looked at her for a long time and finally shook his head. You never knew about people. Technically, she was his employee, hired on his behalf by the law firm. But there was no attorney/client privilege. She could even be working for the prosecution, or the cops might have her wired. "No, I didn't try to kill them."

"Right," she winked. "Whatever. Anything else for today?"

"A question—are firefighters busy on the Fourth of July?"

McGinty nodded as she gathered up her things and pulled on her yellow fireman's jacket. "Of course. One of the busiest days of the year, but I'm sure you knew that."

He smiled. "I figured."

"Lots of little fires, especially in the local parks," she said. "We'll get some serious calls—there's always somebody that decides to hold a firecracker in his hand to see 'what happens.'"

"What happens?"

"They end up in a hospital like this."

She turned and left, and he was alone. He rested on the bed, looking and feeling tired, and waited another half hour before getting the phone out from under his leg. Joe switched it on and called the only number in the "contacts" list.

"Hello?"

"Trapper?" Joe leaned forward. "Good job," he smiled. "Okay, let's get started. Take this down. I've got more things for you to work on."

CHAPTER 35
A Day Off

Wednesday morning, July 4. Frank was sitting on the bed, looking out the hotel window, thinking about what an odd day it was going to be.

Even without knowing what would happen, it was already strange. Here he was, in a hotel room in Ohio, looking out the tall windows at the back of a Walmart and the highway beyond. He had nothing to do today and nowhere to be, other than hang out with Laura and Jackson and enjoy the holiday.

Frank showered and dressed. Since he had time to spare, he got in an early-morning workout before showering, doing sit-ups and push-ups on the carpet. It was a nice hotel, especially the floor-to-ceiling windows. He could see his rental car, a nondescript Ford, in the parking lot below.

Locking up his room, he made his way down to the lobby, seeing several cops. The jury was also staying here, and the cops were busy managing them. It was more work than it seemed, babysitting a jury. They usually rented a batch of rooms for the group and the cops worked hard to keep them separated from the public. The cops likely escorted the jury as a group to meals and the courthouse. In more high-profile cases, each member of the jury was individually escorted by a policeman to and from their room every day.

Frank got a Dayton paper and waited out front. At three minutes after 9:00 a.m., a car pulled up in front of the hotel.

"Hey, mister? You want breakfast?" It was Laura, yelling at him with a smile from her ratty Toyota. She had a whole day planned for them.

"I would," he said, climbing in. Jackson was in the back seat, practically jumping up and down.

"Awesome," she said, pulling away from the hotel. "We're going to breakfast and then to one of Jackson's favorite museums."

"Airplanes!"

"You know it," she said with a glance in her rearview mirror. "You ever been to the Air Force Museum?"

"Can't say that I have."

Laura headed south on the I-75, passing the exit for Cooper's Mill and continuing into Dayton. It was already getting warm, even at this early hour. Frank sat back and relaxed, enjoying the drive. The last time he'd been a passenger on this highway, he'd been racing with Chief King and Deputy Peters to assist with a deadly situation at Dayton General Hospital.

"You're quiet today," she said.

He glanced over at her. "Just thinking. That's all. It's weird to be in town for only a couple of days."

"I know," she said. "Usually, you're around long enough to get shot at."

He smiled. She had his dark sense of humor, one that Trudy had always struggled with. His ex-wife had thought his dark jokes were a sign of depression. Actually, they were just cynical. There was a difference. And being snide was the only way he and other cops could hold on to their sanity.

They got off the interstate to switch over to highway 35, and headed east. Laura got off and headed south through Dayton. He pointed at a hospital on a hill overlooking the city. "That's Dayton General."

"Yup. We're near the college." A minute later, she slowed. "And here we are."

Laura parked in front of an old house that had been converted into a restaurant called Sunny Side Up. Jackson and Frank got out and they headed inside.

Breakfast was amazing—Frank had an omelet that was so light and fluffy that it nearly floated off the plate. Jackson had blueberry pancakes and Laura had French toast and bacon. They chatted and drank coffee, and Frank lingered over every sip, tasting each bite of the omelet and the home fries and the rye toast. He reveled in the conversation with Laura, even though absolutely nothing important or world-changing was discussed. But he was happy.

After breakfast, they headed east, passing through parts of Dayton that Frank had never seen before. It looked like most Midwestern cities, with tall buildings and old churches and older, residential areas surrounding it. They passed over neighborhoods and city streets, and Frank commented on what he saw. Jackson pointed out a few things along the way, but soon dozed off.

"So, things going well in Birmingham?"

"Yeah, I think so," he said. "I did want to talk to you some more about that."

"Shoot."

Repeating some of their phone conversation, Frank went into the discussions he'd had with his boss at the ABI and his future there. He shared with Laura how the cases just weren't that exciting anymore and wondered aloud what he should do next—and where. "Birmingham has been home for a long time. Now, I'm not sure."

"What do you want to do?"

"I don't know." He looked out the window as they exited the highway at some place called Kettering. They were driving through a busy area and came out from behind some trees into a vast, open field. Across the field he saw four massive, curved airplane hangars in the distance, arrayed across two large concrete airstrips. "Is that it?"

"Yup, best museum around," she said, changing lanes. "And it's free. Jackson loves the planes."

"It's nice," he said. "Growing out of the dinosaur phase?"

"No, but he loves planes, too."

She found a spot in one of the large lots and woke Jackson, and the three of them sweated their way across the wide lot, passing a grassy, park-like area before reaching the front doors.

Inside, it was much cooler. Frank saw an IMAX theater off to his left and a huge gift shop to his right. "Where's the museum?"

"Through the gift shop," she pointed. "Admission is free, so they gotta make their money somewhere, right?" She walked Jackson to the bathroom and Frank waited, watching scores of people stream in and out of the museum. Laura was right—this place must be popular on a sweltering day like today.

Once they walked through the gift shop, things got good. The first huge hangar was filled with airplanes from the two World Wars, many hung from the ceiling and decked out with era-specific flags or other decorations. Each plane told a story, and each story was more interesting than the last. Jackson ran from plane to plane, pointing out everything weird about each flying machine.

"Look, Grandpa, that one's made out of *cloth*! Who flies a plane like that?"

Frank nodded. "That is pretty cool, huh?"

He and Laura settled back into their conversation as they strolled through the museum, Laura keeping an eye on Jackson and Frank admiring the displays as they moved from room to room.

"Well, like I already said, you're more than welcome to move up here," she said. "We'd love to see you more."

"You say that now," he said. They were passing a modern B-2 bomber, and he was awed by the sheer size of the monster plane. "But visits are different. I don't think you want me around twenty-four/seven. I'm sure you'd get sick of me pretty quick."

She stepped in front of him. "No, I don't think so. Mom lives down in Cincinnati, and we don't see much of Kyle anymore, thank God. It would be nice to have family around, especially for Jackson. Honestly, I could use the help. And Cooper's Mill is nice, right?"

"It is," he agreed, thinking about the friendships he'd made with Chief King and Deputy Peters and others. "But I wouldn't want to cramp your style."

"My style," she laughed. "That's rich. Well, think about it. But, honestly, we wouldn't mind," she said, looking at Jackson. He was climbing up the stairs to the entrance of a plane and waving at them to hurry up.

CHAPTER 36
Alone

Joe's Fourth of July was not pleasant. He was usually fine with being alone—in fact, he often preferred it. But today, the hospital was running on a skeleton staff, and they had apparently forgotten his lunch. Most of the nurses and doctors either had the day off due to the holiday or had been reassigned to the ER.

As it got darker outside, Joe heard several ambulances passing by on the highway, a sure sign it was the Fourth. Probably more idiots blowing their own hands off, he thought.

Joe wanted to get up and walk, but he couldn't risk it—McGinty was supposed to be here any minute. He had called her for some food when the nurses didn't answer his repeated requests for lunch.

He was glad he waited, because a few minutes later McGinty came bustling in the door with a bag of McDonald's cheeseburgers and some coffee. It seemed like she was always carrying something or struggling with a package. Today she made two trips. After she handed him the food, she went back out to her car and returned with two large boxes of folders and paperwork, setting them on his nightstand within easy reach.

"Those are the copies of the discovery files you wanted," she said, breathing heavily. Joe glanced at the boxes. "Tomlinson said it's everything they got from the prosecution, plus biographies and CVs for their team members."

"Jury, too?"

She nodded. "Yup, whatever the cops gave Tomlinson." She looked around the room and sighed. "So, how are you doing today, Mr. Hathaway?" she asked. It was always the same. She was thin and pretty and full of energy—in fact, she would have been the perfect girl for him if he weren't smitten with May Mercato. Besides, McGinty was part of his plan, and part of that plan meant betraying her in the end.

Or killing her. Joe hadn't decided yet.

"Fine, fine," he said, digging into his cheeseburgers.

"Anything else bothering you?"

"Yeah, I'm going to jail soon," he said sharply. "And I'm surrounded by idiots. They skipped my lunch, and I'll probably miss dinner too with all the rubes that work here."

"It is so hot out there. You're lucky to be inside, where it's air conditioned."

He nodded. "How are my flock?"

Digging some snacks out of another bag she'd brought in, she filled Joe in on his fan club. "Sweating. A lot. The hospital at least moved them to the shaded side of the entrance. Before, they were sitting right in the sun. The whole group of them smells awful," she said, making a face. "I guess I shouldn't say that, but it's the truth." She handed him a box of Pop-tarts. "Just like you asked."

He smiled and set it aside.

"Don't eat them all at once, or the nurses will kill me."

"Yup."

She looked around the room. "Okay, I'm going to go. Need anything else?"

"No, not really. I'm going to call Tomlinson and chat with him."

"Okay, see you in the morning," she said quietly. He nodded and watched her leave, then dialed his cell phone.

"Hello, Joe?"

"Yeah, I'm here," he said, muting the TV. "Have to say I'm pretty disappointed with the case so far."

It was silent on the other end of the line for a moment. "Sorry to hear that, Joe. I feel like we've got a good case planned, once we start getting our people up there. We can go to town on the chain of custody. Their ballistics people were good, and our people found the same details, but the scene of the crash was wonky. They have collection issues, especially the slugs found out on the ice. Those could have come from anywhere."

"Are you ready for tomorrow?"

"Yes, Joe. Stop worrying. This isn't my first case. We've got two character witnesses that the prosecution doesn't know about, people from your old workplace."

"Okay. But I still think I should testify."

"We've gone over this," Tomlinson said. "You might come across as sympathetic, or you might sound patronizing. And the prosecution would grill you, get in your face, try to upset you."

"I'm fine with that." Tomlinson clearly didn't realize who he was talking to.

"I know, I know. You say that—hell, my clients *always* say that. But then they get up there on the stand and someone calls their mom a whore and they lose it."

"I can't go to jail," Joe said. "I won't." It was a moment of clarity, a rare moment when he was being honest. And he meant it—there was no way he was going inside. He'd managed to avoid jail by being injured, but he had a 162 IQ. Joe didn't belong in jail. He was a member of Mensa, for Christ's sake. Or he had been, up until he'd received their tersely worded (and grammatically perfect) expulsion letter last month. They didn't feel like it was a "good fit" anymore.

"I hear what you're saying, Joe." In the background, it sounded like Tomlinson was outdoors. Joe could hear kids playing.

"You're at a picnic?"

"Uh...yeah. Cookout. You know, for the holiday."

Joe shook his head. "Great to hear you're taking things seriously. You need to get me out of here. That's why I hired you," Joe said loudly, then stabbed at his phone, ending the call.

Christ. The man was at a cookout? CHRIST! He wasn't meeting with his people, practicing his remarks, going over the case again? The lawyer had gotten a gift from heaven, an extra day in the middle of the trial. It was a free day to prep, not a free day to eat hot dogs and watch his stupid kids play with firecrackers.

Joe set the phone down and breathed, in and out, slowing his racing heart. It didn't do any good to get upset. Plans were in motion, things that had nothing to do with Tomlinson or the trial.

He glanced over at the boxes of files. Tonight, he would review them, scanning for potential problems and opportunities. There had to be something in there he could use, either about the prosecution's evidence or the staff members. Maybe he could blackmail someone or get Trapper to lean on a juror's family. Anything to get free.

But before he started with the files, Joe leaned back into the pillow and closed his eyes. He visualized a sturdy tree, branching with possibilities. The trunk represented the starting point, the present, and a myriad of possibilities branched away into the distance. Soon, every possible outcome formed branches on the tree that took shape in Joe's mind.

The chances were very high that Joe would be found "guilty." He could see the branches extending from those outcomes...they ended in jail, or worse. But even if he were found not guilty, he'd be under the double murder investigation for some time. He could foresee possibilities where he got off on the attempted homicide charges. That would infuriate the police, redoubling their efforts to put him away.

However, there weren't many scenarios where he didn't end up in prison. Or dead.

But there were always more options. He saw ingenious jailbreaks and escapes, and he saw his band of hippies hiding him. There were scenarios that involved secret makeovers where he dressed as a woman and made it all the way to Canada and freedom, riding in the back of some ratty, trash-filled van with young women mooning over him. He liked that one.

Joe kept his eyes closed and explored all the options, playing out the next few weeks like a massive 3-D game of chess. Moves and countermoves and counter-countermoves. Joe would do something, and the police would respond, or the Court, or the prosecution.

McGinty disrupted some of the scenarios. He could count on her only so far before her morality would step in. But she helped him accomplish things he could not on his own. In his mind, she could be convinced to pull fire alarms, drive getaway vehicles, even get him to a small regional airport and help him steal a plane.

There were many options, and in some of them, she died. He didn't feel bad about that—it was all a means to an end. He needed to use McGinty as long as he could, right up until the moment she stopped being useful.

Joe relaxed, visualizing additional outcomes. Endless branches and endless possibilities. He searched for one that made sense to him. One with a positive outcome for him. Other people's lives hung in the balance, but he didn't shy away from collateral damage. He could kill McGinty, or a few of his fans. Or the prosecution team or the defense team or the judge or Frank Harper and his family.

None of it mattered, as long as Joe got away.

CHAPTER 37
Burn Them Out

Tyler and his father were back, gathering honey from the hives in the field near the abandoned farmhouse. Tyler watched as his father smoked the bee hive, and then opened the lid, pulling out the frames. They worked together to break off combs and put them in jars, but they hurried—it was starting to get dark.

After they were done, they trekked back across the field to his father's truck and Tyler asked his father more questions.

"Can the wasps kill someone? I mean, if they swarmed you?" The kids at his school loved to hear these stories.

His father nodded as he worked, cleaning the bottles and labeling them. "Sometimes. If people are allergic to bees or yellow jackets, one sting can kill them. People who are severely allergic usually carry epinephrine in stick pins for emergencies."

"What if you're not allergic?"

"They're still dangerous," he said. "I've read of a few cases where someone dies from the sheer number of stings. But it's rare. Worse with wasps and yellow jackets, though."

"Why?"

"You know how a bee stings, right? It's in the tail. When they sting you, it pulls the stinger out, and the bee flies off to die somewhere. They only get one shot. But wasps don't lose their stinger—they can sting over and over again, especially if they're agitated."

"Why do they get agitated?"

"Well, the queens are the most important part of a hive. Remember when I told you that bee queens overwinter alone, usually in a protected place?"

"Yup," Tyler said. "They live all winter on stored fat. They find a log or someplace, then come out in the spring and start a new hive."

"Right. Same goes for wasps and yellow jackets—the queen overwinters and then comes out in the spring. They build a new hive and start having babies, first to help them grow the hive, then guards to keep it safe. All girls, by the way—the boy drones come along later to gather nectar. Anyway, the guards can be vicious, especially wasps and yellow jackets."

"That's crazy," Tyler said.

"Yup, wasps are the worst. They're carnivores. Feed on anything. They love trash and picnic grounds and garbage cans—that's why they're always bothering picnics or buzzing around trash. And they love bee hives. They feed on the dead bees around the hive. If the guard bees don't protect it, the wasps will invade. They clean out a whole hive, leave you nothing but dead bees on the ground."

They talked about wasps and bees and yellow jackets while Jim Danvers finished wrapping the glass jars with labels, adding a bit of gingham and string around the tops of some of the bottles to spruce them up.

"One time, I burned one of the nests right as it was getting dark," his father said. "I wasn't paying attention and it was starting to get dark before I even noticed. Anyway, I put the gasoline in and then ran a line of it back a ways and lit it. The line of fire raced away in the gathering dark and disappeared down into the hole." Tyler listened, fascinated. "Flames shot from the hole, followed by fifteen or twenty wasps. They were on fire."

"Geez," Tyler said.

"They looked like fireflies at first, tiny flames dancing in the sky. But then I heard them sizzling, like little sparklers. It was gross."

CHAPTER 38
Fireworks

Heading home from the Air Force Museum, Laura insisted that Frank come over to her apartment for a late dinner. The fireworks at City Park didn't start until 10:00 p.m., so they'd have plenty of time to walk over and enjoy them.

Frank agreed, and she dropped him off at his hotel in Troy so he could relax for a bit before heading back to Cooper's Mill.

Frank headed up to his room and sprawled out on the bed to read the paper. Housekeeping had come, and he suddenly understood why rich folks liked to stay in hotels so much. While you were out, someone came in and took care of tidying up and changing the sheets and removing the trash. The daintily-folded towels and tiny bars of soap were just a bonus.

He was too wired to nap, and it was too hot to go outside, so Frank flipped on the TV. He caught the local news, which started with the sweltering conditions. A heat wave plagued the entire middle of the country, with rolling blackouts and "cooling" locations for those who weren't lucky enough to have air conditioning.

Next, they reported on the former Salem Mall. Up until a few months back, it had been the secret headquarters of the Northsiders gang, all of whom had either disappeared or been killed or arrested. Now, the local government was trying to find a new use for the sprawling complex. Behind the reporter, Frank could see the abandoned mall—and the metal roof he'd scampered across during his escape earlier this year.

The news went to commercial and Frank suddenly wanted a beer— like *really* wanted a beer. But he didn't have any. There was a hotel bar, and he thought about heading down there to slake his thirst, but he wasn't interested in dealing with people right now.

The news came back on with an update on the Hathaway case. The prosecution had rested after witness testimony from a Mr. Frank Harper. It was weird seeing his face on the TV, with a caption that read "Former Police Detective." Of course, the caption could have been worse. It could have said "Former Drunk," or "Left in Burning Field," or "Couldn't Save Young Boy in Atlanta." The best option might have been "Abandoned His Family" or something like that.

Frank listened as the reporter summarized his testimony, along with others. The reporter wrapped up by saying the defense would take over tomorrow and begin their case.

After the news ended, Frank flipped through the channels. He couldn't find anything interesting and decided to head to Laura's place early.

After he arrived, Frank sat down with Laura and Jackson in her small apartment and enjoyed a great meal of spaghetti and meatballs and garlic bread. Laura told him about her jobs and Frank talked about his flight up to Ohio.

After dinner, they watched TV for a while and then walked to the park. Even as the sun was setting, it was still ridiculously hot and humid. Frank carried a blanket for them to sit on, and Laura carried a basket of snacks and a six-pack of water bottles. Her apartment wasn't far from City Park. Families and kids were out, walking toward the park or playing with sparklers in their yards. A few people had lawn chairs set up in their own yards.

"They'll see it from here?"

Laura nodded. "You can see it from anywhere in the downtown, really, but City Park is best."

"Mommy, can I run around when we get there?"

Laura nodded. "Yup."

When they got to the park, Frank was surprised at how many people were there. Some set up chairs and sat on the grass, while others streamed into a small football stadium located next to the park. He was taken aback by how many people he recognized.

"Mr. Harper!" Frank turned to see Jake Delancy, a landlord he'd met on previous visits. Frank had helped Jake out of a sticky problem but had also managed to make another situation of Jake's much worse. They hadn't really spoken since.

Frank put out his hand warily. "Hi, Jake," he said. Frank wasn't looking forward to this—

"Hi," Jake said, shaking Frank's hand. "Nice to see you!"

"Really?"

"Oh, yeah. I was mad at you for a while, but I got over it."

"Oh," Frank said. "You're...I'm sorry about what happened. Especially with the Washingtons."

"Don't worry about it. They're fine. They moved to Toledo. And something good came out of it," he said, nodding behind Frank, who turned to see Rosie, the owner of a local bar, walking toward them.

"Hi, Mr. Harper," she said, smiling and sliding her arm around Jake. "Good to see you again."

Frank smiled at them. "Yes, it is. So, you two are a thing now?"

Jake looked embarrassed, but Rosie only nodded. "Yup. In town for the trial?"

Frank nodded.

"Yeah, that's crazy," Jake said. "I was still sore at you, and then I was reading about what happened with you and the Northsiders. Jesus, man. You definitely got the short end of that stick," Jake said, glancing at Rosie. "I couldn't stay mad."

"Well, I should have apologized anyway," Frank said. "I didn't handle things well."

Jake and Rosie were nodding when Laura walked up. Frank introduced them, and it turned out they already all knew each other. "It's a small town, Frank," Laura said. "I know Jake from the farmer's market. He sells his cheese there sometimes."

They chatted for a minute, and then Laura reminded Frank they needed to find seats in the bleachers. Jake and Rosie said goodbye, and Frank followed Laura and Jackson to the steps, climbing the stadium seats. They found a bleacher and put down the blanket, but Jackson was far too excited to sit down. He asked if he could run and play down on the field, where groups of kids were running and chasing each other. Frank suddenly remembered where they were. He'd been to this field before. It was the drop location for the second ransom in the Martin kidnapping case last fall.

Laura gave Jackson permission to play, and he scooted off.

"So, good day?" She looked at him.

Frank turned to her. "The best. Seriously."

She nodded and looked at Jackson, playing near the 20-yard line. "I don't want to pester you or anything, but I meant what I said. We would love to have you up here."

"Thank you for that," Frank said.

"No need to thank me," she said. "I could actually use the help. Babysitters are expensive," she said with a smile. "What do you charge?"

"Hmm, I'll have to come up with some rates. Maybe one spaghetti and meatball dinner per week?"

"Might get tired of it."

"Nope," he said. "Or you could alternate between that and lasagna. It's been a while."

They chatted and waited, watching the stadium fill with townsfolk. Frank watched the kids on the football field playing and running around in circles with sparklers, waving them in the air. It was nice.

When it got dark, someone came over the loudspeaker, asking everyone to stand for the national anthem. Jackson ran up the stairs and joined Frank and Laura as they stood and listened to a group of young people sing the national anthem. When it was over, people cheered and hooted, and then the first of the fireworks went off, racing into the darkening sky. He and Laura and Jackson watched the show, and at some point, Jackson got scared and wiggled his way on to Frank's lap.

"Don't worry," Frank said to Jackson. "It's just a lot of noise."

"It smells funny."

"That's just the smoke from the fireworks. It can't hurt you." Frank looked over and saw Laura was looking at him. Even in the darkness, he could see her dabbing tears away from her eyes. Frank didn't think her tears were from the smoke.

CHAPTER 39
Defense

Thursday morning, Joe and McGinty were transported to the courthouse for the first day of the defense's case. Joe rode in the back of the police van, thinking. The case wasn't going well, and everyone knew it. In some ways, it might have been a better idea for him to defend himself. It probably wouldn't have worked, but it opened up the case to more appeals. Courts frequently discounted a person's ability to defend themselves.

Tomlinson would get his chance today. Even so, Joe needed a sympathetic jury to get off. He needed them to feel sorry for him, like those idiot kids did outside the hospital. He needed the jury to feel like this poor old man was being railroaded by the courts, so he'd been doing his "feeble" best to look sickly and weak whenever the jury was in the courtroom.

It was also the reason he wanted to get up on the stand. He wanted to play the "sick" card, really talk it up to the jury while the lawyer questioned him. Act confused, act out of his element. And on cross-examination? That's when Joe could really shine. Acting confused and hurt and railroaded would work even better with Whitlowe barking questions at him. Joe had gone through all the scenarios in his mind—Whitlowe was a pit bull. Of course, he'd be a bully to the defense witnesses.

The van stopped, and Joe looked up to see a small group of his followers parting to allow the van through into the courthouse parking lot. The crowd held up signs—one read "Give Him a Rest," while another had a black and white photo of him, blown up, with the words "Victim" written underneath. In the picture, he looked gaunt and terrible.

Inside, they made their way up the elevators and into the courtroom, which was already full. Joe got settled as the bailiff asked everyone to stand while the judge entered.

"You may be seated," the judge said. "It's good we're back—the Court apologizes for the awkward break for the holiday, but it couldn't be helped." He looked up at Tomlinson, Joe's defense attorney. "Are we ready to begin?"

Tomlinson nodded. "Yes. I move to have the case dismissed."

There was a murmur in the courtroom, but Joe had known this was coming. It was a standard court tactic and almost never worked.

The judge nodded, not looking up. "On what grounds?"

"The defense moves to dismiss the charges in this case. The prosecution has failed to produce enough evidence to support a guilty verdict." Tomlinson had made several other procedural motions like that in the past few days to dismiss the trial. Often, they were just motions dropped into the record that could be relitigated during any later appeals.

Judge Wilson glanced up. "Motion denied. Anything else?"

"No, Your Honor. We're ready to begin."

The judge motioned to the bailiff, who brought in the jury. Joe slumped down even more and messed up his hair to look more disheveled. It was immature, but so was this trial.

The defense began its case by calling five character witnesses to speak for Joe. They were friends and acquaintances, people Joe had good relationships with. Two were members of the coffee klatch, and one was a neighbor. The last two were old coworkers. All five of them spoke glowingly of Joe and their friendships. Tomlinson had coached them on exactly what to say, working with Joe to highlight sympathetic aspects of their relationships.

The coworkers were surprise witnesses—the prosecution didn't know they were coming. They spoke about how Joe had been successful and compassionate at work, helping his fellow employees. It was bullshit, mostly, but they recounted a few incidents that could be seen in a positive light.

Joe also noticed Frank Harper was in the gallery—was the prosecution going to recall him?

The cross-examination for each of the character witnesses did not go as Joe had expected. Whitlowe only asked a few questions, and in some cases even confirmed what the defense was saying: that the witnesses liked Joe and that he was easy to get along with. When the prosecutor excused the witness, Joe was even more confused. What was Whitlowe doing?

The defense called two more witnesses before lunch, both of them EMTs from the crash scene. They testified that Joe had apparently tried to cross the tracks ahead of the train. The vehicle had been struck and thrown thirty to forty feet through the air, where it had come to rest in a wide depression in the ground.

They also spoke about his serious injuries and what had been done to save him. They both said the same thing—that the car driven by Frank Harper, an old Camaro, was a civilian vehicle and did not have police lights or anything else to suggest it was an "official" car used by the authorities. Joe knew Tomlinson was setting up the primary argument that Joe had just been driving along and gotten scared by being chased by a "random guy in a car." It was a good argument. Joe didn't think it would work, but who knew?

Before he could ponder it further, the judge called for a lunch recess. Joe was wheeled to a waiting room off the courtroom. He'd spent all the lunches in there with his team. Tomlinson had food brought in from a place across the street, and it was usually pretty good. They often talked strategy as they ate.

"So far, so good?"

Joe looked at McGinty, who was wearing jeans and her yellow EMT jacket.

"Yeah, I think so. Good witnesses today," he said, glancing at Tomlinson. "What's up for this afternoon? Will we be done?"

Tomlinson nodded, dabbing a bit of mustard from his tie with a napkin. "Three more witnesses, all similar. Another neighbor and two other folks from town. Then we'll wrap up. Prosecution gets a short rebuttal phase, and then closing arguments. Judge might start those or break for the day and start tomorrow."

Joe nodded, calculating. Once he was in jail, life would get a lot harder. He needed a plan.

"The EMTs came across as very trustworthy and honest," Tomlinson said. "That's what we want—to plant the seed of doubt."

"We only need one," Joe said, picking at his sandwich.

After lunch, things went even faster. Joe watched as three more witnesses testified about what a "great" guy Joe was, making him smile. He tried to be a little more animated for the jury, nodding and smiling when the witnesses said nice things about him. Two women on the jury kept glancing at Joe, and one of them was the foreman. Joe hoped at least one of them felt sorry enough for him to vote "not guilty" and create a hung jury, forcing a new trial.

Whitlowe didn't challenge any of the witnesses. In fact, Joe came off as a solid citizen of Cooper's Mill. Joe wasn't sure what Whitlowe was playing at, but it made him nervous.

After the final witness, the defense rested. There was a murmur in the courtroom—apparently, most of his followers expected Joe to take the stand. Two members of the media got up and left the room, probably to report that Joe hadn't spoken in his defense.

The judge glanced at the clock. "Mr. Whitlowe, do you want to recall anyone or present any rebuttal?"

Whitlowe stood. "No, Your Honor. We have no rebuttal and are ready to proceed to closing arguments."

The judge nodded, ignoring another round of murmurs in the gallery. "We have time to begin today, or we can adjourn for the day and start fresh tomorrow. Opinions?"

Before either of the attorneys could speak, the jury foreman raised her hand. The bailiff went over and spoke with her quietly, then walked over and spoke to the judge, who covered the microphone in front of him with his hand. He listened for a second and nodded before addressing the courtroom.

"Okay, we're going to end for the day. Please return in the morning for closing arguments."

CHAPTER 40
Heading Home

Frank spent Thursday morning watching the trial, waiting in case he needed to be recalled by the prosecution to refute something the defense suggested.

It happened often enough for there to be a "rebuttal" phase in most trials, where the prosecution has a second chance to put up witnesses or reexamine earlier ones. But Hathaway's team had a particular strategy, apparently. They weren't going after the evidence much or working to refute the prosecution's theory that Hathaway was at the lake. The defense called mostly character witnesses, trying to make Joe out to be a saint and paint Frank as a random civilian trying to carjack Joe.

During the lunch break, Whitlowe surprised Frank.

"You can head home," Whitlowe said, gathering his papers. "We're not going to need you."

"You don't need me to testify again? I can refute what he's saying about being a civilian."

Whitlowe shook his head. "I expected this, and we're fine. Let them have their little win—it doesn't matter. And actually, what they're saying is the truth. At least that's the way the jury will see it. You were driving your personal vehicle, with no lights or sirens. There was no way from the outside that anyone seeing you could know you were working for the CMPD."

Frank shook his head and started to say something, but Bridget cut him off.

"He's right, Mr. Harper. But it doesn't matter."

"No?" Frank was starting to get a little angry. "It's not important that I was chasing him for trying to kill me and two other people?"

Whitlowe looked at him and lowered his voice. "Of course, it matters, but it won't matter in the long run. They're trying to sow reasonable doubt, and my closing will take care of that. Easy peasy lemon squeezy."

Frank shook his head. "I hope so."

"We've got this. Thank you again for coming to town. I know it was a hassle." He patted Frank lightly on the shoulder. "You did good."

Frank didn't know what else to say to Whitlowe, so he said nothing.

He turned and talked to Chief King and Deputy Peters, letting them know he would be leaving. They shook hands and the chief invited him to lunch with them, but Frank didn't feel like hanging around.

Outside, he wended his way through the crowd of hippies and walked to his car. It was so hot outside, Frank could see waves of heat coming off the concrete. Even the metal crosswalk buttons were hot to the touch, and the power lines strung over the downtown sagged in the heat.

Leaving Troy wasn't nearly as exciting as arriving. But at least he'd flown to town with a purpose. He'd come to town to help put a madman behind bars or on death row. Now, he felt like the trip was a waste. The way Tomlinson had left things, it seemed like Frank was extraneous, and flying home to Birmingham felt like a defeat.

At the hotel, he packed up his things and got checked out of the hotel and drove to the airport. On his way, Frank stopped in Cooper's Mill at Laura's salon. They hugged and said their goodbyes.

The airport looked just the same as it had before. He turned in the rental car and signed for it. Then it was time to check in, a trip through security, an hour waiting at the gate, and some coffee from the Starbucks.

At the gate, Frank killed some time on his phone, reading the local and national news. The heat wave blanketed the nation, making it even worse for the more than a million people suffering through the heat without power due to last week's storms. President Obama and Mitt Romney were both talking about Obamacare during the run-up to the 2012 election this fall.

When they called his flight, Frank stood, waiting. He was flying coach and ended up being one of the first people on the plane. It took a while for the plane to board, and Frank's mood didn't improve. As the plane taxied and finally took off, he looked for Cooper's Mill but couldn't find it. Not that he really knew what he was looking for. It all felt so pointless.

Once they were in the air, the flight attendants passed through the cabin, taking orders for drinks and food. Frank hesitated for the briefest of moments, then waved the young man over.

"Bourbon, kid," Frank said, waving a twenty at the man. "Make it a double."

CHAPTER 41
Home and Alone

Getting home from the airport in Birmingham presented a challenge. Frank had drunk more on the plane than he'd planned. One double had turned into several, and the meager snacks had done little to soften the impact of the alcohol.

By the time the plane landed, Frank was feeling fine, awesome, completely mellow. And that would not do. He stumbled off the plane, thanking the flight crew, and walked to baggage claim to get his suitcase. He stood with the other saps and watched the bags travel around and around like a toy train set.

Frank stood there for ten minutes before he remembered that he hadn't checked a bag at all—he'd put it in the overhead bin. Cursing under his breath, he walked to the baggage claim attendant and explained the situation.

It took them another half hour to track down his bag. The maintenance crew had found it while they cleaned the plane and left it at the gate, and then the airline personnel brought it over. He thanked them with as few words as possible—even he could tell he sounded drunk.

Frank got his bag and started for the parking garage but then thought better of it. He was drunk, and self-aware enough to know it. He decided to get a cab, exercising the cautious part of his brain for once, and walked out to the cab stand, flagging one down. He'd have to come back out to the airport tomorrow to get his Camaro.

A taxi stopped next to him.

"Where to?"

Frank gave the Middle Eastern driver his address and climbed in, settling back into the seat. It was nice, not having to drive. It was no wonder rich people had drivers and got chauffeured everywhere they went.

"Good flight?"

Frank looked up. "Yeah, though it was just as hot in Ohio as it is here."

The driver nodded. "Hotter tomorrow, they are saying."

Frank shook his head. "Great."

The driver didn't say anything else and began fiddling with the radio.

Frank checked his phone for messages from Laura or the prosecutor's office, but there was nothing.

The cab came to a stop and Frank realized he was home already. He paid the driver and thanked him, then made his way inside and up to his apartment. It was after 10:00 p.m. and quiet in the building as Frank entered his apartment, setting his stuff down on the small dining room table and closing the door behind him.

He started for the kitchen to make himself a drink before he realized that would be a problem. He'd made a pact with himself several weeks ago—no alcohol in the apartment.

Shaking his head, he walked over to the windows and looked out on the night streetscape of Birmingham. The town was bustling, and he watched the cars below, racing to and fro. A few blocks over, there was a police car parked, the lights flashing around the nearby buildings, painting the darkness blue and red.

Frank leaned against the window. He was dreading going in to the office tomorrow. What if he just never went back? The thought of it made Frank smile. No more cold cases, no more slogging through musty boxes of evidence.

Frank stared at the cop car. That cop wasn't wasting time on old cases—he was probably helping someone or investigating a crime. He was helping people who were alive, right now.

Frank thought about that kidnapping case he'd worked up in Cooper's Mill, remembering the look on the one girl's face when she realized the whole thing was over. She'd told Frank later that she'd been sneaking out of the house by climbing onto the roof and walking around the rooftop. Apparently, she wasn't afraid of heights. Charlie, the young girl, had told Frank that she'd first climbed out there to find a way down to escape, but finding nothing, she'd continued to climb out onto the roof every night. "I just felt free," she'd said.

Free. That's what Frank wanted. He was tired of feeling trapped in a job he hated. In a town he didn't like. He could stay here and be miserable, or he could strike out on his own.

While he'd been in Cooper's Mill, he'd gotten two paying gigs without even making much effort. Could he be a private investigator? Would it be enough to cover the rent? He didn't know, but the prospect excited him. And Laura seemed fine with it. Better than fine. She'd offered to let him crash on her couch until he could get on his feet.

It's what he wanted, Frank suddenly knew. He'd been tiptoeing around it for so long, it felt like he was helpless to make a decision, but it wasn't true. In a moment of unbridled clarity, standing there and looking out over the city, Frank knew what he wanted to do.

It was time to go.

CHAPTER 42
Goner

Frank was nervous, more nervous than he'd been in a long time. It was Friday morning, July 6, and he was back at work after his trip to Ohio. Even with his nerves, he'd managed to avoid drinking this morning. No. He needed to do this with a clear head.

Frank sat at his desk, cleaning up files and paperwork and waiting for Collier to arrive. He was killing time by organizing the twelve in-progress cases, making lengthy notes on each folder explaining exactly where the case stood. When each file was done, he turned to his computer and typed in the same information into the case file that he'd written and attached to the file jacket. When he was finished, he put the file folders in one of the sturdy cardboard boxes to go back to the police archives.

Collier came in just after 9:00 a.m. and Frank stood, asking for a meeting. Once Collier got settled, he called Frank in.

"How was Ohio?"

"Good," Frank said. His hands were sweating, and he was rubbing them on the legs of his jeans. "Case is going well. They should get a conviction."

"You said the defendant is also up on homicide charges?"

"Not yet." Frank filled Collier in on the case, explaining that the local prosecutors had prioritized the attempted murders.

Collier nodded. "Makes sense. Get him behind bars, then take your time with the other cases. So, how can I help you?"

Frank opened his mouth, and nothing came out. He wondered if this was the right thing to do. Should he really be quitting a job that had paid the bills for several years and kept him from being homeless?

"Frank?"

He looked up at Collier. "Um, sorry. I wanted to talk to you about something."

"I figured that out," Collier said. "When you said you wanted to talk about something when I came in."

Frank nodded again and rubbed his hands on his pant legs.

"Is this about your trip to Ohio?" Collier asked. "Did you get shot at again?"

"No, nothing like that," Frank said with a smile. He glanced around at the framed pictures of Collier with famous people. "I'm not happy here. Anymore."

"I know that," Collier said, lowering his voice. "We've discussed it. At length."

"I've been thinking about what you said, about the pension. I've enjoyed my visits to Ohio so much, and I feel like I've already contributed everything I can around here."

"You want to leave," Collier said.

Frank nodded, feeling selfish. More selfish than he'd ever felt before.

"I just don't want to be here," he said finally.

Collier nodded. "Good," he said. "Neither do I."

Frank looked up. "What?"

"I want to leave," Collier said. "This might surprise you, but I'm not excited by the prospect of sitting here for the next five years, yelling at you and Murray," he said, leaning back from his desk. "You're not the only one with plans, Frank. Murray told me last year he's burning out. I also spoke to the chief of police. He would love to shut this division down and save money. The reduced number of cold cases could get rotated through his existing staff with no trouble. He actually said it might work out for the better—he's got people down there on the first floor with nothing to do."

Frank nodded, not sure if he should be saying anything or not.

"I told him he should make the cold cases a reward," Collier continued. "When his men want a break, they get a cold case and a month to work it. Sometimes it's nice to just have one case to work for a while."

Frank nodded. Clearly, Collier had been thinking about this.

"That's a good idea," Frank said. "Lots of different eyes would help, too. What about you?"

"I'll be fine, Frank," Collier said. He glanced at the photos on the wall. "I've always wanted to run for office."

Frank wasn't sure what to say. Was it a compliment to tell someone they'd make a good politician? It didn't seem like it. But he knew Collier would be great at it.

"So, let's talk this through," Collier continued. "How quick can we wind things down? A month? Two weeks?"

"That's...I guess that's up to you, sir," Frank said. "We'd need to close out the twelve current cases and transfer everything back to the archives. And you'd need to coordinate with the chief—you know, for the furniture and stuff. And this space, I guess," he said, looking around at the office. This was all happening so fast.

"Good," Collier said, grabbing his computer mouse and bringing up the departmental calendar on his screen. "Two weeks? I don't think it would take that long, but if Murray's okay with that, we can be shut down by July 20," he said, looking at the screen. "It's a Friday. We'll have a party and celebrate. The chief will want to spin this and let people know we're closing down. It sounds like progress."

Frank nodded.

"Good. Wrap up all the cases and update everything in the database. I'll talk to Murray and the chief, get the paperwork rolling. You want to retire, right? Take the half pension?"

Frank's head was spinning. "Yep."

"So, Ohio?"

"That's what I've been thinking."

"Good for you, Frank. Good for you," Collier said, his mind already moving on to the next subject at hand. "Everyone deserves to be happy," he said, half to himself. "Why isn't Murray in yet?"

"Not sure."

"I'll call him. I want to be the one to give him the good news. Oh, and make a list of what else we need to do before we're done."

Frank nodded and left. Were they really doing this?

Murray got in a half hour later, coming from a last-minute doctor's appointment for his kid. Collier called them both into his office and brought Murray up to speed and they were both happy and Frank felt like his entire life had come unglued. All the time he spent dreading his job—and it turned out these men were hating theirs as well.

The three of them talked about the future of the office and what needed to be done to wind things down. Collier would handle the administrative areas, and Murray and Frank would wrap up the current crop of cases they were working.

"What about trying to close any of our current cases?" Frank asked at one point.

Collier made a face. "Are any close?"

"Not really," Frank said. "There are a couple leads in one. I'm waiting on DNA to come back from the lab on seven of them." Murray agreed, noting that two of his cases were coming along, but neither of them thought any of the cases could be finished in the next two weeks.

Collier thought about it. "That's okay. Whatever we have that's still active on the twentieth, I'll pass along. The ABI can work those first. Send all the others back to the archives."

"There really aren't that many left," Frank said.

"I know. You guys have done a great job. And that's why the last thing you're going to do is type up *how* to work the cold cases. You guys have some great insights and unique ways of tackling them. Try and capture all that in a document that we can pass along."

Murray was smiling. "This is going to be fun."

"You know it," Collier said. "I can't wait to pack up and go."

After the meeting, Frank asked Murray to drive him out to the airport on their lunch break to get his car. Murray drove, and grilled Frank about why he'd finally decided to leave. "It took you a lot longer than I thought."

"Really?"

"Yeah," Murray said. "It's been a while since you've been happy. But your trips to Ohio always seem to cheer you up. How's the drinking?"

"Better," Frank said, leaving out the part about being too drunk to drive home from the airport last night. "I think I'm getting a handle on it now."

"You gonna retire?"

"Not sure," Frank lied. Even though he'd worked with Murray for years, for some reason he didn't want to speak his heart. "I was thinking about maybe picking up a few jobs here and there. P.I. stuff. You?"

"Can't wait to retire. We'll move to Carabelle, down by Tallahassee. We've got a vacation place down there. The wife has been begging to relocate, and my sister lives down there. We've actually been talking about it for a while."

They drove and chatted until they got to the airport and Murray dropped Frank off at the parking lot entrance. Frank waved as Murray drove away, then walked to the Camaro and got in and started the car. It rumbled to life like a sleepy demon.

Frank drove back to the ABI, deep in thought. Now that he'd officially put in his notice, it seemed like things were moving too fast for him.

He needed to make a list, or a list of lists. Frank had things to do at work to wrap up, plus home stuff and packing lists. Not to mention all the logistical stuff involving a move, things he'd need to do before leaving Birmingham for good. He needed to rent a trailer for his stuff. He needed to do the retirement paperwork and talk to his old boss at the NOPD and get the half-pension going.

As for Ohio, he'd need to move his banking and close the accounts he had here. Once he was moved, Frank needed to talk to Jake Delancy and find an apartment or house to rent. He needed to figure out what it took to get a P.I. license in Ohio and to get a concealed carry.

There were so many thoughts swirling through his head that he ended up pulling off the road and into a McDonald's parking lot. He grabbed a pen off the seat and found one of his little yellow notepads. He shook his head and began scribbling down notes. It was going to be a busy couple weeks. And to think, last night on the plane, he'd been so depressed.

CHAPTER 43
Closing Arguments

On Friday morning, the courtroom waited. Whitlowe chose to sit for a few seconds and regard his notes after the judge called on him.

Finally, he nodded and stood.

"Ladies and gentlemen of the jury," he began. "You have taken upon yourselves a sacred duty. You are the line in the sand, the law, the ones who decide what we will tolerate in this open society we all cherish."

He paused and walked to the front of the courtroom, standing near the jury box.

"In this case, it is you who will decide the guilt or innocence of this man," he said, turning and pointing at Joe Hathaway.

There was a sound in the full courtroom like a low mumble, and he took that as a compliment. It was important to gather up all the energy in the room and direct it at the jury. And it was important for them to understand the complex issues and solemn importance of their duty.

Whitlowe continued speaking, his voice echoing around the silent courtroom. This was always his favorite part of any trial, the closing arguments. All the discussion was over, all the witnesses done. Now, it was just down to him and the jury.

He walked them through the prosecution's case again, reminding them of key points and refuting some of the defense's suppositions. Whitlowe quickly reviewed the ballistics and the witness testimony of those who were shot at on the ice. Whitlowe also recounted Frank Harper's mad dash across the ice, running toward the sound of gunfire. The prosecutor kept things moving.

Next, he reviewed the defense's argument, systematically destroying it. They were coming at the jury with the "chased by a carjacker" theory. If Joe had just fired the guns, shouldn't he be expecting to be chased? Why did he leave the parking area in such a hurry? Didn't he see the man coming after him, and wasn't it reasonable to assume that the car chasing him was the same person? Whitlowe went through each step of the defense's case and explained why it was ludicrous.

But he didn't linger. The key to any good closing argument is speed. As soon as the jury got bored, you lost them. You had to remind them of the evidence and then move on. The last thing you wanted was for people to start fidgeting in their seats. Whitlowe watched the jury closely, and their body language directed his cadence. Short, punchy sentences worked best.

He also kept an eye on the judge and those in the gallery. Once they started yawning or checking their phones, it was a lost cause. Whitlowe kept it light and quick. He guesstimated how long most people would assume his closing arguments should take, then aimed for half that. Soon, he was wrapping up and looked at the jury one final time.

"So, you have the power. And the responsibility. It's up to you to put this man behind bars for what he did. If you choose not to punish Mr. Hathaway for his wrongful actions, what is the incentive for others to follow the law? This man, who meticulously planned the murder of two men, one of them a member of the police force. He carried out his plans, going so far as to set a trap that would result in the drowning of his two victims."

He paused and walked over, standing in front of Hathaway.

"When that didn't work, he tried to shoot them, hoping that would put an end to the investigations into his involvement in other heinous crimes. More than anything, this man is guilty. Guilty of betraying the rest of us, guilty of thinking himself above the law. Guilty of trying to kill three people, people with families and lives and children and careers. All so that he could escape justice."

He turned and looked at Hathaway for a moment. "But he cannot escape justice, ladies and gentlemen. He cannot escape justice because you, *you* are the justice. Coming for him. Coming to make him pay for what he's done. Because he's guilty."

Whitlowe turned and nodded at the judge.

"Thank you, Your Honor," he said, then went to his table and sat down. No one at the prosecutor's table smiled or patted him on the back. He'd chastened them on several occasions to avoid any type of celebratory gestures. Whitlowe hated that kind of congratulatory crap. This wasn't a football game—a man's life hung in the balance. Justice hung in the balance.

CHAPTER 44
The Defense Rests

Joe was surprised the judge didn't call for a break for lunch. After Whitlowe raced through his closing statement, Joe had expected Judge Wilson to give the jury a break. Whitlowe had kept things pithy, probably to keep everyone interested. Disappointingly, it seemed the jury paid attention to his whole argument.

But the judge didn't break for an early lunch—instead, he waved at Tomlinson.

"Counselor, are you ready?"

Tomlinson seemed surprised, as well. He stood and nodded.

"Yes, Your Honor."

He walked around the table and began delivering the defense's closing statement. Joe settled into his wheelchair and tried to look pathetic.

Tomlinson went on a tad longer than Whitlowe, hammering home the whole "reasonable doubt" angle. Joe wouldn't have bought it if he was sitting in the jury box. He really only needed one rube, right?

After a few more minutes, Joe found his mind wandering, thinking about that day on the lake. Joe didn't know why he fired at them—probably out of frustration. It wasn't the smart thing to do.

Joe realized that Tomlinson was still talking. Should Joe signal him, get him to wrap things up? If Joe was getting bored—and it was his neck on the line—would others be getting bored as well?

Finally, Tomlinson began to wrap up. He summarized the scant exculpatory evidence and then made a plea to the jury to keep a "travesty of justice" from taking place. Tomlinson was really bringing out the big guns, playing on the jury's fear of making a wrong decision.

He finished, smiling at the jury and walking over to Joe. He clasped Joe's hand and shook it as he sat down, another show of strength designed to stoke jury sympathy. Joe did his best to look sad and put-upon, but inside, he thought the hand shake was too much. Too theatrical.

It didn't really matter. The jury would almost certainly find him guilty. Joe had resigned himself to that. In fact, he was counting on it—the next few steps in his plan required it.

CHAPTER 45
Jury

Whitlowe had sat back and listened closely to the defense attorney as he wrapped up his closing arguments. There were no surprises. By the time Tomlinson had wrapped up and thanked the jury, Whitlowe was able to relax. You never knew about closing statements—they were supposed to summarize the case. But Whitlowe had been in a case or two where the defense attorney had pushed things too far to defend the "reasonable doubt" hypothesis.

Once, a defense attorney had even tried to introduce new evidence during his closing, which is a serious violation. Whitlowe had objected, something he'd never done during a closing statement, and he and the judge had to listen as the defense attorney apologized and broken down, crying over the fact that his client was going to lose. Whitlowe had been smart enough to say nothing. Fortunately, the judge had chastised the crying man and then instructed the jury to ignore that portion of the closing argument.

Tomlinson's closing was standard—go over the parts of the prosecution's case that weren't 100% solid, poke holes at the overall case, and remind the jury they were responsible for "deciding the fate" of Joe Hathaway. What a bunch of bunk. Hathaway had decided his fate when he'd decided to try and kill people.

Whitlowe was feeling confident. Judge Wilson rapped his gavel on his desk, quieting the gallery.

"Okay, the prosecution and defense have both rested," he said, glancing at the clock. "It makes sense to break for lunch, but I'm going to go ahead and give you your instructions now so that you can begin your deliberations. Counselors, can you come forward?"

Whitlowe joined Tomlinson at the judge's bench, and they discussed the final set of instructions to the jury. When they were done, the judge excused them and turned back to the jury.

"Foreman, are there any issues or questions you need answered before you may begin deliberations?"

The jury foreman shook her head at Judge Wilson. "No, Your Honor."

"Good. Members of the jury, you are tasked with deciding the guilt or innocence of the defendant." The judge went on to quickly describe what the jury members were allowed to consider and not consider while rendering their verdict. He also reminded them that they needed to be unanimous, then excused the jury to begin their deliberations.

When the jury had exited, the judge turned to the courtroom. "Okay, while the jury deliberates, we'll stand in recess. Counselors, do we have your contact information?"

Whitlowe nodded, as did the members of the defense team.

"Good," Judge Wilson said. "When the jury reaches a verdict, we will reconvene here. Court adjourned."

They stood as the judge and bailiff left.

"Think they'll come back today?" Bridget asked Whitlowe.

"I doubt it," he said, gathering up his papers and stuffing them into his ratty briefcase. "It's Friday lunchtime. They'll take the weekend, come back on Monday with a verdict. Who wouldn't want a free weekend in a nice hotel on the government's dime?"

Bridget nodded while Bartlett and Dorothy joined them.

"I thought it went well," Bartlett said. "He followed my estimated case nearly to the letter." It was obvious the guy was looking for a compliment or some validation. "Now what?"

"Yup, you did good, kid," Whitlowe said. "Now, we wait."

CHAPTER 46
We Wait

Joe waited until the judge was gone to ask.

"Now what?"

His attorney looked over at him. "Now, we wait. They could come back in an hour or four days. No way to know."

Joe nodded at the empty jury box as the spectators filed out of the courtroom. "No, I know that. But how long do you think it will take?"

Tomlinson shook his head. "Juries usually take their time. And it's Friday—I'd guess Monday or Tuesday. They'll take the weekend to deliberate."

Joe nodded, agreeing. "What if it's not guilty?"

"You'll be free to go, once you've recovered," Tomlinson said, nodding at the wheelchair. "Your home was released by the cops a month ago, and McGinty had a cleaning service in to freshen up the place. She's stocked it with food. She's been staying there off and on."

McGinty was standing nearby and nodded. "Yup, all ready. I thought it might be good luck to get the place all fixed up. All the crime scene stuff is gone as well, and I gassed up the car."

"Thanks," Joe said. Great to hear someone was keeping an eye on the place. "And what if I'm found guilty?"

"Oh, don't say that," McGinty said, but Joe ignored her and looked at Tomlinson.

"Well, in that case, it will go to sentencing, so another hearing in three or four weeks. Judge Wilson will ask the jury for recommendations before he decides. At the hearing, witnesses can speak on both sides before the judge announces his sentencing instructions."

"Until then?"

"You'll stay under arrest, and—"

"Would they increase the number of guards at the hospital?"

Tomlinson shook his head. "Oh, no, nothing like that. You'll still be in recovery. Once you're healed, you'll be transferred," he said. Joe noticed he left off the most important piece of information.

"To jail, you mean. Prison."

Tomlinson nodded, not saying anything else.

Joe was deep in thought as McGinty wheeled him out of the courtroom. He ignored her questions, and the reassuring words offered by the defense team. He looked at his hands in his lap and pondered what to do next. He ignored the shouting fans until one young woman pushed a flower into his hand.

"You go, Joe!" she shouted.

Joe looked up and nodded, thanking her, but his mind was occupied as he pondered outcomes, calculating next steps and possible results even as they loaded him into the police van and headed back to the hospital.

Getting the jury to find him "not guilty" had never really been in the cards, but pleading out had never been an option either. He'd needed the long jury trial to recover from his injuries. And now, he was more recovered than anyone knew. He could hop up and drive this police van if he had to. He could run while everyone else, including the physical therapists, thought he could barely walk. There had been a thousand laps around his hospital room in the dead of night, quietly orbiting his bed like a silent moon.

When the time came, he'd be ready.

But how to get away? He was working on several angles, and another two weeks would help. There was always a chance the judge had his sentence already worked out, but Tomlinson didn't think that was likely. Joe had read in some of the paperwork that, in the state of Ohio, victims' rights were a hot topic, and judges made sure the victims were heard in open court before a sentence was passed.

Joe had two weeks, probably. It wasn't a lot of time to work with, but he had plans in place, people working on things. And he had the element of surprise.

CHAPTER 47
Verdict

Whitlowe sat back and sipped his margarita. They were at Los Pyramidas, a local Mexican restaurant in downtown Troy, just a few blocks down from the courthouse. It had a great rooftop bar and cheap margaritas and was one of Whitlowe's favorite places to blow off steam.

He brought guests here all the time, and the service was crazy fast. No matter what he and his guests ordered, it was always on the table and piping hot in minutes. Maybe they had psychics working in the back who knew what you were going to order even before you did.

It was nice to be out with the rest of the prosecution team, unwinding after the tense case. Whitlowe hadn't heard anything back from the Court. It was nearly 8:00 p.m. and he was certain the jury would be out all weekend.

Bridget smiled at him. "What are you thinking?"

"Oh, just wondering what the jury is discussing."

Winn Bartlett spoke up, leaning over his plate of fajitas. "Based on my analysis of them, it's a good group of folks. They'll come back guilty, I guarantee it."

Bridget shook her head. "There are no guarantees."

The others set out to pick apart the defense argument. Whitlowe was happy to concentrate on his food and drink. The waiter came back around, and Whitlowe ordered another margarita and some more tortillas for his fajitas. He loved coming to this place and always got the same thing: the "Alhambra" fajitas, steak and chicken fajitas topped with bacon, jalapenos and cheese. They were to die for.

"I don't feel sorry for Hathaway," Bartlett said. "It was a good case, and I don't think the defense did much."

Whitlowe waved his fork at him. "Don't get cocky," he said. "And it's bad luck, talking about the defendant while the jury is deliberating."

"Why?"

"I don't know. Just always heard that," Whitlowe said. "Something about putting sympathetic vibes out into the universe."

The waiter had just set Whitlowe's second margarita in front of him when his cell phone went. He fumbled for it in his pocket, nearly knocking over his drink, which came in a glass that looked like a fish bowl. He glanced at the display.

"Judge Wilson. Guys, quiet," Whitlowe said, answering it. "Hello?"

"Mr. Whitlowe? It's Will Duff, the bailiff. The judge asks you to return to chambers. The jury has reached a verdict."

"Oh. Okay, sure," Whitlowe said. "When?"

"One hour. They need time to transport the defendant."

Whitlowe thanked him and hung up.

"They came back with a verdict, didn't they?" Bridget asked and Whitlowe nodded. The team didn't cheer or anything. Still, this was an incredibly positive sign.

"Okay, let's wrap things up," Whitlowe said. He and the others ate quickly and got the rest of their food to go. Whitlowe reluctantly avoided drinking much of the second margarita. It looked so good, but it wouldn't do for him to stumble into the courtroom drunk.

Winn Bartlett gave Whitlowe a ride back to the courthouse. He went to his office, splashing water on his face and changing into a clean suit he kept there. The other members of the prosecution headed home to change clothes—they had all gone out to dinner in casual clothes, assuming it would be days before a verdict came in.

At the appointed time, Whitlowe headed downstairs. There were far fewer people in the courtroom tonight then there had been this morning. Only two members of the press were there, and Whitlowe counted just four of Hathaway's groupies in attendance. They looked like they had been camped on the grounds of the courthouse. Just after Whitlowe and the rest of his team arrived, the bailiff held the doors open for Joe Hathaway and the defense team and Joe's female assistant as she pushed him to the defense table.

A few minutes later, the bailiff asked everyone to rise as the judge entered.

"I call this court to order," he said, sitting down. "The jury has reported to the Court that they have reached a verdict."

The defense attorney stood. "Your Honor, I'd like to move for a mistrial."

"On what grounds?"

"The defense contests the validity of this proceeding and asserts that the prosecution has failed to prove their case. The defense moves that the case be vacated and that all charges dropped."

"Denied," the judge said quietly. "Bailiff, bring in the jury."

The jury filed in and sat down. Whitlowe couldn't tell anything from their facial expressions. Usually, when a defendant was found guilty, the jury looked sad.

"Members of the jury, have you reached a verdict?"

"We have, Your Honor," the foreman said. She handed the bailiff a small piece of paper, who passed it along to the judge. He read it, making no expression, then looked over at Hathaway. "Defendant, please rise while I read out the verdict."

Everyone at the defense table stood except for the defendant. Joe Hathaway also started to stand and then stopped—it was as if he'd forgotten he was stuck in that wheelchair.

The judge looked back at the paper. "I will now read the verdict. 'We, the jury in the aforementioned case, find the defendant, Joe Hathaway, guilty on all charges.'"

Whitlowe expected gasps and noise from the courtroom, but no one seemed surprised. He always expected more drama than what actually came about—maybe he'd seen too many lawyer shows on TV.

Judge Wilson thanked the jury for their service and dismissed them. When they were gone, the judge turned to address the courtroom.

"The jury has found the defendant guilty of three counts of attempted murder." He stopped, waiting.

On cue, the defense attorney stood. "Your Honor, the defense makes a motion to request that you override the jury and acquit the defendant. If that isn't possible, we request a new trial."

"Motion denied. We'll set aside two weeks and reconvene this court on Monday, July 23. We'll hear from the victims and relatives at that hearing, and then I will pass sentence. This court is adjourned."

CHAPTER 48
Whirlwind

For Frank Harper, the next two weeks were crazy.

Frank suddenly had so many things to remember, he'd finally even made a list of his lists. This move to Cooper's Mill seemed to affect every aspect of his life. And as his work lists got shorter and shorter, it seemed the lists related to his move to Ohio grew longer and longer.

The day he'd put in his notice, he'd called Laura from work to let her know. She was the first person he wanted to tell. She was ecstatic and let him know as much. She yelled for Jackson to come to the phone, so Frank could talk to him for a few minutes. Jackson didn't believe him and made Frank repeat it several times. He also asked three times if he'd be able to ride in Frank's car, the "one with the headlights."

Laura offered again to let Frank crash on her couch for as long as he needed. "I'll put you to work. Dishes or babysitting."

"Gotcha," he said. "Sounds like a good trade."

Over the next few days, Frank started the process of moving by making a list with the title "Old Apartment." He began by cleaning, boxing up items for donation, and paring down his furniture so it could fit in a trailer. He gave his notice to his mean-spirited landlady, telling her he was leaving on the twenty-first of July and the place would be ready for a new tenant on August 1. She responded with a terse "Good, we don't need any druggies in this building." He'd started to correct her—he was clean and sober now—but it didn't seem to matter. She also barked at him to clean the place "real good" before he left if he wanted his $300 security deposit back.

At first it had seemed overwhelming, but once Frank had gotten everything written down, it was far more manageable. In fact, the finite lists of things to do made it all seem somewhat anticlimactic. Frank went down the lists, crossing items off as the weekend of his move approached.

Frank had thought he might need to get a moving van, but it turned out he had so little stuff that he'd be able to pack it into a rented U-Haul. He had the bed and his couch and just a few other pieces of furniture, along with two or three dozen boxes of personal effects. Once he'd described the size of his apartment to the man at the U-Haul dealership, they'd been able to pick out the right trailer.

At work, Frank wrapped up his files and teamed up with Murray to write the set of detailed instructions on the most effective ways to pursue cold cases. The document ended up being nearly eighty pages long and included suggestions on the best ways to work with laboratories and federal agencies. Collier reviewed the document several times, suggesting tweaks and additions. When it was done, Collier turned it over to his boss, the chief of police.

Williams, Frank's friend down in arson investigations, was sorry to hear that Frank was leaving town, but was also happy for him. Frank took him out to lunch a couple of times in those final two weeks. The lunches were quiet affairs, as neither of them were very talkative. Frank invited him and his wife up to Dayton for a visit if they were ever in the area.

Collier's mood improved in the final two weeks that the cold case division existed. He smiled and laughed as he packed up his office and seemed genuinely happy. Murray was all smiles, planning his move. He and his wife were excited.

On Friday, July 20, the ABI Cold Case division held a party to close the office down. People were invited from other floors, and the atmosphere was festive. It was also a combination going-away party for Frank and a retirement party for Collier and Murray. It was a fun affair with Collier stealing the show, talking about his plans. To Frank, it sounded like the man was already running for office—he had that cadence in his voice, where he wanted people to remember what he was saying.

All three of them received gold watches as their gifts, and Collier gave Frank a new holster for his gun. Murray got Frank some DVDs— the collected episodes of *The Rockford Files*—and a gift certificate for an online printing company. Williams got Frank a stack of expensive-looking books, titles they had discussed over the years, including a hardcover copy of *The Art of War* by Sun Tzu. Williams pointed at that last one and smiled—they had been discussing Joe Hathaway lately, understandably. "Believe it or not, there's some good stuff in there."

"Mine are for your new business," Murray added as they all chatted. "Now you can learn how to be a real private investigator," he said, pointing at the DVDs. "And get some business cards."

Frank thanked them, not knowing what to say. He had always had trouble making friends, and Murray and Williams had been his best friends in Birmingham. He would miss them.

Collier toasted Murray and Frank and wished them luck in their future endeavors. His speech turned into somewhat of a roast, recounting some of Frank's worst moments on the job. Frank kept his mouth shut and smiled along with the laughter. By the end of the party, Frank was sorry to see it end.

CHAPTER 49
Pacing

Two weeks had passed since his conviction, and Joe's anger had grown daily. His lawyers all assured him the sentence would be light, but he didn't believe them. What did they know? Why should he believe anything Tomlinson said? They'd also been sure he'd go free. Now, he was sitting alone in his hospital room, waiting to find out how long he'd be going to jail. That wasn't going to happen.

All he could hear was the distant beeping of machines in the nearby rooms. Dozens of little monitors and pumps, working tirelessly to keep their humans alive.

Joe stood and started his laps, counting as he went. His legs were strong now, stronger than anyone knew. He paced back and forth, glancing out the window at the highway with each lap around his room.

After a while, he took a break, resting his butt against the wall. He had one hand on the portable IV stand and had been pulling it around the room with him. That was his eighty-eighth circuit of the room tonight. He was also mixing in some squats and jumps while he was at it—as many movements as his portable IV would allow. But his mind wasn't on the exercise. Some small part of his brain was counting the circuits, while other parts listened for the nurses or people walking out in the hallway. But most of his brain was working on the plan for tomorrow night.

Joe turned and walked. He was getting out of here. And once he was gone, he'd set a few things right. Joe's little helpers were working overtime, gathering items. Plans were in motion.

The cops and the prosecutors might be scheduling a sentencing hearing for Monday morning, but Joe wouldn't be available. So sorry, but he had other plans.

CHAPTER 50
Time to Go

Saturday morning, Frank was up early and ready to get going. It was the big day, the day he'd been working toward for weeks. He had finished boxing everything up the night before and was waiting on the movers. He could have asked for help from coworkers, or hired a couple of kids from his street, but he didn't like having people in his business. Instead, the guy at U-Haul had gotten Frank set up.

Two large men arrived promptly at 10:00 a.m. They smiled the entire time they helped Frank schlep his couch and bed and dining room table and stacks of boxes down to the U-Haul. They made very quick work of Frank's stuff. They were so efficient that everything in his apartment was carried downstairs and packed into the U-Haul in less than thirty minutes.

Frank gave them a generous tip and thanked them. After they left, he went back up to his empty apartment and looked around. The place was quiet now, no sounds but the low hum of the refrigerator. All the appliances stayed since they were part of the apartment. He walked around the interior one last time, checking the bathroom for anything he might have forgotten. The bedroom and living room were empty. It was just a lonely, empty apartment, but he was feeling emotional about leaving it. He and this place had gotten along, ignoring each other's foibles. He'd miss the tall, floor-to-ceiling windows that overlooked downtown Birmingham.

Frank tried to remember how many times he'd had people over. He struggled to come up with more than a few occasions when Williams or Murray had visited. Frank knew he was an intensely antisocial person, but now he wondered if he'd missed out on something by not making many friends.

Frank set his key on the kitchen counter next to the note he'd left the landlord with his cell phone number, in case she needed to get in touch. The note also reminded her to return his deposit by check—he'd already had the mail forwarded to a post office box in Cooper's Mill.

Frank walked to the door and looked around one more time and smiled. He closed the door behind him, leaving it unlocked, probably the first time he'd ever left this place unlocked on purpose. It would certainly be the last.

CHAPTER 51
A Cut Above

Saturday afternoon was busy at A Cut Above, the downtown salon where Laura worked as an assistant manager and stylist. Laura was hopping from station to station, assisting three other stylists with their customers, while also running the register and answering the phones.

Located on South Second Street, behind O'Shaughnessy's, the salon occupied part of a former grocery building. Laura liked the salon well enough, but she didn't get along with the owner. Laura was getting some great managerial experience, but most of the staff were often upset with the way the owner ran things. Their main complaint was that the owner took too long to pay their salaries and tips, often citing "cash-flow problems." Laura did the books and didn't know about any cash-flow issues, but she kept her opinion to herself.

She and Jackson had arrived around noon and things finally started settling down after 4:00 p.m. Saturdays were always busier toward noon. The salon sported seven chairs and a private massage room, along with a nail station and three sinks for washing hair.

Jackson was there more often than Laura liked—she hated bringing him to work, but she couldn't always find, or afford a babysitter. He was hunkered down on the floor behind the front desk, playing with his collection of toy cars and plastic dinosaurs. Laura was seated on a stool nearby, tapping at the main computer. She was doing scheduling—easily half of their work was trying to schedule and reschedule appointments that were already booked. There were always messages on the machine from customers who needed to reschedule, and sometimes it was hard to find another open slot with the same stylist. Laura had suggested an online scheduling system, but her boss, so far, had resisted the additional expense.

"You doing okay?"

Jackson looked up and smiled. "Yep."

She smiled. He was a great kid, and great at rolling with it. Whatever she threw at him, he handled it. But she was about to get some much-needed help. Just the idea of her father moving to town made her smile. He was an interesting guy, and had his share of problems, but she was eager to see more of him. They were rekindling their relationship, starting nearly from scratch. She was curious to see where it would go.

Would they be friends, after everything that had happened?

Having a strong male figure in his life would help Jackson. And there was the whole babysitting thing. She hated that she couldn't afford to put Jackson somewhere every time she needed to work. Frank was supposed to get in late tonight, and he'd be crashing on her couch for the foreseeable future. Things were about to change in her apartment, and as strange as it sounded, she was looking forward to it.

That reminded her—she needed to run to Target. She needed to pick up a few groceries before Frank arrived. A friend of hers had texted Laura to see if she could swing by after work—she lived in the country and was on the way.

One of the stylists walked her client over to the front counter, and they chatted with Laura for a minute while she rang the customer up. The stylist and the client also worked out a new appointment that Laura added to the schedule. Once the credit card had been run through, Laura handed the customer a receipt and an appointment card and wished her a nice day.

The stylist waited by the counter as the customer left, walking out into the heat. "She's nice," the stylist said. "Thanks for booking her again."

"No problem," Laura said. "You had a couple people call in to reschedule, so I moved them to your next day." Most stylists worked a fairly regular schedule, and it was standard practice to avoid switching stylists, if possible, to honor customer preference.

"Thanks. Sometimes I think you're better at running this place than the boss," she said, heading back to her station to clean up.

Laura sat back on the stool and relaxed. For the moment, everything was taken care of: the stylists were all busy, Jackson was happy, and the phones were silent.

Laura went back to her *People* magazine. She loved catching up on celebrity gossip. Lately, one Hollywood starlet had been in the news a lot. Jessica Mills had starred in several films as a young girl, but she was having trouble making that transition from teen star to leading actress. She was always in the tabloids, showing up drunk at a movie premiere or worse.

Laura felt sorry for young women like Jessica. She obviously had no one looking out for her. The young woman had been rich and famous for as long as she could remember, and it had turned into a downward spiral. Plenty of other youth in Hollywood had followed the same path, and many of them had not lived to see the end of that road. Laura figured Hollywood was like a machine that sucked people in and chewed them up. If you came out the other side in one piece, you should count yourself lucky.

CHAPTER 52
Good Times

They finally had a cause for celebration. The conviction in the Joe Hathaway trial had been a huge deal. Detective Barnes and the others had worked hard, gathering evidence, and Chief King had decided to show his people what he thought of their work.

On this Saturday afternoon, he'd invited all the off-duty folks in and organized an honest-to-goodness office party. Even though the conviction had come down two weeks ago, it had taken King some time to pull this party together. He was horrible at planning social events, but he needed to get better. He wanted the CMPD to feel more like a family. To do that, he needed to make a point of interacting with the troops and their families more often. Hamburgers and hot dogs were being grilled outside, and he'd brought in corn on the cob and the "good" potato salad from Food Town, the nearby grocery store. After all the stuff that had happened over the last few months, the guys—and their wives—needed a chance to blow off some steam.

King looked around the interior of the police station, where nearly the entire department was gathered. Someone had put on dance music, playing it from computer speakers, and half the people in the room were moving to the beat. King had dimmed the lights and encouraged everyone who wasn't on duty to indulge. There was champagne and beer and cake in the glass-walled conference room that faced the back of the grocery. Beyond the glass and trees outside, King could see waves of heat coming off the black parking lot.

"Great party, Chief!" It was Deputy Stan, who gave King a high-five. "Thanks for the champagne."

King nodded. "Just go easy on it."

Stan wandered off. The man was trying to put his life back together after his divorce, and King wondered what he was doing to get his temper under control. He'd heard the man had taken up boxing. Good for him.

People were having fun, but King needed to say something before folks started to leave. He walked over to the computer and turned down the volume, then climbed up on the desk. Someone groaned as they gathered around.

"Is it speech time?"

King nodded. "Yes, but I'll keep it short. I just wanted to thank you all for the hard work you've put in on the Hathaway case. You guys helped secure a conviction in all three attempted murder charges."

A hearty cheer went up around the room, and several cops and their wives held up glasses of champagne. Detective Barnes leaned over and kissed his wife with a flourish, and the cops around them clapped and smiled.

King put his hand up. "I also heard from Prosecutor Whitlowe this evening," he said. "He's the head of the prosecutor's office for Miami County, for those who don't know. The sentencing hearing for Hathaway will happen Monday morning, and Whitlowe will be asking for the maximum sentence of forty years. He's confident Judge Wilson will take the recommendation under advisement."

Another cheer broke out, and King saw someone else he wanted to thank and nodded at her.

"And thanks to Bridget Turner for dropping by," he said, pointing at the assistant prosecutor.

Bridget raised her glass. "Thanks to you guys! Great job catching him and excellent job with the evidence."

"And good job, Luke," King said to Barnes. "You really pulled everything together. And thanks for advising and assisting with the prosecution."

People clapped, and Detective Barnes looked sufficiently embarrassed.

"Okay, everyone, enough with the speeches. Enjoy the party," King said, and there was another round of applause as he climbed down and turned the music back up. People went back to dancing and socializing, and King wandered around, thanking folks for coming. He ended up at the double doors that led out to the lobby. Glancing around, he exited, hoping no one would notice. He walked up the short corridor and turned into reception. Lola was on the phone, as usual. King walked up behind her and put his arms around her.

"Okay, that's fine. I've informed dispatch, and they are en route," she said into her headset. She jumped when he slid his hands around her waist and turned and gave him a look. "Over," she said into her headset, then clicked at it with a finger. "Jeff, you scared me!"

King smiled. "You're out here working and everyone else is drinking and having a good time."

"It's a nice thing that you're doing for them," she said, nodding at the door. "They worked really hard. Barnes has been burning the midnight oil on the Mercato investigation. I don't think even you know how many hours he's putting in."

King nodded and dropped his arms. "I'll talk to him about it. With this conviction, Hathaway will be behind bars. Barnes can relax and take his time pulling together all the evidence and witness depositions. Oh, and thanks for helping me plan all this. The food is a hit."

"I told you getting the good potato salad was crucial," Lola said. "People love it. I think it has bacon in it or something."

"So, when will you be joining us?"

She glanced at the clock. "My shift is almost over," she said, smiling at him. He was standing a little too close. "Hey, back up, mister. Nobody knows."

"Not yet," he said, stepping closer.

She put a hand on him and eased him back. "I like this job. You know that. And you like yours. We need to keep this quiet."

He finally nodded and smiled. "Okay. For now. But you need to come and get some cake. I'll cover the phones."

"You? You couldn't handle what I do."

He rolled his eyes. "With one hand tied behind my back."

Lola smiled. "No, I'll knock off early. Let me just switch it back over to the 911 center." She grabbed her headset and made the call that officially stopped the incoming 911 calls.

"Good," he said, walking out. She followed him, and he put his hand out for her to take it and she slapped it away. The sounds of the party washed over them, and she hesitated at the door. He could tell she wanted to kiss him but couldn't—too many people were around. Instead, she ducked under his arm and out into the room beyond.

CHAPTER 53
North

Frank was on the highway, heading north. It was just after 2:00 p.m. and he'd gotten away later than he'd planned. His heart was heavy—it felt strange, heading out of Alabama knowing he wasn't planning on coming back. Ever.

The Camaro purred through the Tennessee sunshine, pulling the U-Haul trailer with a temporary hitch Frank had had installed. It would be dusk soon, probably before he made it into Kentucky. He'd decided to drive in the afternoon, after the temperatures started to cool off.

Now, he was cruising north on I-65, circling Nashville's outer loop. The city's tall buildings were off to his left. He studied them as Sonny Stitt crooned on his CD player, singing "Blues Greasy," one of Frank's favorites. Nashville slid away and into his rearview mirror as Frank pondered what he would do once he got to Ohio.

First, he needed to find a place to stay. Crashing on Laura's couch would be fine in the short term, but he liked his own space too much. Jake should be able to point him in the right direction.

Frank drove on, passing around Nashville and north out of Tennessee, crossing into Kentucky and passing east of Bowling Green, deep in thought. He'd had a six-CD changer installed recently, so Sonny Stitt and the others could keep him company. Stitt led into Miles Davis and Stan Getz and McCoy Tyner, a pianist from Philadelphia who'd played with Coltrane in the mid-1960s.

Frank thought about being a private investigator. He wanted to get back out there. Frank needed to be helping people, and being a PI would let him do a host of investigatory activities, once he'd passed the exams and gotten his license from the state of Ohio. Over the past two weeks, he'd investigated the requirements. It would be good to get his hands dirty again.

CHAPTER 54
Laura and Jackson

Trapper found the woman easily.

She worked just where Joe said she did. He seemed to have spies everywhere. Through the windows, Trapper could see she had the little boy with her. Trapper and his friend Petey waited in the parking lot for a little over an hour. The place closed at 8:00 p.m.—he'd called ahead and found out.

He'd also made another phone call—actually, a text. Petey was smarter than he looked and knew how to spoof a phone number on a text. One of Joe's people had learned this woman had a friend who lived out in the country between Cooper's Mill and Huber Heights. Trapper hoped it was enough to get her to drive out of the city—it would be easier than trying to take her in town.

Ten minutes after 8:00 p.m., the lights in the salon flicked off, and she came out of the front doors. The woman walked across the lot with her little boy in tow. They climbed into a dingy car and started off.

At Main, she turned right, heading past First Street and Canal Lock Park and down the slope out of town. Trapper relaxed and settled in, following her. Petey sat in the seat next to him, asleep. The man could sleep anywhere.

Trapper followed the car along 571, passing the Freeman's Prairie on his left and cornfields on his right. Both cars headed east, passing the gravel pit and then over the bridge at the Great Miami River, approaching the light at the intersection of 571 and 202.

She slowed down and put on her blinkers to turn right, and Trapper sped up, rear-ending the back of her car.

It wasn't much of a bump, but it made a loud crunching sound, and her car started to slow, pulling off the road.

She stopped on the shoulder, a quarter mile from the light ahead of them. He stopped behind her, getting out. Petey woke and sat up, staying in the truck.

She was already out of her car, looking at the nasty dent in her bumper. Walking up to her, Trapper put up his hands. "I'm so sorry about that—you slowed down and I wasn't paying attention." He saw no cars coming from any direction.

The woman looked at him, aghast. "Jesus, man, that's not good. Look at that," she pointed. "You're gonna have to pay for that."

She turned to look at him and saw the gun in his hand.

"Don't freak out, Laura," he said quietly, glancing around again. This needed to happen quickly—he was too exposed out here. "Get your stuff and Jackson and get in my truck." He pointed back at the truck. Petey opened the door and climbed down.

She seemed surprised that he knew her name, and her son's, but didn't budge. "I'm not going anywhere with you, a-hole."

"My boss would like a word with you, that's all."

"I don't care. And I have a friend waiting for me."

Trapper shook his head. "No, you don't. We sent that text."

She didn't say anything.

"Okay," Trapper said, waving the gun at her car. "If you don't get in the car, I'm supposed to kill the kid right here. And you. In that order," he said as Petey joined him. "But look, I don't want to do that to Jackson. No one wants that, believe me. But if a car drives by and sees me here, I won't have a choice."

Laura bit her lip, looking at both of them. Trapper could tell she had already decided. Joe said she was smart, smart enough to figure out the situation. "Let me get my stuff."

"Hurry. And give him the car keys," he said, nodding to Petey, who put his hand out.

Laura stepped closer and handed over her keys, then turned and walked back to her car. Petey followed, helping her gather her things and taking her cell phone. A moment later, she was walking back to his truck with Jackson in tow. He looked scared. Petey got in Laura's car and started it up, waiting.

"Hi," Trapper said to the little boy. "You're Jackson, right?"

The boy nodded.

"Good," Trapper said. "I'm just giving you and your Mommy a ride. Don't worry."

He walked them to his blue truck. Jackson climbed in without hesitation, but the woman gave the truck a long look before getting in. Trapper went around and got into the driver's side and pulled out.

"What's going to happen to my car?"

"My friend is going to follow us. You'll get your car back when my boss is done with you." Trapper stopped at the light, then turned north, hurrying. According to Joe, this was the riskiest part of the plan. She might decide to fight back, and if she was going to do that, it would be while Trapper was driving. Of course, she knew he had a gun, but you never knew about people.

The other risky part was when they reached their destination—there was a small chance she might recognize it. Surely her father had talked to her about the place, maybe even describing it. If she did recognize the place, she'd probably lose it and start screaming.

CHAPTER 55
Joe Checks Out

Late on Saturday night, Joe was up, pacing. The hospital was quiet. He knew that nights were when the staff caught up on paperwork left from the earlier shifts. It was also when most of the cleaning and maintenance took place. Push carts of supplies were parked in corridors as nurses' stations and medical supply closets were restocked for the next day. All the floors in the public areas were also mopped and sanitized each evening to cut down on infection. On rotating evenings, the staff used a powerful floor scrubber and polisher, cleaning the different floors and wings.

By now, he knew the nurse's schedules by heart. Barring some unforeseen medical issue with one of the nearby patients, he should go undisturbed for the next seven hours. The last nurse had swung through his area just after 10:00 p.m., peeking in each room. They didn't check on people, in this wing at least, until the early shift at 5:00 a.m.

Joe got to work.

First, he needed to open the window. If he screwed that part up, he would wait for the alarms to go off and then claim he just wanted some fresh air. He found the manicure kit and gum among his belongings. McGinty had brought them, getting the kit cleared by the cops. Opening the kit, he took out the nail file. He also grabbed several sticks of gum, unwrapping them and throwing away the chewing gum.

Joe crossed to the window and set his items down, then studied the window. Metal contacts on the window and window frame would set off an alarm when he opened them. Joe unplugged the lamp on the desk next to the window, flipped it over, and cut off the power cord, using the nail file to saw through the cord and cut it into a three-foot length and to strip the insulation from both ends. It took a few minutes.

Next, he folded up two pieces of metal gum wrapper, folding them over each end of the wire. Last, he wedged the end of each gum wrapper into the metal leads on the window and the sill.

Joe breathed and pulled the window open, breaking the contact between the two pieces of metal. The current connected through the gum wrappers and the wire. He pulled the window all the way open and listened, but didn't hear any alarms. Warm air from outside huffed into the room, moving the curtains and the flowers.

Okay, that was done.

He picked up a plant from the windowsill and padded quickly across the hospital room to a table near the door that led into the bathroom. On the table were boxes, gifts and more flowers. Joe dug through the pile of boxes and found what he was looking for—McGinty had brought in a change of clothes. He found the pair of jeans, a black polo shirt, and shoes in some boxes near the bottom.

He took his clothes and the plant into the bathroom and changed quickly in the dark. Joe slicked his hair back, then took the potted plant and dropped it into the sink. He pulled the plant out and tossed it into the bathtub, then dug his hands into the pot. Taking handfuls of the moist, black dirt, he smeared it on his face and hands to darken his skin.

Joe went back out into the room and wadded up an extra blanket and some pillows and stuffed them under the sheets to make it look like someone was sleeping. The lump wouldn't pass any kind of inspection, of course, but someone glancing in the window might be fooled.

Taking a last look around, Joe grabbed the small bag he'd prepared earlier in the day—cash, his stash of medicine bottles, and his two cell phones—and returned to the window. He climbed up onto a chair and shimmied his way out, careful to not disturb the wire. On the ledge outside, he spun around and dropped to the ground.

It was warm outside. He ignored the urge to stand up and sprint away. Joe could see the large field that separated the hospital from the highway. Now that he was outside, he could see lines of trees to the north and south, probably marking the edges of the hospital property.

Joe crawled along on all fours, staying below the edge of the other patients' windows. He made his way to the side of the hospital he'd seen in previous sojourns outside in his wheelchair, pushed by McGinty to "get some air." He reached the northern end of the wing and continued crawling, moving across twenty feet of open grass before he reached the first of the cars in the parking lot. Crawling was slow going, but he would be nearly impossible to spot in dark clothes against the dark ground.

Still, Joe felt exposed. The whole time he was crawling, he felt like a spotlight would suddenly light up the grass around him. But this was a hospital and not a prison. There was only one police officer, and he was back near Joe's room, snoring lightly in the hallway, if the past few nights were any indication.

Once he made it to the parking lot, Joe felt comfortable standing. He walked quickly through the lot, moving between the parked cars, and crossed to the tree line, brushing the dirt from his shirt and pants. His legs felt great. He turned left, following the tree line to the highway.

A few minutes later, he reached a low fence that separated the field from the highway. A few cars raced by, their headlights bright in the darkness. Joe got out his burner phone and powered it on. He waited for the screen to light up and for the phone to connect to the cellular network, and then he pulled up WhatsApp, a messaging application—it was encrypted and untraceable—and sent a single text.

"Ready."

He waited, his nerves growing. But his mind offered up the comfort of large numbers. He'd done the calculations a thousand times. While it wasn't guaranteed, this course of action was the one most likely to succeed. He was setting himself up for success. Fortune favors the bold—and the prepared.

Joe checked the fence to make sure it could hold his weight. Not everything could be assured ahead of time, no matter how much planning you put into it—and hoisted himself up onto it. He clambered over, dropping to the ground. He headed down into the ditch that separated the fence from the highway and squatted down to wait. His legs felt good, strong. No problems there.

He watched the highway. A minute later, an old brown car turned on its signal and pulled off onto the shoulder, approaching him. He took a chance and turned on his phone, holding up the screen and pointing the display at the car.

The car slowed and came to a stop right in front of him. Joe stood and ran to the passenger door, opening it and climbing in. The driver nodded at him and smiled—it was Trapper.

"We good?"

Joe nodded. "Let's go. Keep it at the speed limit. Is the place ready?"

Trapper slowly applied the gas and pulled smoothly away, merging without issue back onto the highway. "It is, sir. The house had been abandoned. There's a long driveway through some woods, so no one noticed when we moved in. We have a few people staying there, and there's a lookout."

Joe nodded again. "The barn? The field?"

"Barn is nice. Huge. Looks like they burned the field out back."

Joe turned and looked back at the hospital disappearing into the darkness and began to relax. In between watching for police cars, Joe took out his burner phone and deleted the text he'd sent, along with all the contact information. He then powered the phone off and slid the SIM card out, putting it into his pocket. He also removed the SIM from his personal phone and powered it off as well.

Trapper reached in the back and handed Joe a package of wet wipes. Joe pulled a few out and got to work, cleaning his face and hands. When he was done, Joe settled back into his seat and watched the cars passing them on the highway. He'd been locked up in that hospital room for so long, it was good to be outside again. They still had a long way to drive tonight, but he was confident he would end up exactly where he wanted to be.

CHAPTER 56
Frank Arrives

Dayton, Ohio, Frank thought as he passed through the city. It was after 10:00 p.m. and the city was lit up, a few skyscrapers painted with neon colors. It was small for a metro area, and Frank found the highways confusing. Well, he'd better get them figured out soon.

The highway wound around downtown Dayton and over a river, then turned north. He passed several large factories and warehouses and a smattering of restaurants. The highway split into a huge cloverleaf that was under construction, the interchange with I-70. Signs marked where to go, and the lanes were bumpy and uneven. Three lanes went off in each direction, with several of the flyovers and roads unfinished, some of the ramps ending in midair.

He saw the familiar exit for the small town of Vandalia, home to the airport and that donut place Deputy Peters loved, although Frank had forgotten the name of it. The next exit was for Cooper's Mill, and he exited the highway with a new set of eyes. This was to be his new home, and he looked at it differently. Immediately, the place seemed dirtier, grungier, as if the shine had come off the place. On previous visits, the town was just a place to visit. Now, it would be home.

He exited the highway and headed east into Cooper's Mill, passing banks and the McDonald's where he'd introduced himself to the coffee klatch months back. It was the first and only time he'd ever spoken to Joe Hathaway. Frank had gotten the impression the old man was smart and compassionate. Sometimes you couldn't tell.

Frank passed the Dairy Queen and crossed Hyatt and turned to get to Laura's duplex apartment. Frank pulled his Camaro to a stop in front of the dark home. There were no lights on. He looked at his watch. He was disappointed that Laura and Jackson hadn't stayed up to greet him.

He got out and grabbed his suitcase. Frank walked up to the door and knocked, but there was no answer.

"Laura?" He said it quietly. Jackson was probably already asleep, and she didn't want to wake him. But there was no answer and he knocked again, more insistently this time.

Still nothing. And there were no sounds coming from inside. Maybe she was stuck at work?

Confused, Frank took out his cell phone and called her. Weirdly, the call didn't connect. It went straight to her voice mail.

Frank set his suitcase down and tried calling again. He didn't have a key or any way to get in. She had probably fallen asleep.

Ten minutes later, he was getting frustrated. He'd walked around the side of the apartment and looked in the windows for Laura's half of the building. There were no lights and there was no movement. Not sure of what else to do, Frank took his suitcase back to his car and sat in the vehicle, dialing again.

No answer.

CHAPTER 57
A Long, Strange Trip

Joe rode in silence, occasionally speaking up to direct Trapper. The kid knew the plan, but Joe had made a couple of minor changes, just in case.

They drove north, exiting the highway at Wapakoneta, a mid-Ohio town forty miles north of Troy. Joe dropped Trapper off at the pre-arranged location near the Neil Armstrong Museum, it's odd dome easy to spot even in the darkness. A blue truck waited for Trapper, and he got in and followed Joe at a distance.

Joe found the gas station with no trouble—he'd been directed where to go. This busy station was right on the main drag in Wapakoneta and was lit up with neon lights. Joe stopped at the pumps and made a show of gassing up, making sure to glance around a lot. This station had at least four security cameras, according to Trapper. Joe would be easy to spot.

Joe went inside and paid cash for the gas and drove away with a smile. Bread crumbs. Moments after leaving the gas station, Joe saw a car drop in behind him and knew it was Trapper.

They drove for another twenty minutes, heading west toward the Indiana border. Joe stopped at another gas station in downtown Celina, taking his time and making sure his face was on the camera as he bought a bottle of water and a ham sandwich from the sleepy clerk.

Outside, he dropped the burner cell phone into the trash, keeping the SIM card.

He turned south and left Celina, and Joe saw the lake stretching off into the darkness to his left. Trapper pulled around him and took the lead, turning off the main road and winding through the forested areas. They passed a sign for West Bank Park and drove inside, finding a secluded parking lot that faced the lake. There was a boat ramp, the end of it disappearing into the dark water. Joe pulled over and parked.

"Cameras?"

Trapper shook his head as he and Petey climbed from the blue truck. "None around here or at the dog park," he said, pointing north. Trapper, Petey and Joe worked together to put the car in neutral and push it down the ramp, where it splashed quietly into the water.

"You sure that car is clean?"

"Not clean, really," Petey spoke up. "I stole it two weeks ago."

Joe nodded. "From where?"

"Dayton."

"Good."

They watched as the car disappeared into the dark waters of the lake.

Joe followed the kid back to the blue truck and they all climbed in. Trapper drove, heading back in the direction they had just come.

Another hour passed, and Joe dozed. Trapper got back to the highway, heading south, back in the direction of Troy, but he exited at Piqua, the town just north of Troy on I-75. Joe didn't want them driving back past the hospital, in case his escape had been discovered and the police had already set up roadblocks.

Trapper drove east, taking progressively smaller roads through dark forests and corn fields that stretched for miles. They crossed several bridges, and just after crossing one marked "Great Miami River," the kid turned south. They wound through more back roads, crossed the river again, and slowed. The truck turned up a dark driveway that wound into some thick woods.

"There's Clive," Trapper said, nodding at a figure standing in the dark next to the driveway. Trapper turned on the overhead lights in the truck and waved. Joe was alarmed to see the young man outside was pointing a shotgun at the truck. Clive nodded and lowered the weapon, waving. Unsure of what else to do, Joe waved back.

The narrow, paved driveway wound through a stand of trees and exited into a large grassy yard. In front of them, on a rise above the driveway, stood a large farmhouse, with a circular drive that looped in front. None of the lights were on, and the place looked abandoned, just as Trapper had said.

Next to the dark farmhouse loomed a huge barn. Joe could see the outline of the roof against the summer stars. Trapper drove to the right and started up the circular drive in the direction of the farmhouse, stopping right in front of the dark, wide porch.

"Happy?"

Joe nodded in the darkness. "It's perfect."

CHAPTER 58
She's Nowhere

Frank was beside himself.

He'd expected to drive to town and find Laura and Jackson waiting for him. Instead, he'd arrived at the house to find it locked. Her car wasn't out front. A call to the cops had brought Deputy Peters and another cop to her house. Peters had been happy to see Frank, but obviously concerned for Laura and Jackson. Peters and the other cop, Deputy Stan, circled the duplex and then contacted the landlord to get a key. Twenty minutes later, the man arrived and let them into Laura's apartment.

There was no sign of them.

The investigation turned to Laura's last known location, and Chief Jeff King met them at the downtown salon where Laura worked. The owner was called in and the police searched the location, looking for any signs of foul play. The owner, a short rotund woman with a southern accent, also checked the computer and security camera—everything looked normal. She showed them the video, and Frank could see Laura on the black and white screen, closing up the shop and walking out to the parking lot. She got into her car with Jackson and drove away.

"That's it?" Frank asked.

The owner nodded. "She closed at 8:00 p.m. I don't have anything after that."

"All right. What's next?"

Chief King and Deputy Peters looked at each other. Frank could tell they weren't sure where to go next. Check for the missing person at their home and work—straight from the playbook. What else?

"Did she say she was going anywhere? Maybe a friend's house? Shopping?" Peters asked.

Frank shook his head. "This late? No, or I wouldn't have bothered you guys. She knew I was getting to town tonight. There's no good reason for her not to be home," he said.

Another car pulled up, a civilian model. Detective Barnes got out, walking over. "What's going on?"

King filled him in—Barnes had been off duty and happened to be driving by. Chief King got a call on his cell phone and excused himself.

Deputy Peters had one of his yellow notepads out and was writing things down. He finished catching Barnes up and then turned back to Frank. "Maybe we should talk to some of her friends. Know anyone in the area?"

Frank didn't, and said as much. He realized suddenly how little he knew about Laura's life in Cooper's Mill. Did she have lots of friends? Frank mentioned that she might be friends with some of the other stylists, and Peters nodded, walking off to find the owner to ask.

Detective Barnes shook his head. "Good news, then bad."

"What do you mean?"

Barnes pointed at Chief King, who had their back to them. "We had a party at the police station today. For the Hathaway conviction. Now, we've got another disappearance."

"Two, actually."

Chief King came back over to them, scowling. "Barnes, call everyone in. Joe Hathaway is 10-20," King said, using the police code for an escaped prisoner. "The nurses went in to check on him around 11:00 p.m. and he was gone."

"What? How?" Barnes asked.

King shook his head. "Get up there to the hospital and help. They've got the MCSO and Troy PD out looking. Coordinate with me."

Frank felt a sudden chill overtake him.

"He's got them."

King looked at him. "What?"

"Joe. He took Laura and Jackson."

Barnes shook his head. "That's a stretch, don't you think? We just found out he's 10-20, and you think he came here and abducted your—"

"I don't know," Frank said, suddenly angry. "I don't know, okay? All I know is that they're missing. Can you BOLO her car?" he said, using the term for a "be on the lookout" request to local police stations.

King looked at Barnes. "Go, get up there. We'll handle this. Check back in one hour."

Barnes nodded and left, and King looked at Frank.

"Okay, don't get ahead of yourself, Frank. Remember, a working theory is something that you work off of—"

"I know that," Frank said. "Don't you think it's a strange coincidence?"

"Yes. But Barnes is right—why would Hathaway risk coming back here? He's probably halfway to Chicago or Toronto by now."

Frank shook his head. "Unless they find him near the hospital, he had help. A car, a driver, something. Probably picked him up and drove away. So, if he's got people working for him, one of them could have taken Laura and Jackson after they left work. Maybe on their way home."

Frank could tell what King was thinking—how much of this was real and how much was in Frank's head?

"Okay, I need to go to the hospital, too," King said. "I'm going to leave you Peters and Stan. We'll rotate people back and forth. Floyd can continue the search, keep me in the loop on anything he finds."

Frank wasn't sure what to say. King was abandoning the search for Laura and Jackson. Although, to be fair, where else could they look tonight? There weren't a lot of clues to follow.

"Let me come with you," Frank said. "Look around. Maybe he left a clue for me."

"Just for you?"

"He hates me, Chief," Frank said. "You should have seen the way he was looking at me in the courtroom. I'm telling you, he's got something to do with Laura and Jackson."

King thought about it for a moment and then finally nodded. "I'll have Peters and Stan wrap up here and meet up with us. You stay with Peters until he's done, then drive up. You know where it is?"

"I'll find it."

King walked off to find Peters. Frank saw them talking and checked his phone again, probably for the fiftieth time since they'd arrived at the salon.

Nothing.

CHAPTER 59
Farmhouse

Trapper parked the truck in front of the farmhouse and Joe climbed down, stretching his legs. It was quiet here. He closed the truck door and it made a loud sound in the darkness.

"This is perfect," Joe said. It looked just like he'd imagined it would, based on what he'd read in the papers. He and the members of the coffee klatch had spent many weekday mornings discussing the famous kidnapping case over 'senior' coffees and Egg McMuffin's. "Where is everyone?"

Trapper nodded at the house. "Everyone's using candles and flashlights. No power. We told them not to shine them on the windows."

Joe looked up at the house and saw low lights flickering in the upstairs rooms, lights he hadn't noticed before. "How many?"

"Twenty-five of your closest friends, sir."

"And our two guests?"

"Doing fine," the kid said. "She's a handful, but the boy is nice. He's been playing with some of the other kids. We had to move her to the barn—she was making too much noise."

Joe nodded. They headed inside, and it was like coming home. The young people greeted him like a returning king. They looked like they belonged at a Woodstock revival, or a high school production of "Hair," but they served a purpose. If the cops knew the place was full of civilians, they might think twice before raiding it.

Calculations, always. Figure out the best way to do things, then rethink and add to the equation. Feign weakness, push the odds in your favor.

"Has anyone been around?" Joe asked as they toured the farmhouse.

"No, not yet," Trapper said, introducing Joe to the men and women. He led Joe through the house, showing him the kitchen and the upstairs and a bedroom they had set aside for him. Joe nodded, and they left the house, finally heading out into the backyard. There was a tall fence with a closed wooden gate in the middle.

"Burned?"

"Looks like it to me," Trapper said. "Cops torched the crop." He unlatched the gate and pulled it open and Joe stepped in. The tall wooden fence stretched away into the dark, surrounding the burnt marijuana plants.

Joe stepped back out and Trapper closed and latched the gate behind them. He then led Joe past a barren set of playground equipment and walked toward the barn. As they approached, Joe could hear someone shouting inside.

"Wow."

"I know, right?" Trapper walked to a door on the side of the barn and opened it, and the shouting got louder. "Like I said, she's a handful."

CHAPTER 60
Drunken Noodle

Deputy Peters walked over to Mr. Harper, a man he nearly idolized. They were still in the salon parking lot, and Peters could tell the old man was scared just by the way he was looking around. He didn't envy him. Laura and Jackson were wonderful, and Peters hoped nothing had happened to them.

"What should we do now, Mr. Harper?"

"'Frank,' I keep telling you, Peters. It's Frank, okay?" He sounded agitated.

"I know, sir. But I was taught to respect my elders." He couldn't even think of Mr. Harper as "Frank," not even in his mind.

"Do you call your cousin 'Jeff' or 'Chief'?"

Peters thought about it. "I call him 'Jeff,' but that's because he's family. And only when we're off duty—usually, I just call him 'Chief.'"

Mr. Harper nodded like he was making a point. "We're heading to the hospital next. Anything on the salon employees?"

"Nothing, sir. The business owner said they all work together, but she didn't think that your daughter socialized with any of them on a regular basis. Sometimes they went out for drinks at O'Shaughnessy's, but that was it," he said, pointing next door.

Peters could see the wheels turning in Mr. Harper's mind. Peters had no idea what to do next—if this were any other complainant, they would check again in the morning. "Where should we look next?"

Frank shrugged. "She's my daughter, but I have no idea what she does outside of work. I know she got another job."

"Where?"

"The Drunken Noodle, up near the liquor store."

"Okay, let's check there on the way to the hospital."

Peters followed Mr. Harper to his car, telling Deputy Stan to wrap things up here and clear the scene and meet them at the hospital.

The Drunken Noodle was a bust.

Mr. Harper had gone inside without waiting for Peters to arrive, but all they'd found was a group of folks sitting around the bar inside, drinking. The Asian Fusion restaurant was closed, and had been for nearly an hour, and the staff were hanging out and enjoying a drink or three while they cleaned and closed down the kitchen. None of the staff had seen or heard from Laura.

Two of the women grew worried, concerned for her safety, and they both got on their phones to call friends who might know Laura. Peters took statements from the staff and the manager while Mr. Harper brooded in the corner, repeatedly checking his phone over and over. Peters didn't know what to tell him.

Peters felt hopeless, and helpless, much like he'd felt last fall in Kyle Park when he'd overseen the search for those two missing girls. That was before anyone knew it was a kidnapping. He'd never forgotten that feeling of hopelessness, of not knowing what to do next. There was always another field to search, or another forest or park, but were the searches really accomplishing anything? Sometimes, the searches just felt like busywork, a mere distraction designed to make people feel like they were doing something helpful.

Mr. Harper walked back over to Peters, who had just finished his last short interview and released the staff.

"Anything?"

Peters shook his head and nodded at his yellow pad, which was covered with notes. "No, sir. She hasn't been in for several days. I looked in her locker—each employee gets one. Empty."

Mr. Harper shook his head. "Okay, I'll follow you to the hospital. Maybe there's something there."

Peters nodded and headed outside, and Mr. Harper followed. Peters hoped they would find Laura as well. She was a lovely young woman, and someone he could see himself getting close to. Outside, in the parking lot, he saw Mr. Harper heading to his car. The vehicle was packed full of boxes and clothes.

"Is that all your stuff?"

Mr. Harper nodded. "Moving day, remember? I had a trailer attached to the back. I left it at Laura's."

"Do you want to ride with me?"

Mr. Harper shook his head. "No, let's drive separately. See how things go at the hospital. If we don't find them, I'll come back to her house. The landlord gave me an extra key, so at least I can get in."

Peters didn't know what to say, so he just nodded. Mr. Harper got into his car and started it up, waiting, and Peters realized that Mr. Harper didn't know where he was going. Peters walked to his own vehicle and drove west, getting on the highway and heading north with Mr. Harper following.

CHAPTER 61
Barn

Inside, the barn seemed even larger. Joe walked past empty tables stacked with equipment he didn't recognize. They walked out into the large, open area of the barn. A pretty woman was tied to a chair, a gag hanging around her neck. Another woman was standing next to her, trying to get her to drink some water. Joe and Trapper walked up to them, stopping a few feet away. The standing woman turned to them, exasperated.

"She won't drink any water. Or shut up."

Joe nodded. "Leave us."

Trapper nodded and took the woman's hand. "Come on, take a break."

As the two of them left the barn, Joe went and found another chair and sat it down facing Laura's. He crossed his arms as she shouted at him, demanding to know who he was and what he wanted. After a minute, she took a breather.

"You done?"

"Not by a long shot, a-hole," she said.

"You're colorful."

Laura struggled with the ropes that tied her to the chair. "Where's my boy?"

"Jackson? Oh, he's fine. He's playing with the other kids here, I'm told. You should calm down. Then you could see him."

She stopped and looked at him for a second. "You're not one of these hippie dippies, are you?"

Joe couldn't help but smile at that term. "No, no. I'm not. But they are fans of mine."

"Then what do you want from me?"

Joe looked at her. "Oh, I don't want anything from you. Or Jackson."

"Then what do you want?"

He wondered when she would figure it out. "I need to speak to your father."

"Frank? What do you want with Frank?"

"We need to chat."

She looked at him for a minute. "Do I know you?"

"I doubt it," Joe said. "You would remember me, I think. Most people do."

She didn't say anything.

"Frank knows me," he continued. "I think he'll be anxious to talk to me, once he figures out you're gone. He'll come racing up to Ohio, and I'll be waiting. Will someone call him?"

"He'll be here quicker than you think," she said quietly. "He arrived tonight. He's moving to town."

"Really?"

She strained against the rope. "He drove up today."

Joe smiled and clapped his hands. "Oh, that's excellent. I didn't see that coming. I figured he'd hear about you going missing and race up here. He could drive all night if he's still on the Oxy."

"He's clean, now," she said, her voice barely above a whisper. "And yeah, I bet he'll want to talk to you. Or maybe he and his cop friends will just shoot you."

Joe chuckled. "I'm a better shot than any of them. Haven't you heard? How much did Frank tell you about me?"

She shook her head and glared at him. "Why would he talk about you? Who are you?"

"Frank will remember. He practically killed me in that car accident."

Recognition dawned on her face, and he felt a thrill run up his leg, like that newscaster, Chris Matthews, who got a thrill up his leg every time he thought about President Obama.

"You're Hathaway. Joe Hathaway. I thought you were in the hospital, or in a wheelchair."

He stood and twirled around before sitting again with a grin. "Was. Checked myself out. All better now."

"You tried to kill Frank," she said quietly.

Joe nodded. "Not my fault. He shouldn't have stuck his nose in my business. Now I need to speak with him. The easiest way to do that on my terms is to have him find me. Your father loves a good chase, doesn't he?"

Laura didn't answer. Seemed like she was done talking.

"Oh, now you're quiet? Good. So, here's how it's going to go. My friends are here to take care of you and Jackson. They will feed and water you both and you will eat what they give you. And you'll be quiet. I'm an old man and I can't take all that yelling. Agreed?"

She looked at him, and he could tell she was trying to figure out if he was telling the truth or not. Not that it really mattered.

"Okay, how about this," he continued. "You start yelling again, and you'll put me in a bad mood, and then you'll hear a gunshot and know that Jackson is dead. We're in the middle of nowhere out here—there are fields all around. No one will hear you if you keep shouting, and no one will hear the gun go off when I finally run out of patience."

He looked at her and didn't say anything else. He let his words soak into her, and she finally agreed.

"I'll be quiet."

"And you'll eat."

"And I'll eat."

"Good. You're not going to be here long. As soon as Frank knows you're missing, he'll come looking. I'll leave him clues. Once he and I have talked, you and Jackson will be free to go. I promise."

CHAPTER 62
St. Mary's

The disappearance of Joe Hathaway from his hospital room sent the combined police departments of western Ohio into a tizzy. By 1:00 a.m., the manhunt had begun in earnest, a search that would eventually monopolize much of the law enforcement in that part of the state.

The responsibility for tracking down and recapturing Joe Hathaway fell to the Miami County Sheriff's department. They pulled in resources from several other surrounding counties, including Montgomery County to the south and Darke County to the north. The MCSO offices on West Main Street in Troy served as the headquarters for the search, ironically operating out of the same building where Hathaway's trial had been held and where the Miami County Prosecutors' offices were located.

The first priority was to get the word out to surrounding jurisdictions with a detailed description of Hathaway. The Ohio State Highway Patrol (OSHP) was also involved and was setting up roadblocks on the border between Ohio and Indiana. Not only were they watching the highways, units had also been dispatched to check cars passing over the border on smaller rural roads.

The Troy Police Department had been removed from the case and relegated to traffic control. As often happened in a case like this, the local department would be looked at for possible collusion or wrongdoing. They were tasked with helping out with roadblocks for the OSHP and assisting other local jurisdictions with policing duties.

The MCSO's second priority was to get a tip line set up, which they got up and running around 3:00 a.m. Calls started coming in right away after an electronic alert was dispatched to area radio stations, phones, and other internet-connected devices. The alerts included a description of Hathaway. A temporary call center for the tip line was set up in a conference room at the MCSO offices.

The third priority was to establish a time line of exactly what had happened at the hospital. Chief King and the CMPD assisted, working out of a hospital conference room. In the early morning hours on Sunday, King was interviewing nurses and other patients to nail down the timing of Hathaway's departure.

When Deputy Peters and Frank Harper arrived, King had nothing to tell them. They were no closer to finding Hathaway, and there was no sign of Laura and Jackson. King had to admit, the timing was odd. King took Peters aside and had him call in two off-duty CMPD deputies to help. After that, Peters and Frank left. It made King feel helpless, but there was really nothing anyone could do.

After they left, King got back to work. A report came in around 5:00 a.m. of a possible Hathaway sighting at a gas station between Wapakoneta and Lake St. Mary's, about forty miles north of the hospital. The OSHP was dispatched and soon reported footage of Joe Hathaway at the gas station, along with a cash transaction and a car description and license plate.

Using that, the OSHP and MCSO tracked another transaction in Celina. It looked like Hathaway was headed west, out of the state and over into Indiana. The gas stations were both along a busy route that would lead drivers over the border in the direction of Fort Wayne.

As the sun was coming up, King wrapped up his interviews. There had been no reason to check on Hathaway before 11:00 p.m., when the nurse looked in on him after checking on another patient who had suffered some vomiting. The nurse grew concerned when he wasn't moving and found the balled-up sheets under his blanket. And the open window.

The nurse in charge seemed confused about how Hathaway had been able to move around so well. She mentioned sometimes patients were "more healed" than they let on, but that was usually a ruse to get more pain medications. King asked her if she'd ever seen a patient pretend to be less mobile than he really was, and she shook her head.

"Nope, never. For him to be able to get around like that? He must have been walking on his own. I'm surprised no one caught him."

King was assisting a Sergeant Wilkerson of the MCSO and reported his findings to him during an update meeting at 6:00 a.m. King also learned that investigators had tracked Hathaway's path from the hospital to the highway. It was clear the "injured" patient had covered nearly a mile between his room and the highway—and in good time.

Wilkerson nodded. "He was in a wheelchair for the trial?"

King nodded. "I was there. Maybe he was playing up his injuries for the jury."

The OSHP and MCSO were searching for Hathaway east of Wapakoneta, between there and the Indiana border, pouring in hundreds of policemen and coordinating with the Indiana State Patrol. Indiana also had a BOLO out on Hathaway's car, and had started a ring of roadblocks out from the Ohio border east of Fort Wayne.

"Also, we're getting reports of a bunch of credit card transactions in Hathaway's name," Wilkerson said, holding up another sheet. "All in the Detroit area. Started yesterday around noon. Shops, restaurants, and other locations. I've got officers headed up there to coordinate with Michigan State Police."

King nodded and made a note of it. How could Hathaway be in two places at the same time?

The conversation turned to the stolen car and any accomplices. It was clear Joe had had help. "The car was taken from Dayton and reported missing on the eighteenth, so someone's been planning this for a few days," Wilkerson said. He held up a printout. "Hathaway had to be communicating with someone, setting up the pickup."

After the briefing, Wilkerson walked over to King. "What kind of staff do you have here?"

King knew without looking. "Five deputies and my detective, Barnes. Two are interviewing staff members, and Barnes is helping with the crime scene at the highway."

"Good," Wilkerson said. "Some of the men from OSHP are starting the interviews with the Troy PD officers, especially the ones who have been on duty here," he said. "I don't like doing it, but someone has to. But that means we're short handed up west of Wapok," Wilkerson said, using the local shorthand for Wapakoneta. "Can I get you and your men up there to help with the search?

"No problem," King said. "We'll get rounded up and head in that direction. Who's coordinating up there?"

Wilkerson gave King the name of a Sergeant Moynihan with the OSHP. "He's running everything along 33 to the border and coordinating with the Indiana State Police."

CHAPTER 63
Trapped

She awoke and looked around. It was Sunday morning, and Laura could see the interior of the barn much better.

The place was huge, with wide wooden beams and high rafters. She saw a bunch of wooden tables stacked along one side of the barn, and another area with more tables under a lower ceiling. In one corner of the barn, she saw an old, rusting car. The windows were brown and caked with years of dirt, and the passenger door was wedged against the barn wall. On the opposite side of the barn there was a sliding door at least fifteen feet high. It had sat partially open all night, a dark strip of inky blackness. Now, after the sun had come up, she could see outside and make out a tall fence and some trees beyond it.

She'd been tied to that chair all night, ever since they had brought her and Jackson here, and sitting in the chair overnight had made her back and legs hurt. They'd let her out once in the night to go to the bathroom. She'd stumbled in the dark, led by the woman.

This morning, she'd started loudly demanding food and water and a chance to see Jackson as soon as she woke up. Finally, Laura heard a door creaking, and the woman from last night came in, followed by a large man with a shotgun.

"What do you want?"

"I have to pee," Laura said. "And I need to see my son."

"Can't help you with your son," she said, but she walked over and untied her. The man stood off to the side and pointed his gun at Laura. The woman turned and led Laura past the tables and she realized this area of the barn had been used as a workshop, with wide wooden tables and florescent light fixtures hanging low over each. On some of the tables she saw old scales along with some other equipment. It looked like someone had used this area for packaging goods of some sort.

"Over there," the woman said, pointing, and Laura saw the small bathroom. They had brought her to use it overnight, but now, in the daylight, she could see it was built into the corner of the work area. Inside, Laura did her business quickly and then pressed against all the walls and ceiling, looking for soft spots in the wood or a loose board. She found nothing.

When she came out, the woman pointed at the table behind her. There was a plate of eggs and toast and some wet wipes for her hands.

"Eat."

"I want to see Jackson."

The woman shrugged. "Again, can't help you. Take it up with the boss."

Laura sat and ate, and the woman sat across from her. The man sat on a table nearby, his gun across his knees.

"So, why am I here?"

The woman shrugged. "Not my deal. Boss says it's going to happen, it happens."

"Hathaway? You work for him?"

"We all do."

"Why?"

There was movement off to her left, and she saw the man walk in. He waved the two others away and sat where the woman had been sitting.

"Because they believe in me. I'm the keeper of truth."

Laura looked at him. "You have a cause? I thought you just liked to freeze people. And kill pregnant women."

Hathaway looked at her. "You're just like him, aren't you? You have the same expression when you make your salty comments," Hathaway said. "Did you know that he interviewed me?"

"No."

"Came to the McDonald's where my friends and I were eating. Asked us all kinds of questions, and he never had a clue. Not one. I sat right there and talked to your *brilliant* father and he never suspected a thing."

She looked at him. "Great. You're so clever. So, Jackson and I are your bait." She lowered her voice. "He'll come for us, you know."

"I hope so. I'm counting on it."

"And then what? He's a cop, and he's got cop friends. Lots of 'em."

Hathaway smiled and looked at the woman standing off to the side. "See? I told you she was just like him."

The woman nodded. Hathaway looked back at Laura.

"Well, most of his friends are busy in Wapakoneta, or up near Detroit, looking for me. They're beside themselves."

"Whatever," Laura said, finishing her food.

"Clever retort. Plus, I'm not sure if I believe you about him being clean. Once an addict, always an addict. He's probably high right now."

She shook her head and sat back, looking at him. He waited, but she didn't say anything.

"Out of witty remarks?" When she didn't reply, he smiled and turned to face the others. "Tie her up," he gestured before turning back to Laura. "And don't worry, Miss. This will all be over soon."

CHAPTER 64
Frank Gets A Clue

Frank wasn't sure how to proceed.

It was Sunday afternoon and the day was half gone. Laura and Jackson had been missing since sometime last night. Frank had been beside himself all morning, driving around town aimlessly, searching. No one seemed to have any idea where they were. And no one seemed as worried as he was.

There was no sign of Laura's car, and his endless calls to her phone were going unanswered. He had investigated the "Find My Friends" and "Find My Phone" apps on his phone and even spoken to a representative at Apple, but they were unable to track her phone's location.

He didn't know what to do next. He'd gone back to Laura's apartment around 4:00 a.m. and tried to get some sleep on her couch. He'd dozed, fitfully, for a few hours. He got up around 10:00 a.m. and driven around before heading back to the police station.

Now, Frank sat in the station at one of the large tables in the middle of the bullpen. There was no one there but him and Peters. Everyone else was either on the streets or up in some place called "Wapakonetty," helping Chief King look for Joe Hathaway.

Frank looked at the table in front of him. There were printed copies of the surveillance photos from the two gas stations—cameras had caught Hathaway's fleeting image. But there were no clues to where Laura and Jackson might be.

Frank felt like he was on his own. Deputy Peters had been left in charge of the CMPD. He was overseeing the day-to-day policing of the small community. No matter what else was happening in the world, the work of cops on the ground never stopped. Peters had himself and Stan and two cops. There was also a Troy Police officer in a patrol car helping out.

"It just doesn't make any sense," Frank said for what felt like the fiftieth time. "It can't be a coincidence that they go missing just as Hathaway escapes." The only other person in the building, Lola, was working the phones out front.

Peters nodded. "At least they have a lead on where he is."

"Don't you think it's strange that he let himself be photographed?" Frank pointed at the photos. "Disappears from the hospital like a ghost and then these? Hell, in this one he's practically looking at the camera."

Frank's phone beeped on the table next to him, and he nearly jumped out of his skin reaching for it. If Laura was calling him...

It came from a blocked number. A text with a single letter "C." He clicked on the text, which took his phone to the messages application. This was a new conversation from an unknown caller.

"Is it her?" Peters was sitting up, looking at Frank.

Frank shook his head and passed the phone to Peters, who looked at it, then looked up at Frank.

"That's weird. What does 'C' mean?"

"No clue. Sometimes you send a single letter to respond to a text, like 'Y' or 'N,' but I have no idea who this is."

He set the phone down, but he kept glancing at it. They talked about the Hathaway disappearance, but he was getting antsy again. Frank wanted to drive around and look for Laura's car, and said as much. As he was standing to leave, his phone buzzed again. Another text.

"H."

He showed it to Peters.

"CH?" Peters asked.

Frank looked at the phone. "The texts were exactly five minutes apart."

Over the next fifteen minutes, Frank got three more texts. With the last one, he felt a chill run up his back.

A letter "K."

"C H E C K," Frank said, repeating the letters. "Someone texted me those for a reason."

"What? What does 'check' mean?"

"It's a chess term," Frank said quietly and handed the phone to Peters. "It means you're in danger of losing the game."

Peters looked at the phone and then at Frank. "Hathaway?"

Frank shook his head. "I don't know."

"Or it could be a prank," Peters said.

Frank was looking at his phone. He took the phone back and started to answer and paused, his thumbs over the keys on his phone. What should he say? What if it wasn't Hathaway but just someone screwing with Frank? What if it meant nothing? What if it meant everything?

"What are you doing?"

"I need to answer it," Frank said.

"No, I don't think you should," Peters said, picking up his own phone. "Let me call Jeff first—he'll know what to do."

Frank waited while he listened to half of a conversation that he could have predicted from the start: Peters told King about the incoming texts; King was curious; Peters said nothing else had happened; and King dismissed it as a prank.

"Jeff said that it was probably a prank..."

"I heard," Frank said, still staring at his phone. Finally, his patience ran out, and he typed a reply.

"WHO IS THIS?"

Frank waited, watching the phone in his hand. But nothing happened. After a minute, he stood up. "I'm going to head out, drive around. I can't sit here. I'll let you know if anything comes up."

Peters nodded. "I'll start a phone records request for the texts. Might take a few hours. And I have three cops on duty, plus the Troy PD officer. Call me if you find anything."

Frank headed out and got into his car and drove away from the police station, deep in thought. He circled town, the air conditioning blasting, revisiting Laura's apartment and the hotel and other places in town he was familiar with, looking for her car. He drove past the salon and even up to the grocery and liquor stores, in case she'd been out shopping and something had happened. Frank drove the side streets, searching for her car.

His phone buzzed again at exactly 3 p.m.

"CHECK"

Frank pulled over and called Peters to inform him of the new text and to ask about the phone records search. Peters said it was still in the works.

Frank hung up and stared at his phone and finally answered, texting again, demanding to know who was texting him and what they wanted. He hit "Send" and stared at the screen, waiting.

Nothing happened.

Five minutes later, frustrated, Frank cursed loudly and set his phone on the passenger seat before putting his rusty Camaro into Drive. He had to keep moving. He felt like a shark in the ocean. If he stopped moving, stopped searching for his daughter and grandson, it felt like he might just die.

CHAPTER 65
Willshire

Sunday afternoon, the search for Joe Hathaway continued. Chief King and his deputies were helping out in Willshire, a small town located right on the border between Ohio and Indiana. They were assisting the locals with interviews, and Detective Barnes and three of King's deputies were going through surveillance footage at local gas stations.

Floyd had called several times to keep him in the loop. So far, everything was under control in Cooper's Mill. There had been a small fire downtown, but it was quickly handled by the fire department. And someone had tried to rob a bank in Huber Heights, apparently taking advantage of the well-publicized police shortage. The shortage, however, didn't mean there were no cops around, and the robber was quickly apprehended.

But there was still no word on Laura Powell or her son, Jackson. Peters said that, other than a series of strange texts, there had been no changes in the case. Frank Harper was beyond worried. King understood and wished he could be down there, helping out.

Instead, he was sitting in his patrol car outside one of the local gas stations. He called Moynihan, the OSHP sergeant in charge of the search along Highway 33, and gave him an update.

"Thanks, King."

"Some of my men are running up against their shift times," King said. "They've been on since midnight. Are we bunking down somewhere around here or heading home?"

Moynihan grunted, a sound King was starting to find annoying. "Nah, nobody's going home. I arranged with a Vacation Inn in Willshire. They've got a block of rooms for anyone who wants to crash for a few hours. Just tell them who you are."

"Okay, thanks," King said, hanging up, disappointed. He knew it was pointless to ask how much longer he and his men would be up here. Now that the OSHP were running things, it was all about manpower, and they were going to fight tooth and nail before letting anyone go home. King shook his head and started up his car, heading for the hotel.

CHAPTER 66
Hostile Chiefs

Nothing for hours. The last text was 3:00 p.m.

"CHECK"

Now it was nearly 8:00 p.m. and he didn't know what to do.

Frank had driven around for hours, searching, and finally ended up back at the police station. Peters had gone home for a break and was back as well, running through reports and remotely assisting Chief King with various tasks. King was still stuck at the Indiana border, helping with the search for Hathaway. Frank had been keeping King and Peters in the loop via text all day.

At 8:00 p.m. on the nose, Frank's phone buzzed.

"MATE"

Frank sat up and showed it to Peters.

"That's new," Peters said. "What do you think it means?"

"Checkmate. The game is over," Frank said.

At 8:01 his phone buzzed again.

"CHECK"

"Great, back to this."

The same messages alternated at 8:02 and 8:03 and 8:04, "Check" and "mate," and then nothing for several minutes. Frank could feel his frustration building.

Peters shook his head. "What are they doing?"

"I don't know."

Frank typed on the keyboard. "WHERE ARE LAURA AND JACKSON?"

Nothing. Frank stared at the screen, gripping his phone too tightly. He wanted to chuck it across the room and watch it shatter against the dark windows, but he couldn't. These texts were the only clue—

His phone buzzed.

"SUN"

Sun? Rising sun, setting sun? What did it mean?

Frank looked up at Peters and showed him the phone. "Any ideas?"

Peters shook his head.

Frank stared at the single word. It had been three minutes since the message had come in. He stared at the text and studied the time stamp. 8:10. Did that mean anything?

He had to answer. If it was a prank, he needed to end it. And if it was Hathaway...the man played games. Someone had to play along, or he'd get bored. Bad things happened with Hathaway got bored.

"I have to assume it's him, or someone working for him," Frank said.

"What does 'Sun' mean?"

Frank had a sudden idea. The man had been obsessed with Sun Tzu and *The Art of War*. It was the only 'sun' Frank could think of that had a connection. He turned to a computer on the desk and pulled up Google to do a search. He found a website dedicated to *The Art of War*—Frank had a copy of the book, but it was at Laura's. The website featured the full text of the book, which consisted of thirteen chapters, written nearly two thousand years ago. Thinking about the time of the message, Frank found the eighth chapter and then scrolled down to tenth verse. Reading the verse, another chill ran up Frank's back.

Peters leaned over and looked at the computer, reading. "You think...?"

"Has to be." Frank took his phone and began typing the verse:

"REDUCE THE HOSTILE CHIEFS BY INFLICTING DAMAGE ON THEM"

Frank hit Send and waited. For a long, excruciating moment, nothing happened. And then his phone buzzed. A reply came back.

"AND MAKE TROUBLE FOR THEM"

It was the next part of the passage.

"I don't understand," Peters said, following along.

"Whoever they are, they're quoting a section on winning a war. Actually, the whole book is about how to win at war. It's cruel and unforgiving and definitely not politically correct. This section is about causing damage on your various enemies to delay or distract them."

"'Reduce the hostile chiefs' sounds like they're talking about the cops and police departments," Peters said. "Keeping them busy."

Frank nodded. "And 'make trouble for them' to keep them occupied."

He turned back to the screen and read the next passage, then typed a few words into his phone, his thumbs flying.

"AND KEEP THEM CONSTANTLY ENGAGED"

He hit Send. In seconds, he had a reply.

"HOLD OUT SPECIOUS ALLUREMENTS"

"The photos from the gas stations," Frank said. "Too much for the cops to pass up."

"Wow, he's following right along," Peters said, looking at the Sun Tzu quotes on the computer. "He's reading from the book?"

"If it's Hathaway, he's probably got it memorized."

Frank's hands started to sweat. This was either Hathaway or someone screwing with Frank. Either way, Frank was going to get to the bottom of it. He looked at the computer, then typed the last part.

"AND MAKE THEM RUSH TO ANY GIVEN POINT"
and hit Send.

He waited, reading back through the whole passage. "The meaning is clear," Frank said to Peters. "Someone knows the police were occupied."

Peters nodded. "We are stretched thin. But what if this is someone just wasting your time?"

Frank shook his head and waited, but nothing came back. The clock on his phone read "8:17." Frank scrolled down the website page. Chapter 8 of *The Art of War* only had fourteen verses. If they were going with time-matching verses, there would be no more messages until 9:00 or 9:01, the first verse in chapter nine.

Frank didn't have time for this crap.

He typed "THIS IS FRANK HARPER. WHERE ARE LAURA AND JACKSON?" and hit Send.

Peters stood and went and got another notepad. Frank stared at his phone, fuming. The anger in him felt like a tide, threatening to overwhelm him. Peters came back and sat down.

"Maybe he wants to play a game," Peters said. "He answered your quotes with the next section. But before that it was a chess match. What if he's just sitting there with the phone in his hand, waiting for you to play? He's finally got someone to play with."

"Play chess? I don't know how. Plus, he's got Laura and Jackson," Frank said. "He knows he's got me over a barrel. I'd do anything to find them and get them back safely."

Frank started to say something, and his phone buzzed.

"CHECK"

"Great," Frank said. "This again."

CHAPTER 67
Canal Road

"How's he doing?" Chief King asked.

Deputy Peters looked over at Mr. Harper, who was sitting at the long table that ran down the middle of the bull pen. He had a pad of paper in front of him and was scribbling something.

"Not sure," Peters said quietly into his phone. "He's trying to communicate with the person that's texting."

Peters could hear his cousin sigh so loudly that it sounded like he was in the room with them. "I don't know what to tell you. What about the searches?"

Peters looked at his own sheet of notes. "We took groups through Kyle Park and City Park this afternoon. Nothing on the BOLO on her car, and no one at work or around her apartment saw anything. I had Stan canvas the neighborhood and talk to her neighbors. Nothing."

"Okay," Chief King said. He sounded tired and frustrated. "This Sergeant Moynihan has us talking to every gas station in the area. And now they're dragging some of the bodies of water. Everything else okay?"

"Yes, we're good," Peters said. "Lola wanted me to remind you to be safe." It had become clear to Peters that Lola and his cousin were dating and had been for a while.

"Tell her I will," King said. "And send Frank home. He needs to get some sleep. If we don't hear anything overnight, call me, and I'll send some people back to help you. Search the river area and canal, especially along Canal Road. A car could go off there and no one would see it."

"Okay. I had Ramirez drive that today, but we'll do it again tomorrow."

"Okay, have a good night. Stay safe."

"You, too."

Peters hung up and looked at his notes. There were no other places left to check in Cooper's Mill for Laura and Jackson. He felt a pang of guilt. She was such a nice person, and her kid was adorable. He'd gotten to know her a few months ago, in that crazy time when Mr. Harper had disappeared. She was a good person, and if she had been hurt...

He looked up at Mr. Harper. "Anything new?"

The grizzled old cop only shook his head.

CHAPTER 68
Pawns

The whole exercise was incredibly frustrating. Frank would type stuff in, and sometimes the person on the other end would answer and sometimes they would not. He couldn't make any sense out of the conversation. Frank scribbled down ideas and tried them, but nothing seemed to work. If Frank didn't type anything for a few minutes, then they would send back just the one word, "CHECK," as if to keep him in the game.

Peters wrapped up a call to Chief King. "Anything new?"

Frank shook his head.

"You said 'check' is a move in chess?"

Frank looked up at Peters. "Yeah."

"What about chess moves? Does he actually want to play chess?"

Frank shrugged. "Can't hurt to try." He turned back to the computer and pulled up another website that listed chess games. He familiarized himself quickly with the rules of the game. He had played a few times in his life, but wasn't sure if he remembered the rules correctly.

The official system they used to describe a move on the chessboard was called algebraic notation. The sixty-four squares on the board were numbered and assigned letters starting in the bottom left corner, so that square was called A1. The top right corner was H8. Pieces were assigned a letter—"K" for king, etc.—and pawns didn't get a letter. Pieces were moved by saying something like "Rook to H4" or "Pawn to B3." Usually there was only one of that type of piece that could legally move to that particular square.

"Looks complicated," Peters said.

Frank nodded. "Let's start with an easy one," he said, putting in what was listed as an opening move in many chess games.

"PAWN TO F4"

There was only one pawn that could move to that spot. Pawns could only move one space forward, usually, but they could move two spaces forward on their first move of the game. And they could move one square diagonally forward to "capture" or remove another player's piece.

Frank waited.

The phone buzzed.

"ROOF"

Hmm, Frank thought. Not what he was expecting. Glancing at the website, he'd expected a counter move in chess code or whatever they called it. That didn't make sense. He put his move in again.

"PAWN TO F4"

The phone was frustratingly quiet for three minutes, then buzzed.

"CHECK"

"Same thing as before," Peters said. "You have to play the game."

"What?"

"You put in your first move. Pawn to F4. Now put in your second one."

Frank shook his head. "How can I know my move without his move? I have to counter against something."

Peters thought about it. "Maybe you're supposed to put in his moves also?"

Frank looked at the screen and opened another tab on the browser, then typed in "list of chess moves." He was in a hurry and typed in "list of cheese moves" first and had to back up and type it correctly.

The first thing to come up was a Wikipedia page called "List of chess gambits." It showed popular opening chess moves, or "gambits," used by famous players of the past. He found one that started with F4. It was something called "Bird's Opening" and had been popular since the fifteenth century. Who knew? But if Frank was suddenly playing chess with an expert, the man would surely recognize it.

Frank typed in the second move in the "Bird's Opening," waiting. He had no idea what he was doing. Nothing came back for a minute and then—

"CHECK"

Frustrated, Frank searched the web, looking for a list of moves and countermoves. Maybe Hathaway wanted him to play both sides of the game. It didn't make sense, but maybe there was another game going on here, one that involved the word "roof."

Finally, Frank found a site with the appropriate information. It showed games from the past played by experts and listed each move and countermove. Frank found one where white (he assumed he was playing white as they always went first) opened with F4, then typed in the first countermove into his phone and waited. A second passed and then:

"ROOF"

Okay, maybe this would work. Frank typed in the second move for white on his phone and hit Send, then waited ten seconds and put in the second move for black.

"You're putting in both sides," Peters asked?

"I guess," Frank said. "You would think he would want to play me."

"You don't know anything about chess," Peters said. "Do you?"

Frank pointed at the screen. "Only this stuff. I wouldn't be much of a challenge, probably. I can type these moves from the internet, but I have no idea how to actually play."

The phone buzzed.

"POT"

"Pot," Peters said, grabbing his pad of paper and writing down "pot" and "roof." "What does it mean?"

"I have no idea." Frank went to start typing the next move when a text came back.

"THREE MOVES LEFT"

Frank swallowed. Three more chances. Three more cryptic words?

He put the next chess moves into his phone and hit Send. Over the next five minutes, he got three more words back that made no sense at all.

"FIELD"

"BAG"

"FOYER"

After that, he kept texting and sending, but there was no response. He waited the amount of time needed and was expecting the word "check" to come back, but even that word did not appear on his phone. After another ten minutes of trying, Frank gave up.

"I think he's done for the night," Frank said.

Peters was studying the list and looked up as Lola came into the room.

"Deputy? I have a call you should know about. We got a 911 on a house fire between here and New Stanton. FDs are scrambling, but we don't have enough personnel to manage traffic. Can you help?"

Peters looked at Frank and then nodded to Lola. "Get Stan in to help with patrol calls. I know it's his night off, but me and the two on-duty deputies won't be enough, right?"

"Not to cover more than one call," Lola said. "I could get another car from the TPD."

"Yeah, do that, also," Peters said, standing up. "I'll head out to New Stanton and help out with traffic around the fire scene."

Lola turned and went back out to her desk.

Peters looked at Frank. "What do you want to do?"

Frank looked up from the list. He was holding the pad in his hand.

"You go," Frank said. "Cover things. I'm going home...well, Laura's house." He held up the list. "See if I can figure this out."

"Let me know if you do," Peters said. "I'll call if we learn anything."

He turned and left, and Frank stared at the list of nonsense words and wondered what they meant. Was he playing some kind of game with Joe Hathaway, or was this just an idiot with Frank's cell phone number?

Frank shook his head and copied down the words for himself on another sheet. He went back to the computer, copying the website addresses from the chess-related and Sun Tzu sites into an email and then sending that email to himself. He wasn't sure if he'd need them again, but it didn't hurt to have them handy.

On his way out, Lola asked him if he needed anything, but Frank just shook his head. He thanked her and wished her good luck. It was obvious that the CMPD and other local police agencies were stretched thin.

Outside, Frank got into his Camaro and started the car. It was nearly 9:30 p.m. and he had no idea what to do next.

He didn't want to go back to Laura's apartment. It felt so empty. Seeing her things on the kitchen counter and little Jackson's toys strewn about his bedroom made Frank want to cry.

Little Jackson had prepared a surprise for his arriving grandfather. Frank had found the dining room set up with all of Jackson's dinosaurs, all arranged around a handwritten sign that read "WELCOME GRANDPA." Frank could hardly look at it.

CHAPTER 69
Blue Truck

Trapper was parked down the street near the CVS. He watched the old Camaro pull out of the police station parking lot. He reached for his phone and dialed, starting the truck and pulling out onto the road to follow the car.

"Hello?"

"He's left the station."

"Okay," the voice answered. "Where is he now?"

"Driving. Looks like he's headed for her apartment."

It was quiet for a second. Trapper could hear Hathaway talking to someone else before he came back on.

"Okay, he's probably going to sleep. He's had a busy day, and he's got a lot to think about. Sit on the apartment for as long as he's there. Any other cops?"

"No, they're busy," Trapper said. He'd been listening to the police band for both Cooper's Mill and Troy. It was clear from the tone of the dispatchers that both precincts were shorthanded. He said as much to Hathaway and gave a count of the number of deputies they had available.

"Good," Hathaway answered. "I've got people calling in fake 911 calls in Troy and Cooper's Mill and New Stanton. In the end, Clive and the boys can handle three or four, assuming Frank figures things out and brings them along."

"Boss, you sure I can't just take him out now? He's tired. It would be easy. I can pull up next to his car and shoot him in the head—"

"No. He's mine."

"Okay," Trapper said, shaking his head.

"Let me know when he leaves. It won't be long until he figures it out, and then he'll be headed here. I want some warning."

"Will do," Trapper said and hung up. He had arrived at Frank's daughter's apartment and drove past it, looking for other police vehicles. It was clear. He drove up the street and turned around, parking where he could watch the apartment. He let the truck idle and charged his phone. This could be a long night.

CHAPTER 70
Monday

Frank managed to get a few hours sleep over Sunday night and into Monday morning. Around 8:00 a.m., Frank gave up trying to sleep and walked around the apartment, organizing his things and ignoring the yellow sheet of words he'd taken from the police station last night. He'd stayed up too late staring at them.

Yesterday, Frank had unloaded his car and put his suitcases and bags in one corner of the living room, unsure of where Laura would want them. He tidied his boxes and other things and found his clothes and took out some clean ones as well as his toiletries. He was still wearing the clothes he'd arrived in late on Saturday and realized he stank. It had been hot outside on Sunday. Too much sweat and worry.

Frank went into the small bathroom and stripped, turning on the shower. He got down on the floor of her bathroom and did some sit-ups and push-ups while the water warmed up. He needed to work out, take the edge off. Project his anger into the smooth operation of his arms and legs, focus the anger on Hathaway.

Clearly, the guy wanted to play games. Frank would be happy to oblige him, for now, but he relished the idea of getting his hands on Hathaway. Frank hurried, going as fast as he could until his arms burned and his back hurt from doing sit-ups on the hard bathroom floor.

He stood and climbed in the shower and rinsed off. The water was too hot, and he turned it cooler. Laura only had frilly, girly soaps, so Frank added Irish Spring to his mental shopping list. He washed with a lavender soap that lathered too much and smelled like sunshine and rainbows. Frank rinsed off, not feeling clean.

Frank stepped out of the shower and toweled off, turning off the water. He put on the fan to clear the steam and got dressed in the jeans and a T-shirt he'd brought in with him.

He came out of the bathroom, hoping that Laura and Jackson had come home. It was strange, how quiet the house was.

Hathaway was holding them as bait. Frank was sure. The man was sick. Look what he'd done to Tom Mercato. He'd kept the man's dead body in a goddamned *freezer*, apparently so he could look at Tom and pretend to play chess with him. And look at the weeks of planning Hathaway had put into luring Mercato's girlfriend all the way to Indianapolis and then faking her car accident, killing her and her unborn child. He'd used fake texts...just like whoever was texting Frank.

Frank needed to do something. He felt like he should be doing something. He went back over to the table and sat down with his list of words and stared at them.

CHAPTER 71
In an Old Car

Sunday night had not gone as Laura had hoped.

She'd demanded a chance to see her son, but the woman didn't care what Laura wanted. As Sunday dragged on, Laura had tried everything: begging, threatening, sobbing.

At one point, the woman and Laura had a long conversation about Jackson. She reassured Laura that he was fine—some of the people staying at the farmhouse had families, and he was bunking with a family with two kids around his age. She also said he was eating and asking about his mother.

Her subdued mood didn't last, however. Late in the evening, she was back to screaming and crying. The woman who was watching her came and went, and this time she finally warned Laura to keep quiet or else.

Laura didn't comply and started screaming even louder.

"Do you want me to get Hathaway?"

"I don't care what you do," Laura spat.

The woman left Laura tied to the chair. While she was gone, Laura worked on the ropes that bound her arms and legs, but it was good rope, well-tied. When the woman returned, she was smiling. And two men were following her.

"Okay, I think we have a solution."

They untied her from the chair and walked her over to the rusty car that hunched in the corner of the barn. Laura had no idea what was happening and felt her temperature rise. The woman pulled the rusty door open and the two men sat Laura down on the dirty bench seat as the woman tied Laura's hands around the steering column.

"Now, you can yell all you want," she said with a smile and closed the door. One of the men pushed a large wheelbarrow up against the driver's door sideways so it wouldn't roll, wedging the door shut.

That had been last night.

Laura had slept leaned up against the car door, her hands tied to the wheel. It felt loose like she might be able to pry it free, but she'd been too tired to try.

Now, it was Monday morning and she was working on the steering wheel. Although, with both doors wedged shut, there was no getting out of here. But she tried anyway. After a couple of hours, the wheel popped off in her hands.

She put it back when she heard someone coming, jamming the steering column back down into the rusty hole.

The wheelbarrow outside moved and the door opened. It was Hathaway.

"How was your night?"

"Screw you."

"Great," he said. "Today's the day, I think. Your father and I played chess last night."

She looked at him. "How's that?"

Hathaway seemed to be mostly talking to himself. He looked up at her and smiled. "Never mind. But let's get you fed and happy for today, okay? He'll be here soon."

"Want to make me happy? Let me see my son."

"Oh, I thought we already did," Hathaway said, turning and waving over his shoulder. The woman came around the car door into view, and with her was Jackson.

"Hi Mommy," he said.

She smiled and immediately started crying. "Hi, Jackson. Are you okay?"

She saw his eyes taking in the scene—her, tied up inside the car; Hathaway, leaning possessively over Laura; the woman with her hand tight on Jackson's shoulder. What must he be thinking? Finally, he nodded. "I made some new friends," he said cheerfully. "We're all sleeping in the same room as their mommy and daddy."

She nodded. "You be good, okay, and if you see a chance to get away—"

"Okay, that's enough," Hathaway said, leaning back over and blocking her view of Jackson. "Get him out of here."

The woman walked away with Jackson, but Laura heard him one more time.

"Bye, Mommy."

After they were gone, her sobbing intensified. She tried to control it and be strong, but there was no stopping it.

"There, there, that's better, right?" He said, watching her like a scientist would observe a particularly interesting species of insect.

"Screw you!"

Joe smiled, making her madder. "Okay, good talk. Behave yourself today."

CHAPTER 72
Five Words

Waiting around Laura's apartment didn't feel right. Frank knew he should be out there looking for her. He shook his head and stood. He grabbed his keys and phone—and the list of words he'd jotted down from the night before—and left with no destination in mind.

First, he headed to McDonald's and went through the drive-through and got some coffee and food. As he waited in line, he could see inside the restaurant and saw the coffee klatch, the table full of old-timers he'd interviewed back in the winter. They were chatting and smiling and looked like they were having a good time.

Frank felt a pang of jealousy. Maybe that's what he needed. His anger and his bourbon—and his guilt—seemed to drive away any friends he managed to make. For a moment, Frank considered parking his car and going inside to talk to them. Maybe one of them would have some insight into Joe's mind. Instead of going inside, Frank got his food and coffee and drove away.

He turned right out of the McDonald's and drove, winding through residential areas, looking for Laura's car. He drove and ate, driving the back streets of Cooper's Mill, seeing parts of the town he hadn't seen before and ended up near a cemetery.

He turned on Hyatt and headed back north into town, recognizing the big houses on the west side of the street as he approached the Dairy Queen. He passed the Martin house, where he'd interviewed Nick Martin during the case surrounding the kidnapping of his daughter. The beautiful house sat back away from the street at the end of an immaculate lawn.

Frank wondered how Charlie and that other girl were doing?

He shook his head and concentrated on looking for Laura's car. A small benefit of all the driving was that he was learning the town. He recognized streets now and had learned where some of them ended up. Downtown Cooper's Mill was a grid, with numbered streets going north to south and other streets going from east to west.

Frank passed through the downtown again, noting the toy store and the church where Jackson had attended preschool. He recognized the red-bricked coffee shop on the left, where he and Peters had worked on their first case together. At the last intersection, he saw Ricky's, the bar where Frank had spent his very first evening in town.

God, a beer sounded so good right now.

Instead of pulling over and stopping at the bar, Frank continued east, passing down the hill and out of town. Heat simmered off the road in waves that obscured the road as it stretched away to the east. He passed Freeman Prairie, where he'd almost died once. Soon, Frank was in the country, driving back roads and taking lefts and rights, randomly searching for her car. He opened the Waze app on his phone and hung it from his windshield to make sure he didn't get lost.

He thought back to little Charlie. She'd climbed out of her room and walked on the roof, looking for a way down. Frank hoped she was getting along okay—it had been nearly a year since their kidnapping.

Roof.

Frank looked over at the yellow sheet of paper.

ROOF POT FIELD BAG FOYER

In an instant, the clues fell into place.

Charlie had climbed on the roof. Pot was part of a growing operation that Sergeant Graves ran with the help of a young man, George, who worked for him and lived at the farmhouse. There was a field out back of the farmhouse where the girls had been taken, a field of marijuana.

Bag could mean the bag of money from the ransom.

Foyer.

Frank had been shot in the back as he walked toward the foyer of the old farmhouse. He'd laid on the floor, bleeding, while Graves went upstairs to kill the kidnapped girls. After running into his accomplice, who'd fired at him, Graves had fled down the stairs and into the foyer, where Frank had shot and killed him.

It was too much of a coincidence. It seemed like someone was talking about the Graves farmhouse, where he and his compatriots had held those two kidnapped girls. All the words were related to the farmhouse. But they were also generic enough that, if you didn't know the story, they would just be random words.

Were Laura and Jackson there? Bait for a trap?

Frank pulled over and stopped his car on a patch of shoulder that overlooked the small river that ran east of town. He studied at the list again and called Peters.

"I think I know where they are, and what the words mean," Frank said, quickly explaining.

He heard Peters whistle on the other end. "You know, you could be right. That list doesn't make sense any other way."

"I need to call Jeff and tell him."

Frank thought about it. "There's no time to organize a big group. I need to head there. Now."

"It's probably a trap."

"I know," Frank said, and he realized he meant it. But nothing was more important than getting Laura and Jackson out of harm's way.

"Okay," Peters said. "Let me talk to Jeff and figure out what he wants to do. Though you know he's going to say to wait until we can get a group together."

"I know," Frank said. "Just send me the address. I don't remember where it was or how to get there."

"Um, okay," Peters said. "But you have to promise me you won't go in alone. At least wait for me—remember that driveway? Don't go up. I'll bring Stan and Ramirez."

Frank promised but then added. "I can't wait forever."

"Okay, I'll call you right back."

Frank hung up. After a second, his phone buzzed with an address. He copied it into Waze and got directions. It was just fifteen minutes away from his current location, near the river he was parked near, but further north. He moved the map around and found a gas station near the farmhouse. He found the address for the gas station and sent it to Peters, saying he would wait for them there.

Frank neglected to add exactly how long he would wait. That was another matter entirely.

CHAPTER 73
East

"East," Trapper said into his phone. "We're near the river."

"Okay, stay on him," Hathaway said. "Let me know when he heads this way."

"Will do," Trapper said and hung up. He was in his blue truck, following Frank's Camaro at a good distance. The old rusty machine was easy to spot—it didn't look like any other car on the road. Trapper stayed back, keeping at least a quarter of a mile between them.

CHAPTER 74
Frank Waits

Frank found the gas station with no trouble. Waze took him right to it, following the river north. He passed at least one dairy farm, the smell of cow manure wafting across the road.

Frank pulled into the parking lot of the station and waited, turning off his engine. He called Peters and let him know he was ready. Peters said that Chief King had requested they wait for backup, but Peters had told him it was too time-sensitive. Peters was on his way there with two other CMPD deputies, Stan and Ramirez.

When he finished talking to Peters, Frank studied the farmhouse location on his phone, pulling it up on Google and Bing Maps. The farmhouse was only yards from the river. Frank remembered the house, as well as the barn next to it and the huge fenced field in the back.

When he was done with the maps, Frank checked his gun and spare. He opened his glove compartment and counted his bullets—he had around forty. And he had a thought. If he were going to go into this private investigating business full time, he needed a better place to hide his guns in his car. And not in the trunk—he needed them where he could get to them. Quick. He felt around the dashboard, wondering if there were places inside to hide stuff.

Frank walked around the back of his car and opened the trunk. He'd brought a shotgun and extra ammo up from Birmingham in a locked gun case, but he couldn't remember if he'd taken it into Laura's house or not. He frowned when he realized it wasn't in his trunk. He must've taken it inside already.

Peters and the others arrived shortly before 11:00 a.m. They greeted Frank and Peters introduced them. Frank already knew Deputy Stan— they'd had a run in once, when Frank had nearly broken the policeman's arm. The other deputy was a Hispanic woman, Ramirez. Peters opened the trunk of his police car and handed out bullet-proof vests to everyone. There were also shotguns and other weapons in the trunk.

"We've been here before," Peters said with a smile.

"We have," Frank said, strapping on a vest and then picking out a shiny shotgun. "Okay if I use my own handguns?"

Peters nodded, putting on his own vest. "Can't believe we're going back to the same place. You really think Laura is in there?"

"I sure hope so," Frank said. He loaded the shotgun and pocketed some extra shells. "The words would only matter to someone like us, someone who knows about the case."

Peters nodded. "You don't have to convince me."

They finished getting ready and got into the two police cars as Frank opted to leave his Camaro at the gas station.

"King called again," Peters said as they drove. "Those credit card charges up in Michigan? They were charged by that McGinty woman, Joe's assistant. They caught her on video in several locations. Local cops arrested her—she said Joe had asked her to drive to the Detroit area over the weekend and make some purchases for him."

"To distract the police, no doubt," Frank said, and Peters nodded.

They crossed the river and slowed a quarter of a mile down from the entrance to the long driveway that led up through woods to the farmhouse. Peters stopped and parked the car.

"You ready?"

Frank nodded. It felt like deja vu all over again. Here they were, back at the farmhouse, but this time they had two more deputies with them. Peters parked on the road, a ways down from the driveway. They got out and went around to his trunk and waited.

"I wonder why Hathaway came here."

"I don't know," Frank said. "But he sure loves to play games."

The other cop car pulled up behind them and the two deputies got out, adjusting their vests.

CHAPTER 75
Driveway

"They're approaching the house," Trapper said into his phone. "Pulling off near the driveway," he said. He was driving west and did not slow down. Trapper passed the two police cars, which had pulled onto the shoulder near the farmhouse driveway.

"How many?" Hathaway asked over the phone.

"I saw four at the gas station, two in each car." Trapper continued on the road, glancing at the cops in his rearview mirror before a curve in the road cut off his view. "They were loading up, putting on vests."

"Then they're coming in," Hathaway said. "We're ready."

"I'll circle back and follow them up the driveway," Trapper said.

"Good," Hathaway said and then hung up.

CHAPTER 76
Won't Budge

Neither of the car doors would budge.

After they'd fed her breakfast and put her back in the car, Laura had waited until it was quiet, cleaning off the dusty windows as best she could. Once the people were long gone, she'd pulled the steering wheel off and freed her hands from the rope that was looped around the steering column. She rubbed at her wrists, which were getting raw, and tried both doors. One was wedged shut with the wheelbarrow, and she couldn't get it, or the door, to move. She laid back and kicked at the window and the windshield, but nothing happened other than it hurt her bare feet. On the passenger side, the car door was jammed up against the barn wall. The door wouldn't move an inch.

Laura crawled around the interior of the car, exploring, looking for anything she could use to pry open the driver's door. The car was full of dust and cobwebs and little else. There was nothing in the glove compartment and nothing under the front seats.

She climbed into the back, a wide bench seat like the front. There were no rear doors, unfortunately, and the windows were solid sheets of heavy glass. She kicked at both several times, but nothing happened. She laid down and kicked at the dirty back windows. Again, the old automotive glass was just too thick.

Laura reached up to the top of the backseat to pull herself up and realized the seat was loose. She felt it give a little. She leaned to the side and pulled back on the seat, hearing it tear free from whatever it was attached to. She pulled again and laid it flat and looked inside.

There was a dark area—the trunk. It was huge. Why didn't they make cars like this anymore, with trunks large enough to camp in? Above was the trunk lid.

She climbed inside and pushed up on the lid. It gave slightly.

Yes.

Positioning herself, she laid on the floor of the trunk and pushed up on the lid with her bare feet. She felt the metal move under her toes and heard a low, groaning shriek.

The lid popped open. Above her, she saw the barn roof and a hayloft.

Laura peeked around the edge to see if the noise had attracted anyone but saw nobody. Not wanting to waste a second, she climbed out of the trunk and carefully lowered the lid, just in case they put her back in there.

Smiling, she tiptoed across the barn floor, looking for a way out.

CHAPTER 77
Approach

"Ready?" Peters asked, holding up his phone and pointing at a Google map of the area. "Okay, we'll go up here. It's a long, twisty driveway through the trees. Ramirez, you're with me on the left. Stan, you go up the right with Mr. Harper. Stay in the trees and stick together, then we'll assess the situation at the top. We're here to recover Frank's daughter and grandson—that's our primary goal. It is also likely that Joe Hathaway is here. We need to be careful. He's a deadly marksman."

The others nodded, and Frank didn't add anything. Frank followed Peters' lead—he was in charge. Frank might be older and more experienced, but in this situation, Peters was calling the shots.

Peters started up the road, taking out his weapon and crossing quickly. He walked along the shoulder and stooped over as he approached the driveway. There was an embankment that ran down and into the thick forest that stood along both sides of the road.

As they got closer to the driveway, Peters turned to say something and—

Gunfire erupted from the driveway.

Peters ran down the small embankment and into the trees. The others followed him, returning fire and working their way along the tree line toward the driveway.

Ramirez got the guy—Frank saw a man fall, dropping his rifle. Cautiously, they approached the man. Peters kicked his gun away and felt at his neck.

"He's dead," he said, then looked at Ramirez. "You okay?"

She nodded.

"Okay, call it in. And get us some backup," Peters said to her. "Let's go."

They reached the driveway and started up. Frank heard Ramirez using the radio on her shoulder, calling in EMT support and mutual aid from the Troy PD. She was probably talking to Lola. Frank stayed to the right with Stan, and Ramirez followed Peters up the left side. They worked their way through the forest, watching for more shooters, but there were none. Finally, up ahead, Frank could see the driveway open up into a clearing. There was the farmhouse, a building Frank remembered well, with several cars parked in front.

"I think we're outnumbered," Deputy Stan said. He sounded nervous. "Are those civilians, or—"

Frank moved his head, turning to say something to Stan, and felt something brush past his face. There was a rush of wind as something flew past him, so close that he could feel the heat coming off it. The sound of the gunshot followed an instant later, and he dropped to the ground and rolled to his right, getting behind a tree.

"SHOOTER!" Frank shouted as he rolled. Three more shots rang out, one after another. One glanced off the driveway's black asphalt a foot from Frank's hand.

He glanced over at Peters and Ramirez, but they were down as well, not moving. They could be alive or dead, as far as he could tell.

Frank lay motionless in the dirt, a few feet off the driveway. He craned his neck and looked behind him. Stan was there, belly-up on the ground. Frank could see the cop's eyes, glassy, staring at the trees above them.

There was a hole in his head.

The bullet had been meant for Frank. Hathaway was a notoriously good shot. If Frank hadn't moved at the last second, that would be him lying on the ground instead of Stan.

CHAPTER 78
Barn Door

The barn was huge. The only two exits were the main door her captors always seemed to use and the large barn door that faced the wooden fence. The first door was locked from the outside. The second was open six inches but secured with a length of rusty chain and an old padlock.

She tried to pry the door open farther and squeeze out, but only her right arm and leg fit through the opening. Giving up, she searched the barn for something to help her out. Maybe there was a key. Laura went over to the workshop area, hoping to find some tools. Maybe like one of those rotary saw things to cut the barn door open. Or an axe.

The main door was where they had come in—that had to be in the direction of the farmhouse. Laura decided not to go that way. She needed to find a way out using the barn door. And a weapon.

Chapter 79
East

Frank turned and looked at the farmhouse as he heard the "crack" of another rifle shot. It whizzed past them, passing overhead and down the driveway. Frank heard it impact a tree. He looked over and saw Peters and Ramirez hunkered down in the bushes and looking at him.

"What's the plan?"

Peters shook his head. "Driveway is a kill zone."

Frank glanced around and then pointed. "You could go west through the woods and circle around and get to the barn. Remember it?"

"Yup, we'll do that. You go east, come out on the other side."

Frank nodded. "How far is the river?"

"Two, three hundred yards," Peters said. "On the other side of that open field. Good luck."

"You too. Stay safe."

Frank glanced back at Stan but there was nothing he could do. Blood pumped slowly out of the hole in his head.

Frank crawled to his right and got deep enough into the brush and trees to stand. He watched the farmhouse and ducked from tree to tree, making his way around the house until he was on the eastern side. He remembered there was a kitchen off the back. He could see it and the rusty jungle gym and the high fence behind the home.

What Frank needed was more information. He stayed low to the ground and watched, waiting. He could see through the windows into the kitchen. No sign of the shooter, but there were people inside, milling about, at least twenty. They looked scared. One woman was holding a baby and crying.

A group of men stood just outside the kitchen door, near the playground equipment. They were clearly arguing. One man kept pointing to the east, and Frank turned around to look. There was a break in the trees and he could see a large open field next to the farmhouse. On the far side of the field, he saw another line of trees and the ground dropped off. Could that be the river?

Frank looked back at the men. He'd seen them somewhere before. Not them specifically, but people who were dressed like them? But where? They looked like a hippie commune. The woman holding the baby was wearing a shawl.

Hathaway's fans. That's who these people looked like.

Frank cursed under his breath—he should have grabbed Stan's radio. He thought about calling Peters, but a phone ringing might give away Peters' position and get him and Ramirez killed.

Frank moved more to his right to get a better look into the kitchen. Two women broke away from the group and ran in Frank's direction, taking the beaten-down path to the field to the east. They passed Frank without seeing him.

"No, this is crazy," one said. "We have to stay."

The other woman shook her head and kept running. "Stay if you want, Patty. I'm not getting killed over that old kook. Now, he's shooting at people."

They ran past him, and he saw the younger one was crying. Beyond the break in the trees, a path ran across the wide field, passing a dead tree in the middle and a small collection of strange white boxes. The women hurried into the field and passed out of his sight.

So, Hathaway had managed to gather a flock of followers, and they'd set up shop in this house. After Joe's escape, he needed a place to lay low. And hiding here, just outside of Troy, was brilliant—everyone would assume he'd fled to Canada or Paraguay. Instead, this place was only a few miles from the hospital.

And the location was important to Frank. It was damned smart and served dual purposes. Joe would understand what this place represented in Frank's life. And when Joe was ready, a few clues would bring Frank racing here. Just as Hathaway had planned.

Another woman came outside, followed by a gaggle of children. They started off toward the field and the river. Frank saw three girls and two boys.

Jackson.

He was dressed differently than the other kids—his shirt had a dinosaur on it—but there was no mistaking it. Confirmation. Joe or his people had taken Laura and Jackson.

Frank started to stand up and then hesitated. Should he follow Jackson or search for Laura?

The woman was clearly protecting the kids, and Jackson seemed okay with her. If she could get him to relative safety, Frank could find Laura. But there was no way Frank could let the woman or Jackson out of his sight, right? He'd found his grandson. Wasn't that more important than finding Hathaway?

Jackson kept stopping and pointing back at the house. Frank bit his lip and stayed still. It was one of the hardest things he'd ever had to do in his life, squatting down in the bushes and watching as his only grandchild was led away into the forest.

But Frank needed to find Laura.

CHAPTER 80
Gunshots

Searching the workshop, Laura found a toolbox behind a cardboard box on a low shelf. Inside, she found a hammer and a screwdriver and grabbed them both.

Gunshots. Even from inside the barn, she could tell what they were.

She ran back over to the barn door and tried unscrewing the latches that held the chain, but gave up after a second. Pocketing the screwdriver, she went to work with the hammer. It was loud but effective, and the fourth or fifth hit broke the latch. It fell to the ground, and she pushed the barn door open, sliding it sideways on the tracks.

She kept the hammer in her hand and stepped out of the barn. In the daylight, she saw a strange, tall fence that lined the back of the property. She dropped to all fours and crawled to her right, not seeing anyone. From here, she could see the back of the farmhouse, where they'd been taken that first evening. It was daytime, and the place looked different. There was a piece of playground equipment at the back of the house, a rusty old jungle gym.

Laura was studying the house when a group of men came out of the back of the farmhouse and gathered around the jungle gym, arguing. They looked like more of the young people who seemed to take direction from Hathaway.

A minute later, a woman came outside, and Laura saw she had several kids with her. The group ran for the next field over, and Laura recognized Jackson instantly just from the way he ran. She would know that goofy, side-to-side gait anywhere. She was too far away to say anything or call to him, but he was getting away. She needed to follow.

Laura heard movement in the barn behind her. Someone was coming, and that was probably a bad thing. Standing, she sprinted for the side of the farmhouse. She heard more gunshots and wondered if someone was shooting at her. She flattened herself up against the side of the house and waited, peeking around the corner. Jackson and his group had run along a path through the field, but they were stopped in the middle. Two of the kids were waving their hands around like mad, and the woman was slapping at them.

Suddenly, a figure ran in her direction from the barn. It took her a moment to recognize him.

"Deputy Peters?"

He flattened himself against the house next to her. Another cop Laura didn't recognize waited at the barn doors—she had her gun out and was looking around.

"We saw you leave the barn and I followed," Peters said. "Good to see you."

"You too," she said, stunned. "Frank?"

"He's around here somewhere. There's a shooter on the second floor. Have you seen Jackson?"

She pointed at the field. "He was with a group of kids. They took off it that field."

Peters peeked around the house, and she caught a whiff of him, a masculine scent of sweat. "They're running for the river," he said.

"How far?"

"Hundred yards. The field fronts the Great Miami. Have you seen Hathaway?" Peters asked. "He escaped custody at the hospital."

She nodded. "His lackey kidnapped me and Jackson and brought us here. Later, Hathaway told me that we were the bait."

"To get Mr. Harper here," he said quietly.

Laura nodded.

CHAPTER 81
Hive

Jackson yelled at the lady in front of him.

"Where are we going?"

The other kids were running ahead. They were crossing a big field.

"Just keep up," the woman yelled. She wasn't as nice now as she had been earlier. Her name was Margaret. She'd given him food and water and then he and the other kids had played games together. But they wouldn't let him see his mommy. Jackson didn't like that.

"I need to go back," he said, stopping. "I need to get my mom."

The other kids stopped running near a dead tree.

The mom came back to talk to him.

"Your mommy is going to be fine, Jackson," the lady said. "She's going to come this way, too."

Behind Margaret, the kids were playing with a bunch of large white boxes that stood in the middle of the field under the broken tree. The boxes were white and had handles and lids. One boy was trying to push a stack of boxes over. A second boy had removed one of the lids and was looking inside.

"I need to save her," Jackson said. "A mean man has her stuck in a car. I saw her hands. They were tied up."

The lady, Margaret, started to say something, and that's when the screaming started.

She turned around and looked. Jackson saw one of the boxes had been pushed over. The air looked weird. Fuzzy. Next to another white box, one of the boys was holding a lid. It was black on one side and the kid was waving it around in the air.

Jackson saw a cloud of bugs around the kids and realized they were bees. He didn't know the word for it, but he knew that they lived in hives and flew together in clouds. They were all over the boxes now and the dead tree, and the kids were screaming and slapping at their arms and running away.

Jackson didn't even realize he was backing up toward the house. All he could do was look at the bees and the mom running in to protect the kids. She was trying to shoo the bees away from the kids, who were all screaming. One boy was rolling around on the ground.

CHAPTER 82
Chase

Ramirez joined them by the farmhouse.

"What next?" she asked.

"We need to clear out these civilians," Peters said. "Get them across the field to the river, then south to the road. I saw a shooter with a rifle on the second floor. It's probably Hathaway, looking for Mr. Harper. Backup?"

"Ten minutes."

"Okay, let's find Hathaway and get him to stop firing. Or pin him down. We'll go in through the kitchen."

They rounded the back of the farmhouse, Laura in the lead. Peters could see she was impatient—she wanted to go after her son. Peter stepped around her and led.

There was a group of Hathaway's followers gathered near the back door. They turned and looked at Laura, Peters, and Ramirez strangely when they noticed them.

"Get out of here," Peters yelled, waving his gun. The men scattered, some running back into the house and the others running for the distant field.

"Okay, get inside and stop Hathaway. I'll be back," Peters said to Ramirez. She nodded and went inside, and Peters turned and followed Laura, who was already moving away. They got nearly to the tree line when a figure stepped out.

"Laura," Mr. Harper said with a smile. "Are you okay?"

She nodded and hugged him tightly. "Yes, we are. Thank God. We're chasing after Jackson. He went that way, toward the river, we think. Are you okay?"

He smiled. "Yeah. He went that way with a group of kids," Frank said, pointing at the break in the trees and the field beyond. "I just need to find Hathaway."

"Ramirez is inside, looking for him," Peters said. "I'll get Laura and Jackson headed to safety, then come back and help."

Mr. Harper looked at Peters with an expression he didn't recognize at first. It looked like sadness, but then it melted into pride. Mr. Harper stepped up and hugged Peters. "Thank you. Yes, come back and help. We're gonna need it."

"No, Frank," Laura said, grabbing his hand. "Come with us. Leave him alone. Hathaway is insane."

Mr. Harper shook his head. "He'll chase us, Laura. I gotta end this, right now." He kissed his daughter on the head and then ran for the house.

"Come on," Laura said to Peters, angry.

She ran for the tree line and rounded it. Peters was following her and nearly ran into the back of her when she stopped abruptly.

"Jackson!"

"Mommy!"

She was leaning over her boy. Peters looked past them and saw groups of men and women and kids running for the river banks. Some of them had already made it and were making their way down the embankment to the river. In the middle of the field, near a group of white boxes, people were screaming and rolling on the ground. Insects appeared to be swarming around them.

"Dispatch, this is Peters," he said into his radio. "We're going to need more EMTs in the area, near the river crossing. Active crime scene— Deputy Ramirez and Mr. Frank Harper are inside the residence with an active shooter. They need backup, but avoid the driveway—it's a fire zone. Do *not* allow EMTs to approach the house until you hear from me."

"Copy that," Lola's voice came back. "EMTs on route, along with two more cars." That meant at least four more police officers—they usually didn't give out the exact personnel numbers over the air, as the broadcasts could be monitored. "ETA three minutes."

"Are you okay?" Laura asked her son, and Peters kneeled beside them. For a moment, they looked like a family.

"I'm okay, but the bees are stinging those kids," Jackson said, pointing. "The kids knocked over the hives." Peters looked—he could see a swarm. People, including kids, were rolling around on the ground or running away. He swallowed. Peters hated bees. He was mildly allergic. A sting or two, he could handle. But he'd never been this close to a swarm...

"That's okay, we'll go around," he said to Laura and Jackson. "Let's get you guys to the river."

Laura nodded. "Come on, let's go," she said, and stood, pulling her boy behind her. The field was rutted and the ground uneven. Peters ran after them.

"Mom, let go," Jackson said. "I can run better on my own."

"Okay, but keep up," she said. Peters smiled at that, catching up with them. They ran along the path to the river. The bees were still swarming around the hives. As they ran across the field, Peters saw more bees coming out of holes in the ground. Did bees live in the ground? They were too big for bees—they swarmed in thin clouds, heading in the direction of the bee hives. Wasps?

Running at full speed, Peters stepped awkwardly into one of the holes that he didn't see and fell, hard, kicking up dirt. He rolled and stopped, cringing and grabbing at his foot. It sang in pain. It looked like his ankle was twisted.

"Oh, my God!" Laura knelt near him. Bees buzzed around them, and she slapped at one. "Can you walk?"

"Mom, look," Jackson said, pointing at the ground. The hole Peters had stumbled into was swarming with insects, the ground boiling with black and yellow shapes.

"Come on, Floyd! You have to walk," she said, pushing him up to his feet. Peters realized the ground around them was pockmarked with holes, and more wasps were coming out of each of them, swarming into the air.

"Ow!" Jackson slapped at his arm. Peters saw half a dozen on his face. "Mom, let's go!"

Laura tried to push Peters up. "Jackson, run! Run for the river!" Her shoulder was covered with wriggling black shapes. "Come on, Floyd—get moving!"

Peters looked down at his arm. It was covered with bees. No, they weren't bees—these were longer. "Wasps. Yellow jackets," he said quietly. One flew in his mouth and he spit it out. Peters felt them sting his arms and face and the back of his neck. Jackson was getting stung, too, and slapping at his own face and neck, screaming as he backed away.

"COME ON!" Laura yelled.

Laura finally got Peters to his feet and he felt weird. Hot. He walked and put weight on his foot and it held. "I can walk," he said, and his voice sounded strange to him. He pushed her hands away. "I'm good. Go."

"You sure?"

"Yeah," he said. His skin felt overheated, like he'd been in the sun too long.

His head swam and Peters looked at her and lied.

"I'm fine. Go. I'm right behind you."

She looked at him and kissed his cheek. "Come on, keep up. The water will wash them off."

Laura let go, gingerly, and Peters stood on his own, starting in the direction of the river. The ground crawled, a black and yellow mass. She slapped at her arms and ran after Jackson, who was screaming and crying on the ground. He had fallen. Laura scooped him up and they ran for the river.

Peters followed, stumbling on the uneven ground. He could barely walk. His mouth felt funny, and his throat. He couldn't breathe, and the bugs were biting his arms and his neck and his face. He waved the bugs from his eyes and watched Laura and Jackson, making sure they got to the embankment. His legs stopped working and Peters fell to his knees. The black ground boiled around him. The stings didn't matter anymore. He finally saw Laura and Jackson make it to the water and dive under.

Deputy Peters smiled. He'd done his job.

CHAPTER 83
Target Practice

Joe was pissed.

It had been a great plan—wait in the second-floor bedroom with his rifle, take out Frank and the other cops when they came up the driveway. He'd gotten at least one of them, seeing the man's head explode. It was glorious until he realized it wasn't Frank Harper.

After that, Joe had lost sight of them. They'd dropped down into the trees and disappeared. Joe had run from room to room on the second floor, waving his gun out the window and firing at the trees. He was good with moving targets, but not when they were actively hiding from him. And the Kevlar vest he was wearing under his shirt was uncomfortable. He fished out his phone and dialed.

"Trapper, drive up here, flush them out," Hathaway yelled into his phone. Moments later, the blue truck rolled up the driveway, a gun pointed out the window. But it hadn't done any good—the cops and Frank were gone.

Joe went to his bedroom and pocketed his medicine and as much money as he could carry. He also tucked a handgun into his waist and put two boxes of ammo in another pocket. He left the room, working his way around to the back of the house, checking out each window. There was a bedroom above the kitchen and back stairs. He found a window and looked out. A bunch of his followers were running away from the house, abandoning him.

Oh well, it wasn't meant to last. He didn't have the energy to be a cult figure.

He lifted his gun and looked through the scope at them running away. Suddenly angry, he pulled the trigger, shooting one of the hippies in the back as they ran for the river. The man fell silently. Just for fun, he picked off two more, a man and a woman. They fell to the ground and lay still. Joe smiled.

"POLICE DEPARTMENT! CEASE FIRING!"

Joe turned, and some Mexican woman was standing in the doorway. She was a cop, apparently, and was pointing a gun at him. "DROP YOUR WEAPON!"

He lifted his rifle and she shot him.

Joe felt a wave of fire in his left hand and dropped the rifle to the ground. Looking down, his left hand was bleeding. Joe could see a track along his wrist. The bullet had grazed him, and blood was welling up and dripping to the floor.

"DO NOT MOVE!"

Joe put his hands up, blood running down his arm. "There was no reason to shoot me."

She stepped forward, her eyes boring into him.

"DO NOT MOVE!"

"You don't have to shout, girl," Hathaway said. "I'm old. I'm not deaf."

She moved forward to kick his gun away, and he was considering going for the gun at his waist when he saw movement in the hallway behind her. A gun came up and fired. Joe didn't know what was happening until the woman fell, grabbing at her back.

Trapper walked into the room, his gun out.

"You okay, boss?"

Joe smiled. "Yeah." He took the pistol from his waist and aimed it at the woman sprawled on the floor. He pulled the trigger.

"NOBODY."

He pulled the trigger again.

"SHOOTS."

He pulled the trigger again.

"ME."

The woman stopped moving, her eyes staring at the ceiling.

Trapper laughed. "I think you got her, boss."

Joe hissed and looked at his bleeding hand. "Wow, that hurts."

"Let's get you downstairs and get that wrapped up. Where is Frank Harper?"

"Hell if I know."

Chapter 84
Pepperidge Farm Remembers

Frank ran into the old farmhouse.

It looked just as it had before, and it all came back to him in a flash. He was in the kitchen—there was a little breakfast nook, and the kitchen windows looked out on the play equipment in the backyard. More of the hippies were running around, and Frank could hear gunshots going off inside the house.

"Get out of here," Frank yelled at the civilians. "Get clear of this building."

They ran past him as he walked through the first floor, his gun pointed straight up. People kept popping into view and he would point his gun at them. None of them were Hathaway, though, so he held his fire.

Frank walked into the long dining room, noticing the windows. He'd crawled through one of them to make entry to the house last year, skipping the doors and catching the kidnappers by surprise. Now, the floor of the room was covered with cots and blankets, enough for twenty people to bunk down for the night.

Frank continued into the small living room and turned, ending up in the foyer. He could see the doors going outside and the stairs going up, but he heard nothing else. He looked down at the corner by the door, remembering where he'd lain after being shot.

Frank shook his head and walked to the stairs. He'd never been upstairs. For some reason, he was more nervous then he'd been in a long time. Hathaway was smart, smarter than your average criminal. If the guy had a plan—and he always did—Frank couldn't help but feel like he was walking right into it. In spite of the odds, Frank put his foot on the first step and headed up.

CHAPTER 85
Bandaged

"Ow, that hurts," Joe said. Trapper was wrapping his hand in the kitchen. They'd come down the back stairs, and a few of Joe's followers had come in and were helping Trapper attend to Joe.

"We heard more shooting," one of them said.

Joe nodded. "Frank Harper. I saw him outside, shooting at people when I was looking out the windows."

The man shook his head. "We'll help you kill him, boss."

Joe looked at Trapper. "Go upstairs and move that other cop. I'm going to the river—that's where they'll be headed."

Trapper nodded and handed the gauze to another person, then disappeared up the back stairs.

Joe stood. "Come on, we have to find him."

"Who?"

"Frank Harper or his grandson," Joe said. "They won't get away."

One of them handed Joe his rifle—Trapper had carried it downstairs for him—and they left through the sliding doors.

Behind the farmhouse, Joe split his remaining followers into three groups. "You guys, go to the barn and make sure the daughter is still there. She's in the rusty car. Bring her to me. And if you see Harper, just shoot him."

They nodded and shouted, "Keepers of Truth!" before running off.

Joe turned to the others. "You five guys, help Trapper check the whole house. Every room. Harper may have doubled back. And don't let him talk to you—just shoot him. He's not even a real cop. He's one of the ones that faked all that evidence against me," Hathaway stated, using his best "victim" voice. "You have to avenge this miscarriage of justice. You three, you're with me."

Hathaway turned and walked up the path that led to the neighboring field. One way or another, he would have his revenge on Harper and the cops. Joe had already killed two of them, and he was going to kill Harper and his family. When this was over, Trapper would drive him to Canada. He had arranged for a flight to Iceland, and then, from there, Morocco. They didn't extradite to the United States, and he'd already arranged for Trapper to wire a substantial amount of money ahead.

Joe and his three followers ran into the field, and Joe could tell something was going on. There were boxes in the middle of the field, near a large dead tree, and two of the boxes were on their sides. He saw a dark cloud around the boxes and realized they must be beehives.

Joe experienced a rare moment of surprise—in sifting through a myriad of alternative plans and possible outcomes, there had been no way Joe could predict a field full of bees and other insects attacking him and his group of followers. Across the field, he saw several figures running for the river, waving their arms and slapping their skin. Others had not made it that far—Joe saw shapes in the dirty field, fallen men and women. Some writhed on the ground, while others lay still. There was no way to foresee this.

"Come on," Joe said, running for the river. "Watch out."

CHAPTER 86
The Fight

Frank found Ramirez in the last upstairs bedroom.

Amazingly, she was alive. She'd been shot four times, three in her vest and a through-and-through in her calf. Frank plugged the leg wound with a piece of cloth to stop the bleeding, then loosened her bullet-proof vest. She breathed easier. He found her gun and picked it up.

"A-hole shot me in the leg. From behind," she said to Frank, her words rushed. "And then Hathaway. Three times."

"Well, he's a good shot," Frank said. "Got you right in the vest."

"Thank God," she said. "Hurts like hell."

Frank heard a sound behind him and put her gun in Ramirez's hand. "Someone's coming." He stepped behind the door, and Ramirez laid back down on the floor, partially closing her eyes.

A moment later, a man stepped into the room with a gun. He started towards Ramirez, who was watching him. She turned slightly and shot the man, who stumbled sideways. Frank stepped out from behind the door and kicked at him, knocking him to the ground. Frank snatched the man's gun away, then kicked him again, this time in the face. He stopped moving.

Frank leaned back over Ramirez. "Call it in again. Tell them the driveway is clear and you need EMT. Say 'officer down' so they'll hurry up. I'm going after Hathaway. He must have gone down a back staircase."

She nodded and reached for her radio. Frank got his gun and left, finding another set of stairs that led down into the kitchen.

As he reached the main floor, a group of men was coming back in from outside. They were civilians. He didn't want to kill anyone—or at least anyone who didn't deserve it. Frank holstered his gun and spun out of their way, making his way around the kitchen island and into the small breakfast nook.

"I'm here to capture Joe Hathaway," he said. "I'm a cop."

"No, you're not," one man said, picking up a knife. There were five of them, and they were all big. And angry.

Another picked up a rolling pin. "The Keeper of Truth deserves to be free," he said.

"That's not up to you," Frank said.

"Well," the knife guy answered. "We'll see about that."

They rushed him. The first one got in a good kick to Frank's side before Frank crouched down and lifted the guy from his feet, throwing him over the table. Frank prioritized the targets by weapon type, and pivoted to put the guy with the knife between himself and the others. They came around anyway, grabbing at his arms. They wanted to hold him for the guy with the knife to stab. Great.

Frank slapped their hands away and punched one across the face even as he dodged a jab from the knife. Then he grabbed an unarmed man and pushed him into the guy with the knife, sending them both to the floor.

Frank backed away, circling, and the other two came at him. Frank caught the rolling pin between his two hands and spun, tucking the rolling pin under his armpit and trapping the man's hands. The other guy, unarmed, punched Frank hard in the head. Frank saw stars and backed up—the guy with the rolling pin was trying to pull his hands free, so Frank used that momentum to pull him off his feet. As the man fell, Frank stripped the rolling pin out of his hands and grabbed it, bashing the unarmed man hard across the chin and sending him flying. Frank turned and brought the rolling pin down on the other man's back. The guy crashed to the floor.

Frank stood, woozy, and looked around. Two of the men were down, and two had fled outside. Only the guy with the knife was left.

"Put that down," Frank said, huffing. His face hurt. "You don't want to die for that crazy man."

The guy with the knife smiled, and Frank realized Hathaway wasn't the only person around with a screw loose. This guy looked happy, excited, like his whole life had been leading up to this moment.

"Oh, I'm fine, copper," the guy said, approaching Frank with his knife ready. "Don't worry about me. I've been looking forward to this. Finally get to fight the man, one on one. You cops are always ganging up on people. Now I have a chance—"

Frank knew he had to act quickly. He drew his gun and shot the man.

"Sorry," he said as the hippie shrieked and fell to the ground, holding his shoulder and starting to cry. "I don't have time for this."

Frank checked on the others and used cords from the kitchen curtains to tie them up. He left the house, running toward the open field. Frank skirted the tree line where he'd been hiding ten minutes before. He came around the corner and saw the open field.

He'd seen Laura and Jackson and Peters run this way.

Bee hives stood in the middle of the field, five large white boxes sitting near the base of a broken, old tree. Two were tipped over. The hives were painted white but covered with patches of blackness that oozed and dripped. Frank realized he was looking at bees or wasps on the outside of the hives. Thousands of them, crawling and buzzing over each other, attacking and boiling and bubbling like living tar. Closer, the ground around him moved, and he saw bees swarming in the air, attacking each other.

Across the field, he saw Hathaway and three other men with him. He ran after them, crossing the field. There were several people on the ground, not moving.

Frank ran in the direction of the river while he loaded his guns. He'd lost his shotgun somewhere along the way, but he had three handguns, two in his holster and back, plus a third, his trusty backup, at his ankle.

Bees swarmed around him, and he swatted at his arms and face to shoo them away.

Frank nearly tripped over something and stopped, looking. It was a person, lying face down in the field. He flipped the person over.

It was Deputy Peters.

His eyes were swollen shut, and his arms were swollen and misshapen. Huge red welts covered his arms and neck and face.

"Deputy. DEPUTY!" Frank shook him and felt for a pulse.

Nothing.

No. This couldn't be happening.

Frank waited. There was no pulse. He waved away more bees and realized they weren't bees. The bodies were too long. Wasps, or yellow jackets? Peters must be allergic.

He must have been allergic.

Frank was stunned. He felt for a pulse again, torn between chasing after Laura and Jackson and Joe and staying here to care for his friend. But it looked like Peters was past being cared for. If he was allergic, did he carry that Epi-pen that some people did? Frank slapped at bees on his arms and felt through Peters' pockets, finding nothing that could help. Car keys, pocket knife, five full gun magazines. They were long and metallic and for a second, he thought they were one of those stick pens, but they weren't. No medicine, no gun.

Frank looked around, swatting wasps away from his face, looking for an Epi-pen or Peter's gun. He could have dropped both. Something stung the back of his arm, and he slapped it away. Frank stood, slapping at another wasp just as it stung him on the cheek. It hurt, and Frank grabbed at the insect and crushed it between his fingers.

Two more landed on his face, and he slapped them away and started running. He needed to get farther away from the hives. He found the gun eight feet from Deputy Peters' body, buried halfway in the ground with the brown handle sticking up out of the dirt. Frank grabbed it, made sure the safety was on, and pocketed the gun. But there was no sign of any shots or Epi-pens.

Frank glanced back at Peters. He was covered with yellow jackets. And the ground was like a living, moving carpet. They were also coming out of holes in the ground. Did wasps live in the ground? Were they attacking the hives? That was what it looked like.

He shook his head and turned and ran for the tree line. Hathaway and the others had disappeared. Frank could see the ground on the other side of the trees sloped down to a small river.

He only prayed Laura and Jackson were still alive.

CHAPTER 87
Riverside

"Come out!" Joe shouted.

He was standing by the Great Miami River. At this point, the river was probably thirty or forty yards across. "You can't hide from me!"

He'd sent his three men up and down the river.

These people had to be hiding somewhere. There was a group of his "followers" walking along the shoreline, heading south, downriver. He lifted his rifle and looked through the scope, scanning the group, looking for any of the Harpers, but it was all morons from the farmhouse.

Beyond them, Joe could see a bridge crossing the river. Parked on the bridge were an ambulance and two cop cars. A quarter mile, he guessed. He took a few shots at them, seeing his bullets ricochet off the side of the ambulance. The hippies scattered as bullets flew over their heads. Adjusting for wind, he shot at a cop looking over the railing and delighted to see him fall. Joe also took out one of the lights on top of a patrol car and the driver's side window of the ambulance.

He turned and scanned the riverbank on the other side, moving his scope along, looking for people. He reloaded and shot at trees randomly, watching the bark explode. The woman might be fearless, like her idiot father, but the little kid would be scared and might betray his position.

Joe kept searching. They couldn't have gotten away.

"I can see you! You can't hide!" he shouted as he scanned the river, thinking they might be hiding in the water. Could they do that? Would a kid that age be able to control his panic and hold his breath? Joe doubted it. He did the calculations in his head and confirmed it. There was no way they could have gotten away. They were near, right now. Somewhere. He just had to find them. And when he was done here, he could go back and find Frank Harper.

Joe turned and saw movement at the top of the embankment. Speak of the devil. Harper's head appeared. Joe lifted his rifle and aimed.

CHAPTER 88
The River

"I can see you! You can't hide!"

Hathaway was shouting from somewhere ahead.

Frank crested the embankment and saw Joe Hathaway standing near the edge of the water, looking right at Frank. He had a rifle out and was already pointing it right at him.

Frank didn't hesitate. He dropped his weapon and put his hands up.

"Joe! Why are you yelling? I'm right here."

Hathaway smiled and kept his rifle pointed at Frank, who could see that Joe also had a pistol tucked into a holster on his hip. One of Hathaway's hands was bandaged.

"Finally, we get a chance to talk again," Hathaway shouted, holding the rifle. "Remember that time we had coffee? You asked me so many questions. But you never figured it out. And Tom was at my place all along. Didn't that make you feel stupid?"

"Like yesterday," Frank shouted, his hands up. "Look, you've got me. I'm the one you want—I figured out your chess moves and the Sun Tzu quotes. My daughter and grandson were just bait to get us to this moment," Frank said. "Let them go."

Behind Hathaway, Frank saw Laura poke her head out from behind a tree. She was hiding on the opposite bank. Frank didn't see Jackson—she was probably keeping him hidden. She looked right at them but didn't move. What was she doing?

"Those clues were too easy," Hathaway said, walking slowly toward Frank, the rifle flat in his hands and pointed at Frank. "I know that now. Even that moron you worked with could have figured them out. Did you see him? Now he's dead, swollen. What an idiot."

Frank wasn't going to get angry. Not yet. The second gun in his undershirt holster itched. Frank hoped he would get a chance to use it.

"I knew you'd figure out where I was," Hathaway said. "Although I expected you to bring more people, a SWAT team, guns blazing. Why else would I have surrounded myself with pitiful civilians?"

"I guess the chief didn't care," Frank said. He needed to keep the man's attention on him. Laura was crawling to Frank's right, downriver, and now Frank saw Jackson crawling behind her. They were hidden, all right, but not very well. If Hathaway turned around, he'd spot both of them easily. "Maybe if the chief liked me more, he would have listened to me."

"What do you mean?"

Frank looked at Joe. "I told him you'd taken Laura and Jackson. Nice job, by the way, sneaking out of that hospital. How'd you do that?"

Hathaway smiled and took another step toward Frank. "I don't have time to tell you right now. Too much going on. Maybe some other time. Let's just say it wasn't that difficult. And I don't really care about your daughter and grandkid. I've got you here now. You and I are going to play some chess. You're going to love it."

Frank shook his head and lowered his arms slowly. "No, I won't. I don't like chess. It's pointless."

"Pointless?"

"Yeah, pieces moving around a board. Too predictable for me."

"You don't know what you're talking about. There are infinite combinations—"

"A kid's game. A simpleton could play it."

"It's not," Joe said with a smile, stepping closer. "It takes years to master. And I know what you're doing, by the way. You're just trying to make me mad."

"Oh, I don't care either way," Frank said. "I was just saying I don't like chess." Frank stared at the gun in Hathaway's hands. The long barrel was pointed right at Frank's face, unwavering. Frank remembered how many shooting competitions this insane nut had won.

"Let's just say you won't have a choice in the matter. You'll learn to like it."

"Did Tom?" He was waiting for a distraction, anything. "You can't take me back to your house and stuff me in your freezer, Joe. You've got to flee, right? Canada? Asia?"

Hathaway snorted at the mention of Tom. "He was an idiot. Tom had everything and didn't appreciate it. Couldn't just be happy with a wife. No, he had to run around on her."

Okay, maybe a different tactic.

"His girlfriends were pretty, though. Especially that young one in Indianapolis, the one that was pregnant. Better looking than May Mercato, at least."

Hathaway stopped. "Take that back," he said, his face suddenly serious. "May has a lot of things going for her. When this is all over, she'll come visit me—"

Behind him, on the embankment, Frank saw Laura stand suddenly.

She was at least sixty or seventy yards downriver by now, and Frank couldn't see Jackson anymore. Laura stood and waved her arms.

"Hey, A-hole!"

Hathaway's head turned only a half inch to track the sound and it was all the opportunity that Frank needed. In one practiced move, Frank lifted his shirt with his left hand, pulled the gun with his right hand, and dropped to one knee. He fired at Joe three times in quick succession, and saw at least one bullet strike the old man in the chest.

Frank didn't take any chances. He dropped to the ground and rolled, assuming a barrage of return fire from a man who'd spent years learning how to hit what he shot at.

No bullets came. There was a big difference between target shooting and having the target shoot back.

Frank looked up, his gun pointed in Hathaway's direction. The nut job was bent over his gun, on his knees in the dirt, groaning loudly.

Frank stood. "Drop the weapon!"

Hathaway looked up and smiled, struggling to his feet.

"Stay down!" Frank yelled. "I will fire again!"

Hathaway smiled and lifted his rifle in Frank's direction.

Frank fired again, three more shots in quick succession. At least two struck Hathaway, one high in the shoulder and another in the chest. Joe dropped his rifle and stumbled backwards toward the river.

"Get down on the ground!" Frank shouted at the man.

Hathaway was making for the river, stumbling and coughing. Blood ran down his arm. Frank could hear Laura shouting off to his right and glanced at her. She was running in Frank's direction, but he waved her back. Hathaway got to the edge of the water and started laughing. It sounded so strange. Frank was yelling at the man to stop moving and threatening to fire again, but Joe wasn't listening.

"Sorry, Frank! I gotta go."

Hathaway backed knee-deep into the river. He wavered for a moment, his hand on the surface of the water, and fell backwards, disappearing under the surface before bobbing up to the top, the current immediately carrying him away. Frank ran and grabbed at the man but missed. All Frank could do was turn and watch the dark shape float away.

Laura was down river and she grabbed at Hathaway.

"Be careful!" Frank shouted.

She got a hand on the jacket and held Joe for a half-second before the current pulled Hathaway out of her hands. By the time Frank had run downriver and joined her and Jackson, the shape was moving around a bend and out of their sight. Frank couldn't tell if the man was moving, or if it was just the current. Frank hoped he was dead.

"Are you okay?" He asked Laura. "I'm so sorry you got caught up in this. Is Jackson okay?"

She nodded and threw her arms around him. "Yes, he's fine. I had him crawl that way, and I came down here to yell at Hathaway. You looked like you needed help."

"I did," Frank said with a smile. "But that was dangerous."

"Yup," she said. "I owed him that much. Actually, I wouldn't have minded getting a couple punches in for tying me up in that barn." She looked down the river. "Was he dead? I saw blood in the water."

"I hope so. I shot him at least twice," Frank said, scratching at his bee stings. "Let's get back and check on the other cops and call it in."

Laura looked behind Frank, her eyes searching the other shore. "Did you see Deputy Peters? He was right behind us."

Frank looked at her.

"We got separated when those bees attacked," she continued. "We all got swarmed. He was following us."

"Yeah, I found him," Frank said with a grimace. "He didn't make it."

"What?"

Frank nodded. "He must have been allergic. He was swollen..." Frank suddenly didn't have the heart to talk about it. "Okay, get Jackson. There are EMTs up on the bridge," he said, pointing.

"We should go to him," Laura said. "We could help him."

"It's too late for that," Frank said. "But I'll send the EMTs down to make sure."

Together, they found Jackson hiding under an old log. Frank and the others waded carefully across the river while Laura argued with Frank to go back and help Peters. Finally, they walked south and climbed up to the bridge.

Two dozen of Hathaway's hippies were there, along with several injured cops. Laura took Jackson over to be checked by the EMTs. Frank found Ramirez in one of the ambulances—she was being treated.

"You okay?"

She nodded. They were wrapping her chest. "Peters?"

Frank shook his head. "No, he didn't...he's dead."

Ramirez made a face. "Oh, no. Did you talk to King yet?"

Frank shook his head again. "I'll call it in," he said, reaching for his phone and dialing.

Chief King picked up. "Frank?"

"Yeah, Chief, I'm here," Frank said, suddenly exhausted. "I found my daughter and grandson. And Hathaway."

"You found them? Thank God. Are they okay? Did you guys capture Hathaway?"

"We traded shots," Frank said. "He fell into the river. I got him at least twice—he wouldn't drop his weapon. I shot him, and he fell into the river and floated away. He's headed south, I think," Frank said. He was dreading every moment of this conversation. "You need to get people down river to find him."

"Okay, I'll get on that. Is Peters with you?"

Frank frowned. "He was with me. We ended up finding them all at that old farmhouse in Troy, the one from the Martin kidnapping."

"Peters sent me the address. We're on our way," King said. "Ten minutes out. I'll call the county, get the divers out there to find Hathaway."

"Those clues—Hathaway was taunting me."

"It's okay, we're headed to you."

"Chief," Frank said. He didn't know how to bring it up. The conversation had already gone on too long without talking about the most important element.

"I can't believe Hathaway succeeded in having us chasing our tails all this time," Chief King was saying. "All those cops near Indiana, and in Detroit, for nothing."

"Listen, Chief, I have to tell you something."

"It can wait, Frank," King said. "We're almost there. Just get your family checked by the EMTs. Have Peters run the scene until I can get there."

Frank swallowed. "Chief...I don't know how to tell you this. Deputy Peters...he's dead."

There was no sound on the other end of the line. Frank couldn't even hear the chief breathing.

Frank pressed on.

"We got separated, and he got my daughter and grandson to safety. There were bee hives in the field next door. He was attacked, and stung, over and over. Bees or yellow jackets or something."

There was no answer.

"They ran through the field and the insects just swarmed," Frank continued, desperate to fill the silence. "I'm so sorry, Chief. I can't even imagine what you're thinking right now."

King came back on. "Okay, thank you."

Frank didn't know what to say. "I guess he was allergic."

"He is," King said quietly. "Was."

The line went dead.

CHAPTER 89
Traumatized

"So, now what?"

She looked up at him. They were sitting in Sammy Eggies, a diner next door to the Haunted Bookstore in downtown Cooper's Mill. Jackson was playing at a neighbor's house. It was Thursday morning, three days after the ordeal at the farmhouse.

"What do you mean?" she asked.

"I mean what are you going to do, now that I'm living here," he said with a weary smile. "Maybe it was a mistake. You're going to need to get a personal bodyguard if bad stuff starts happening to you all the time."

"'Starts happening?'" she said. "I think it already started. Jackson is going to have bee nightmares for a month," she said quietly. "I'm not sure what to tell him."

Frank thought about it for a minute. Cops dealt with these kinds of thoughts all the time, learned how to ignore them or drink them out of existence. What did you tell a young woman? Or a little kid?

"I'd tell him not to worry about it," Frank said, shaking his head. "Everyone gets kidnapped at least once in their life, right? So now he's got that out of the way."

"You're not funny, you know. At least I got my car back."

"Good," he said. He ate his breakfast, not sure what else to say. The cops had found Laura's car parked behind the barn she'd been held in.

Frank and Laura ate in silence for a few minutes, only talking to pass the salt. After a time, he spoke up again.

"Actually, he should talk to someone about it," Frank said. "You were right. Talking to the police shrink helped me. I didn't think it would, but it did."

"I told you. But I don't know what to tell him. Can you sit down with him?"

"Sure," Frank said.

"But don't lie to him. Tell him enough of the truth, but don't scare him more than you need to."

He thought about that for a moment and shook his head. "Trudy never wanted to know anything. Then, at the end, she suddenly wanted to know everything. By then, it was too late."

"Well, Jackson's no idiot," Laura said, sitting back to sip her coffee. "He knows bad things happen, especially to cops. I told him we got caught up in a rare situation, and it's not likely to happen again. And, for the record, you could tell me the same things. You haven't even asked how I'm feeling."

"Sorry," he said. "You're right. I should've done that. I guess I'm used to being around guys, or cops, or both. They just deal with it and move on."

"Drinking yourself into a coma isn't 'dealing with it,'" she said. "You could learn a thing or two from us 'weak' womenfolk, Frank. We might obsess about things, or prattle on and on, but our suicide rate is lower," she said with a smirk.

"I don't doubt it. And your blood pressure, too," he said.

"The big question is what are you going to do?"

"Well, I need to find a place to live," Frank said. "My landlord is a real pain."

"Funny."

"Seriously, I'm meeting with Jake next week. Hopefully he can find me a place that's cheap and near the downtown."

"You still thinking about being a P.I.?"

Frank nodded between bites of his omelet. "The requirements aren't too bad. I should be good to go in a month or two."

"Let me know if you need accounting help," she said. "I could use the experience."

"Actually, I have some paperwork from the state I don't understand, if you want to help me with that. I need to get a FEIN, whatever the hell that is. And an LLC."

"I can help with that. I'm familiar with the acronyms," she said with a smile. "Do you think you'll get enough work?"

Frank shrugged. "Not sure. But I don't really want to work down in Dayton. And I can't work for the CMPD, that's for sure. At least not for a while. Those guys are hardly speaking to me, and the chief won't return my calls."

"It wasn't your fault."

"I know. By the way, how are you dealing with all of that?" he asked with a smirk. "See, I'm concerned."

"Thanks for asking. I'm getting along. The worst part was waiting in that barn. And that car they had me locked in—it was claustrophobic. Now I know how you used to feel about elevators."

"Yeah, it's not good."

"The worst part was I didn't know what they were going to do to us."

"How'd you get free?"

"I didn't tell you? I got the steering wheel loose and crawled out through the trunk."

"Good job," he said with a smile. Frank lifted his coffee and toasted her. "Couldn't have done better myself."

"Thanks," Laura said. "Then I only had two thoughts—find Jackson and find a weapon."

"You did good, getting out of there. When I saw you, I was relieved. I had no idea what Hathaway would do to you guys. He was twisted."

"Well, I hope he's dead," she said. The cops had searched the river, but there was no sign of a body. Frank figured they would find Joe's corpse somewhere downriver over the next few days, snagged on some rocks.

"Me too."

"And I'm sorry to hear you're on the outs with the police," she said. "What happened to Peters wasn't your fault, not by a stretch. Or Deputy Stan, or anyone else that got hurt."

"Peters knew what he was doing, and he knew what he was getting into. Same with Stan. It's just part of being a cop. Sometimes bad things happen. All you can do is train for it and hope you're ready."

"It wasn't your fault, Frank."

"I know, but the chief blames me," Frank said. "We were there because I insisted."

"You were saving me and Jackson," she said. "And looking for Hathaway."

"I know," Frank said. "But King hasn't spoken to me since."

"It's not your fault."

Frank nodded.

CHAPTER 90
Funeral

Two days later, they held the funeral for Deputy Peters.

It was a somber event, to be sure. The entire Cooper's Mill Police Department was in attendance, as were Frank and Laura and a dozen other mourners, including some cops from other jurisdictions.

The burial was held in the Maple Hill Cemetery, located on Hyatt at the southern end of town. The cemetery, speckled with tall oaks and edged by roads on two sides, held most of the town's deceased. Apparently, many of the larger headstones and monuments were carved with the names of families that had lived in the Cooper's Mill area for generations.

Deputy Stan had been buried here two days ago.

Frank hated funerals. He looked at the casket and thought about Peters. They had worked well together. Frank had hoped to work with him more after moving to town. Frank would miss his eagerness and his thirst to learn.

On the other side of the casket stood the police department. A few of them had nodded at Frank or acknowledged his presence, but Chief King hadn't so much as looked at Frank. The chief looked like he'd been crying for at least a week straight, and the receptionist, Lola, was standing very close to him, gripping King's arm and crying as well. Based on their body language, Frank got the impression they were more than co-workers.

A priest joined them and began speaking. Frank let the words flow over him, not listening. He knew as much about Peters as he was ever going to know. Learning more now wouldn't help. Nothing could help. Peters had been clumsy and impulsive and reckless and the closest thing Frank had to a partner in a long time. And now he was dead. Killed saving Frank's daughter and grandson.

Frank glanced at King, who happened to be staring at him. The chief's face was tight and angry. It was obvious. King blamed Frank for Peters' death, and there was no going back. He would need some time before he'd speak to Frank again, if ever.

Frank looked down at the ground and shook his head. Ben Stone,

Steve Furrows, and now Deputy Floyd Peters. People he'd worked with, partners. All dead.

The priest continued, and Frank glanced up and King wasn't looking at him any longer. The man had turned away and was being comforted by Lola.

Minutes later, the service wrapped up and Chief King and Lola stepped forward. King produced a folded flag and placed it on the casket. King said something under his breath, nearly silent, and touched the casket before nodding solemnly and turning, walking away. Lola glanced at Frank, and he mouthed the words "I'm sorry" to her before she turned to follow King.

The other cops began filing past the casket, each brushing a hand on it and saying a few words before moving on. When the last of the officers and deputies had passed by, Frank stepped up and rested a hand on the casket and said some kind words for the young man. Even though he'd only known him for a short while, Frank felt like Peters was practically family.

"I can't believe he's gone," Laura said, her hand on Frank's arm. "It's so sad."

Frank nodded and walked away. Laura followed. They headed toward the cars, parked on the small drive that wound around the interior of the cemetery. Frank had hoped to talk to King afterward and get a chance to say how sorry he was, but King was already getting into a black limousine with Lola.

Frank yelled after him.

"Chief," he said, putting up his hand and waving at King to stop.

The chief turned and looked at Frank, his face blank. Frank could see that King was heartbroken at the circumstances and distraught, of course, to be burying a member of his family. But, most of all, riding atop the sea of emotions painted across the man's face, was anger.

Anger at Frank.

King didn't say anything, or smile, or even hesitate. There were no kind words, or a half nod of recognition, one cop to another.

No emotion of any sort.

Chief King just looked at Frank and turned away, sitting down into the limo. He and Lola pulled their doors shut without saying a word, and the car pulled away, wending through the trees and groups of headstones in the rural cemetery before disappearing out of sight.

Epilogue

The man stumbled along the riverbank, heading north. It was starting to get dark, and he could relax a little. He wasn't certain where he was, but he was pretty smart. He could figure it out.

Last night, he'd awakened floating in the dark river, bleeding from a hole in his shoulder, nearly delirious. He'd clawed his way from the water and rested for a while, stuffing wet leaves into his wound. Some part of his mind reminded him that leaves weren't a sanitary wound dressing, but he didn't care. His chest hurt, too, and he'd stood and loosened the Kevlar vest to breathe, then started walking upriver against the current. Joe figured the cops would be looking for him—or his body—downriver, toward Cooper's Mill.

The riverbanks were foreboding walls of sharp rocks and earthen cliffs, broken up by occasional beaches and flat areas of sand or dirt. Trees hung at weird angles over the water, branches dipping to the surface. The dark made it difficult to see where he was going, but he didn't dare work his way up the banks and into the forests that lined the river. Surely there would be trails, and roads, but those led to homes and towns. And people.

At one point in the night, Joe walked under a bridge and recognized where he was. He stumbled ashore and made his way across the wide field that separated the farmhouse from the river. Off to his right, he could see the boxy shapes of a collection of beehives, now dormant. Joe didn't see any cops and found the back door unlocked.

Inside, the kitchen was a mess—it looked like there had been a fight, with broken chairs and cabinet doors hanging askew. On the counter was a first-aid kit, the same one Trapper had used. Joe rummaged through it, finding gauze and ointment and a package of Advil.

He searched the house, scavenging anything that might help him. In the living room, he grabbed a sleeping bag and a backpack left behind by one of his followers. He also found some food and a flashlight.

Upstairs, he grabbed the extra pain medication he'd left behind. From the second floor, he looked down the driveway and saw a lonely cop car. A man was sitting inside, talking on the radio. For a moment, Joe thought about walking down there and shooting the cop and taking the car—Joe still had one of his pistols, the one he'd tucked in his waistband. Of course, there was no guarantee the weapon would work after getting wet. And if he killed a cop, the chase would start all over again. Joe wasn't ready for that, not yet. He needed to get away, get healthy. And plan. He needed to plan.

He'd gotten back to the river and cleaned and dressed his shoulder as best he could, using the flashlight and hiding in a secluded beach area.

That had been last night. Today, he'd walked all day, staying out of the sweltering sun and hiding when he heard cars or people. Joe wasn't sure how far he would follow the river—at some point, he'd have to venture away from the water and start looking for medical help. His shoulder was throbbing and likely infected. There was no exit wound, which meant Harper's bullet was still in there, grinding away.

Joe ignored the pain and smiled and kept walking through the dark water, heading upriver. He had money, and a gun, and a backpack full of supplies. He wasn't exactly sure where he was headed, but Joe knew he was clever enough to figure it out.

He was the smartest person he'd ever met.

ABOUT THE AUTHOR

Greg Enslen has published seven mysteries and thrillers, including the Amazon bestsellers "A Field of Red" and "The Ghost of Blackwood Lane." His four-book "Frank Harper Mysteries" series has received critical acclaim. He also writes original screenplays and has published twenty other titles, including in-depth binge guides for popular TV shows such as "Game of Thrones" and "Mr. Robot." His books are available from major retailers and on his **Amazon Author Page** at http://bit.ly/geauthor.

Greg lives in southern Ohio with his wife, three children, five dogs and an indeterminate number of cats. His interests include travel, reading, film and television, and yelling at various sports franchises. Greg enjoys writing late at night, after everyone else has finally trudged off to bed and the house is quiet. For more information, visit his website at **gregenslen.com** or check out his **Facebook fan page** at http://www.facebook.com/gregenslenswriting.

Books By Greg Enslen

Greg has written and published twenty-six books. Most titles available from Amazon, other major book retailers, and on Kindle:

Frank Harper Mysteries
A Field of Red
Black Ice
White Lines
Yellow Jacket
Welcome to Cooper's Mill (free companion guide, available exclusively at gregenslen.com)

Fiction
Black Bird
The Ghost of Blackwood Lane
The 9/11 Machine

Guide Series
A Field Guide to Facebook
"A Viewer's Guide to Suits," Season 1
"A Viewer's Guide to Suits," Season 2
"A Viewer's Guide to Suits," Season 3
"Game of Thrones: A Binge Guide" for Season 1
"Game of Thrones: A Binge Guide" for Season 2
"Game of Thrones: A Binge Guide" for Season 3
"Game of Thrones: A Binge Guide" for Season 4
"Game of Thrones: A Binge Guide" for Season 5
"Game of Thrones: A Binge Guide" for Season 6
"Game of Thrones: A Binge Guide" for Season 7
"Mr. Robot: A Binge Guide" for Season 1
"Mr. Robot: A Binge Guide" for Season 2
"Mr. Robot: A Binge Guide" for Season 3

Newspaper Column Collections
"Tipp Talk" 2010 Newspaper Column Collection
"Tipp Talk" 2011 Newspaper Column Collection
"Tipp Talk" 2012 Newspaper Column Collection
"Tipp Talk" 2013 Newspaper Column Collection

CAN I ASK A FAVOR?

Thank you for reading this book—I hope you enjoyed it! If you did, I'd really appreciate it if you could take a few minutes to post a short review on Amazon. Reviews of this book on Amazon, Goodreads, or Facebook help new readers find out about my books.

To leave an Amazon review, use the following link: **http://bit.ly/geauthor**. Select the book you'd like to review, scroll down to the "Customer Reviews" area, and then click on the button that reads "Write a customer review." And feel free to be honest in your review—I love feedback, good or bad, and the total number of Amazon reviews affects how Amazon lists book titles. Every review helps increase the "social buzz" of the book, and I truly appreciate it.

While you're at it, you might want to join my newsletter, where I highlight upcoming title releases, discounts, beta opportunities and appearances. You can sign up at **www.gregenslen.com/newsletter**. My monthly newsletter isn't spammy, and I promise not to sell or share your information. Thank you for your support!

— Greg Enslen